DEADLIGHT

A VALBERG NOVEL

Desmond J. Doherty (signature)

DESMOND
J. DOHERTY

GUILDHALL PRESS

ISBN: 978 1 911053 03 3

Author's photo (inside front cover) © Mustafa Oymak

Personal Helicon taken from *Death of a Naturalist* © Seamus Heaney and reprinted by kind permission of Faber and Faber Ltd.

First published October 2015.

Guildhall Press
Ráth Mór Business Park
Bligh's Lane, Derry
Ireland
BT48 0LZ
00 44 28 7136 4413
info@ghpress.com
www.ghpress.com

A catalogue record for this title is available from the British Library.

Guildhall Press gratefully acknowledges the financial support of the Arts Council of Northern Ireland under the National Lottery Programme.

LOTTERY FUNDED

ACKNOWLEDGEMENTS

My heartfelt gratitude for their ongoing encouragement and support to: Gerard Brennan, Jim Curran, Bill Vail, Andrew Eaton, Mark McCauley, Michael Doherty, Richard Moore and Pearse Moore.

Sincere thanks to all those at Guildhall Press and associates for a great professional job as usual: Paul Hippsley, Kevin Hippsley, Joe McAllister, Declan Carlin, Garbhan Downey and Peter McCartney.

My appreciation to the Arts Council NI for supporting this publication.

For Clare

'Deadlight' was the codename for the British Royal Navy operation to scuttle 116 German U-boats surrendered to the Allies at the end of World War II. The operation was to take place off the northwest coast of Ireland. Forty-two of the surrendered U-boats were moored at Lisahally in Derry.

PROLOGUE

Maze Prison and Court Complex, County Down – May 2013

Gerard O'Driscoll finished eating his favourite meal of liver, potatoes, and onions. He would have preferred some red wine to wash it all down but water was fine. He asked for a cup of tea and sipped it slowly as he checked the time. It was ten minutes to eight. Two armed guards then escorted him back to his cell. This was the process every night. The moment O'Driscoll lay down on his bed, he held his breath and heard bodies falling. The guard who put him in his cell and the one standing at the door collapsed in a heap in front of him. There wasn't even time to shut the door. He carefully watched the faint vapour drifting through the ventilation and air-conditioning system. Still holding his breath, he got up and went to the door. All the guards were sprawled on the ground, motionless. The purpose-built, multi-million-pound Maze prison and court complex was silent. He went back into his cell and removed from the cistern in the toilet area a gas mask sealed in a plastic bag. O'Driscoll looked up at the CCTV camera that monitored him, smiled and shook his head. He quickly tore free the mask and put it on. He looked around one last time, then stared directly at the CCTV camera. Then he walked out of his cell and the prison complex.

CHAPTER 1

'Dear Jesus,' Chief Superintendent David Kells moaned as he looked at the sight before him.

A gunshot rang out. Several panicked police officers dived for cover.

More police and army personnel poured into Ebrington Square from the main entry point at Browning Drive. They all sought protection. Many gathered at the steps leading into the square. Commander Ruth Everett and a Tactical Support Unit sealed the area. They immediately tried to identify the naked male, stiff and unmoving in a white wooden chair, in the middle of the square. A crew from the Tactical Support Unit photographed and filmed the scene as it developed from their secure location.

All Kells could think about was heroin, and the escalating drug problem sweeping Derry, which he was keen to keep quiet. Was this the start of a drug war or a feud between drug dealers? A bullet to the head or a knife attack would be easier. And Gerard O'Driscoll was most definitely in prison, so it couldn't be his work.

Confused and stressed out, Kells was glad to greet Detective Sergeant Linda Wilson.

'I know who that is, David,' she told him.

'You do?'

'It's Victor Bostridge. The barrister who was the prosecutor in that fiasco of a trial. The White rape. Remember?'

'Jesus. I see now. He's the guy ...'

'Yeah. The guy who DCI Valberg saved from choking on his Thai chicken sandwich by shaking his throat in Derry

Courthouse last year after the trial collapsed. He's not moving, David. He looks dead.'

'More dead lawyers. Will there be any left?'

'Was that really a shot that rang out, or is everyone overreacting? Where did it come from, David?'

'It seemed far away to me – possibly from across the river?'

Commander Everett approached from the steps and nodded to the Chief Superintendent.

'David, this has the same feel as the Emerald Bank siege, December before last, when that solicitor Rankin was blown to pieces with his own bomb. That's what this reminds me of. Anyway, we've had a good look and I can show you.'

Everett produced an iPad with close-up footage of Bostridge, who appeared to be nailed to the chair.

'David, as you'll see, his eyelids look as if they're stapled open. His feet are nailed to the chair. So are his hands behind him. There's a clear plastic bag fastened around his genitalia some way. And there's what appears to be a rat inside the plastic bag ...'

'It's gruesome.'

'Completely.'

'No bomb?'

'Not that we can see. It's just a big clear bag with a rat running about. It's utterly insane.'

'Insane?'

'Mad. How do you understand the mentality of someone who would do something like this? What we need is someone as mad as the person who set this up. Someone good at lateral thinking but sick and touched by insanity as well.'

The Commander paused and looked at the screen again.

'I can think of someone who fits that bill, Ruth. But he's not here.'

'If he's alive the rat might start ... well, chewing on his bits and pieces. As a way out, that is.'

'What about the shot? Where do you think it's from?'

'We haven't seen or heard any strike marks but we are sure it was a shot. From long range, from across the water. Pop your head up and just look over. Plenty of locations. Pick one.'

'Well, what do we do, Ruth?'

Another shot rang out. Everyone ducked in reflex.

'Christ. Did anyone spot a flash?'

Ruth looked across the river to the city, studying the landscape and thinking rapidly.

'A high-powered weapon. From afar. High calibre. Can't tell the location of the shooter. The sound is echoing up the river and bouncing everywhere.'

Kells took out his mobile and speed-dialled a number. He was relieved not to get an American or European dialling tone.

'Bloody answer will you! Answer! Answer the phone,' Kells shouted.

He let it ring as another shot rang out. Everyone remained undercover.

A police officer yelled, 'Look! He's moving. His head twitched. He's alive.'

Just when Kells went to switch off the phone it answered.

'You're in Ebrington. Aren't you?'

'How do you know that, Jon?'

'I was listening to the radio. There's breaking news from the City of Culture.'

'Where are you?'

'You don't know?'

'Jon, I've no time for this.'

'What do you see, David?'

'A man nailed to a chair, with a rat in a plastic bag about to start eating him. We're pinned down at the steps leading into Ebrington Square. There's a sniper across the river. But it's impossible to tell where exactly.'

'O'Driscoll once said something to me about seven towers and one target. When he was in Carstairs, before they transferred him to his own custom-made prison. Something about when it would all kick off. Can you contact the Maze and get him on the phone and ... if I'm allowed ... I'll be there. Well?'

'Get here.'

'I don't want any bullshit at security lines. Get O'Driscoll on the phone. Sort it now and I'll be there.'

'I'll have Linda and young Bell, if he's about here, sort all that now.'

'I'm on my way.'

11

CHAPTER 2

Valberg arrived at the entrance to the Ebrington site via Browning Drive on a black and silver BMW K1300S motorbike. His leather trousers and jacket were the same shade of black as his motorbike. He identified himself and was waved through the first line of security.

Constable Michael Bell greeted him. Valberg had been cleared for access but that didn't prevent Detective Sergeant Walter McMurray from blocking his path.

'Ah, you're back, then? Evel Knievel, is it? And have you permission to enter this crime scene?'

'That's a lot of questions, Wally. Please go away. I tell you that every time I see you.'

'Now, are you interfering with an officer doing his duty?'

'Wally, go and interfere with yourself. You're an expert on that. Now please, leave me alone.'

'Oh. Your little poodle there has come to get you.'

Valberg turned to Bell.

'Ignore him. Is Linda here?'

'Yes, sir. Where have you been?'

'Don't worry about that. Walk quickly. Come on.'

'Sir. All the same, it's great to see you. God, ages now, sir, since we've seen you. We're well into this City of Culture thing here. It's May already. Can't believe it. You've lost weight, and you've a bit of a tan going there.'

Valberg glared at Bell and shook his head.

'Michael. Did I teach you anything? Keep your thoughts private, will you.'

Valberg and Bell moved as fast as they could through the

lines of police officers. Valberg sensed they were surprised to see him. In the circumstances, that was understandable, he thought.

As they arrived at the corner, just outside Ebrington Square, another shot rang out and everyone flinched or ducked for whatever cover they could get. Valberg saw armed officers entering the buildings around him.

He stood still and examined the scene.

He immediately noted how the white chair had been positioned. It was sitting in the middle of the square and facing at an angle towards Derry's Guildhall on the west bank of the city.

Valberg could see that the person on the chair was secured firmly to it, naked, immobile and bloody. Valberg observed the rat inside the plastic bag. It was too far away to see clearly but it seemed to be scurrying about as if it were doing somersaults.

Valberg's concentration switched towards the city and the possible locations for a sniper. His line of sight was immediately drawn to the spire of Saint Columb's Cathedral. However, a sniper couldn't be located there, he concluded. There was no vantage point and it was too obvious.

'Michael. Can you get me a pair of binoculars?'

'Sir, the Chief says I'm to bring you to him first. He's over there at the steps, on the right, with Commander Everett.'

Valberg ignored him.

'Michael. Get me binoculars.'

Bell hurried away, ducking down now and again.

Valberg started speaking loudly to himself.

'Seven towers. One target. Where are you? Who are you? Why?'

He continued scanning the buildings intently. He took in Saint Columb's Cathedral, Saint Eugene's Cathedral and Saint Mary's Chapel, high up the hill in Creggan.

His gaze fixed on the tower at the top of The Apprentice Boys Memorial Hall in the centre of the city. Was a shot possible from there? He could make out the three openings and vantage points at the top of the tower. Perfect cover as well. But Valberg knew if he pinpointed that particular location it would be strongly rejected. He still hadn't been forgiven for deliberately misdirecting all the police personnel there in pursuit of Gerard O'Driscoll on the day the Peace Bridge opened. He couldn't make out any movement there at all, however. It was just too far away.

'Where are you? Seven towers.'

Bell arrived back, crouching down, out of breath, with a set of binoculars.

'Sir, the Chief is having a fit. He's waving you over to him. He's down ...'

'I see him. Let him settle.'

Valberg took the binoculars and another shot rang out. Bell got flat on the ground behind one of the concrete seats at the entrance to the square. By now everyone was shouting at Valberg to get down as well. He compromised and dropped to one knee beside Bell but the top of his body was still partially exposed.

'Two shooters, Michael.'

'What, sir?'

'Two shooters. That last shot was a different sound than the previous one.'

'It could be the same location, sir, but a different weapon.'

That got Valberg's attention. He lowered the binoculars and looked at Bell who seemed to be trying to bury himself into the ground.

Valberg nodded his head.

'Never thought of that. Nice one, Michael. I need another shot here, now.'

'Another shot? Right, sir.'

'Jesus, Michael, if you keep crawling along the ground there, you'll end up the victim of a Texas heart shot.'

'A what, sir?'

'A Texas heart shot – shot in the behind.'

'In the buttocks?'

'Yeah. But the bullet will travel up to your heart and kill you. But stay down anyway, in case you get into trouble for breaking some PSNI procedural manual for snipers in the City of Culture year.'

Another shot rang out.

By now Ebrington Square was clear, apart from Valberg kneeling just inside it behind a concrete seat. He had a view of all he needed to see. Bell was still lying on the ground beside him.

'Sir, the Chief says you are to go over to him at the steps right away. Right. Okay, sir? Can we go now? There always seems to be a gap in the shooting.'

'Mechanical, almost. I take it you can tell me that uniform are closing down the town and emptying every building over there?'

'I think so, sir. Derry is essentially being evacuated. Heard that being talked about. Logical isn't it, sir?'

'Logical. Yes, Michael. That's right.'

Valberg watched the police marksmen take up positions inside the buildings around him – no doubt, he thought, with better binoculars than he had, and sight scopes to view and measure distances across the River Foyle. All the marksmen were masked and in black, but there was no mistaking a female form in the middle of them. The loose strands of blonde hair that hung below her balaclava caught Valberg's attention. Who was she? He had watched her enter the building and now he could see her in the clock tower. He did not want to look at her through his binoculars. He briefly watched her getting into position. In all likelihood, there was nothing to be concerned about. Valberg also knew that there was nothing unusual about him noticing a blonde female in the middle of chaos and danger.

He decided to go and speak with Kells and see if they could get Gerard O'Driscoll on the telephone from the Maze prison.

Time, as always, was of the essence.

CHAPTER 3

Valberg stood up and, skirting the square, walked towards the steps where Kells was sheltering with several other officers.

'You'll never see anything from here. Shots echo up the Foyle, David, don't they?' Valberg stood out from the steps, looking around, to the alarm of the Chief Superintendent.

'What are you doing? Take cover. Are you trying to get yourself killed? Are you mad? No. Don't answer that.'

'Two weapons. Perhaps the same location.' Valberg looked at Bell. 'Michael spotted that.'

Another shot rang out. Valberg looked across the river again, then at Kells. 'There's another one. Jesus. It's the wild west.'

Kells' phone rang. He looked at it.

'It's the prison, Jon. I've been trying to get them – at bloody last. Do you think O'Driscoll will talk to you?'

With that, Valberg's own personal mobile rang. He handed the binoculars back to Bell.

'Hello.'

'What do you see?'

'No time for games, Gerry. Where the fuck are you?'

It was O'Driscoll. Valberg tried to get the attention of Kells, but he was busy shaking his head.

'Neither have I,' said O'Driscoll. 'In fact, I don't have much time at all. What do you see?'

'A man nailed to a chair. Presumably already dead. Or bleeding to death. Naked, with his eyelids glued or stapled open. And a rat in a bag. But it's not what I see. It's what I *can't* see … and what I hear. Where's the sniper, Gerry? Tell me. There's been enough blood. Come on. What do you know about this? Are you watching this from your prison cell on a secure link? Come on, where are you?'

'What makes you think there is one?'

'Do you mean only one sniper? Or that there is one at all? Jesus, Gerry, tell me.'

O'Driscoll didn't answer.

'You said seven towers and one target when we last spoke. Remember? You rang me when I was in the Savoy in London. Seven towers could be the seven locations I've now counted. Austins Department store? Don't think so. Saint Columb's? No. City Hotel? BT building? Memorial Hall? A shot from Creggan, even …'

'Do you see a target, Jon?'

'I see many targets. We're all targets.'

'Are you confident enough to walk to the obvious target?'

'The man in the chair?'

'Show you're unarmed. Walk to him. You might save him if you do. There might just be time.'

Then there was silence.

'Gerry. Gerry. Are you there? Help me. Obviously you can see what is going on here.'

'Take your clothes off. Well, your top half anyway.'

'What?'

'Are you surrounded by police?'

'Yes.'

'Walk away and remove your clothes. Do it now. Right away. Show that you are unarmed. An act of faith. Quickly. Do it. Open your arms like the good Lord Christ. Do you trust me?'

Valberg began to walk out in the open, away from all those taking shelter at the steps, slowly and carefully.

Kells quickly put away his phone and started shouting at Valberg to get down and take cover. To come back. The Chief Superintendent went quiet when he saw Valberg take off his leather jacket and polo top and throw them on the ground.

'Dear Jesus, Jon. Jon,' Kells pleaded. 'You have to come back. I've just been told …'

But it was too late, Valberg was out of earshot.

17

Valberg momentarily looked back at Kells. His superior was now being restrained by other officers from going out to grab him. For a brief moment Valberg thought that Kells was as mad as he was.

Valberg raised his right arm and walked towards the body in the chair, his phone to his left ear.

'Okay. I've my top and jacket off, and I'm walking to the chair. You've humiliated me enough. I'm putting my trust in you. Or my faith. I'm just now approaching the body.'

'What do you see?'

Valberg stared at what was in front of him and shook his head.

'Gerry, have you, or someone else, made a last-minute entry for the Turner Prize? If so, it's sure to win.'

'What do you see?'

'He's dead ... Wait, his stomach is moving ... What's in his stomach, Gerry?'

'What's underneath him, Jon?'

'A rat in a bag. Tied around his dick. And I hate rats. You fucking know that.'

'Murophobia, Jon? Wow. A real test for you. Release the rat. Test yourself. Can you do it?'

'Why? What's the point? I could just let this performance art continue.'

'Stay put. Don't be hasty. If you release the rat I'll give you a clue. The shooter is close. Probably trained on your head. Sometimes things are so obvious we don't see. I tried to talk her out of it.'

'Her?'

Valberg was terrified. And he felt like a coward. Not because he could be shot dead at any time but because of his fear of the rat. It had him in a trance.

'Have you released our furry friend yet, Jon?'

Valberg got down and examined the plastic bag tied around Bostridge's genitals. He tried to gently pull the bag down with his right hand but it was no good. He was afraid of the rat. He flinched back as soon as it moved.

'Jon. Jon. What are you doing?'

Valberg could see Bostridge's stomach moving.

'He's alive. He's alive. We have to get him help.'

18

'What does a rat do when it's cornered, Jon?'

'I dunno. Eat its way out?'

Valberg was frozen. Flying bullets meant nothing to him, but the rat held him transfixed.

'Have you released Roderick yet?'

'Roderick?'

'Roderick, the rat. Release Roderick. From *The Life of Brian*. Don't you get it?'

Valberg looked at Bostridge's eyes. They were the eyes of a dead man. Wide open and vacant.

Valberg took a deep breath. He didn't feel cold at all. He shivered a little but tried to hide it. It was his reaction to the rat he couldn't control.

'Is there another bomb inside his stomach, Gerry? Another suspect device that I need to run from? More explosive material? And where the fuck are you?'

'Oh, I don't know what they've done. I'm just a shadow anyway. A shadow shedding skin. Picking scabs. Every day. Every day, Jon, I'm fading away. My best years behind me. I'm not the man I used to be. My body is abandoning me. I don't have long, my friend. You better believe that.'

Just then, Valberg spotted more movement at the bottom of Bostridge's stomach.

'It's another fucking rat, Gerry. Isn't it? It's going to eat its way out.'

'I must have told her about our rapist friend, Grimestone. Remember? I was going to do that to him. I came to enjoy her visits. If divine justice hadn't presented itself with that cross falling on his head, I was going to torture him to death. I was going to put a rat inside him. But a rat inside the lawyer will do now.'

'I fucking hate rats.'

'Let it gnaw its way out. Then release Roderick.'

Valberg watched stitching on the lower part of Bostridge's stomach start to come undone, while liquid and small pieces of intestines began to gently ooze out. Whatever was in Bostridge's large stomach was now frenzied and about to escape. Valberg looked on in horror, helpless.

'Jon. Jon. Are you with me? You'll need some therapy sessions by the time this is over and ...'

19

Then Bostridge's stomach opened. Valberg fell back on the ground as a rat tumbled out and scurried away towards the River Foyle.

Valberg could now see the other rat frantically writhing inside the plastic bag as blood, bile and liquid from Bostridge's stomach poured down over it.

Valberg refused to play anymore.

'I'm leaving, Gerry.'

'Careful, Jon. What time is it? *A que hora?*'

'Time?'

'The clock tower. Does it tell the right time? Can you see it?'

Valberg looked up directly at the clock tower in the centre of the square.

'What do you see?'

'What do *you* see, Gerry? You're here. I feel your presence. Did someone let you out on compassionate bail? Where are you? Come on. Somehow you have eyes on us here. Don't you? Where are you?'

Valberg looked closer at the clock tower and could see the female police sniper. Her weapon seemed to be pointing directly at the steps, where Kells and all the other police officers were taking shelter. Valberg could see Constable Bell and DS Wilson there, too.

'Release the rat, Jon. He's harmed no-one.'

'Gerry, what's going on? Don't tell me you've involved Diana White. Is that who you're talking about? Are you controlling all of this? Where are you?'

'She'd make a great sniper. An assassin. Deadly. It's a lonely profession. You'd like it, you know. Better than being a lackey for a law firm. Or being part of that great new police force of yours that you keep an eye on.'

'That can't be her up there. No way.'

'She's hurting. Have you no mercy? Compassion? Where's yours? Get your Gandhi head on.'

Valberg looked at Bostridge again and back up at the clock tower.

'Diana White, Gerry? Have you trained her? The girl Grimestone raped and assaulted. A correspondence course, was it? She's been visiting you. Do you think the police don't know? Is she copying you? But it can't be her.'

'Maybe not. Your eyes just playing tricks on you. Control, Jon. Control. She wants control. We all do. Release the rat and she'll vanish.'

'Look, Gerry, she won't get out of that building if she's in there. You know that. You're fucking about as usual. I don't believe you.'

'Jon, relax. This has been nice until now. Release the rat and end this. And just as I'm ruminating – fucking Irish people spend so much time looking at monsters and demons from their past, they miss the present. Just like you. Get with the programme, Jon, and get up to date. Before it's too late. I'm a dying man. Not long to go. Too many bumps on the head. You need to believe that.'

'Fuck you, Gerry. Fuck you and fuck your state of health.'

Valberg paused again and took another deep breath. He put the phone down and lay underneath the chair and with both hands pulled the bag from Bostridge. Liquid splashed everywhere. The rat scuttled over Valberg and ran towards the river, almost instinctively. It stopped and seemed to Valberg to be looking back at him momentarily, then darted away.

Valberg swore angrily as he stood up. It was his way of releasing the tension in his body and his genuine fear. He looked immediately up at the clock tower, but the female sniper was gone. Then there was more shooting, but this time rapid fire, and the bullets were hitting the ground all around Valberg. He was certain now all the shooting was coming from the cityside.

Valberg watched a massive Culture Year banner that had been draped over the main building in Ebrington Square fall, as if in slow motion, to the ground. He dived for cover behind the bulk of Bostridge, but the shots were coming closer. He looked back again to make sure the female sniper was not behind him in the clock tower. He was pinned down.

He scanned the ground for his mobile phone. A bullet smashed it to pieces. Then a shot hit Bostridge's head and Valberg was covered in brain matter. He rolled over as a multitude of shots riddled Bostridge's body.

Valberg had never been so close to a human body actually being shot. The thud of each bullet got Valberg's attention.

He watched the exit wounds erupt each time. He thought he was lying in a trench in the First World War, hearing the pounding of bullets on human flesh.

Bostridge was hit so many times his body had now fallen over backwards, and to the side, facing Valberg. But he was still securely nailed to the chair.

Voices started shouting that the shooter had been spotted at Foyleside shopping centre.

Then it all stopped and there was complete silence. This was quickly filled with the noise of sirens and more shouting.

The rats were gone.

Valberg lay on the ground and stared at the lifeless eyes of Victor Bostridge close to him. He imagined the terrible squeals of pain and desperate struggles suffered by Bostridge after he had been stripped naked and nailed to the chair as someone perpetrated this horrendous last act of torture. He also saw that Bostridge's mouth seemed to be stuffed with something, but Valberg just shook his head. He didn't want to know what was in there.

He rolled on his back again and sensed himself drifting away while a pool of blood started to seep in his direction. He began to think of the White family and the fact that he hadn't visited them since the collapse of Raymond Grimestone's trial. Now he certainly would.

As he lay there on his back, Valberg noticed some breaking blue sky fighting its way through the heavy, hanging, grey clouds of Derry that were ever present, even in May.

All of a sudden, the song *I've Got The Power*, by Snap, came into his head. He recalled dancing to it one time in a nightclub in Stockholm.

He was there now, momentarily, as the sound of urgent footsteps hurried towards him. It was the last time he could remember being stripped to the waist, totally intoxicated and dancing. He had ended up regaining consciousness in the apartment of a Swedish girl, brandishing a new tattoo of a small skull on the back of his right shoulder. He had no memory of how he got it. All he could remember was dancing in the club with two blonde girls and he wished he could be there now.

Time froze. He stopped the noise of the police and ambulance sirens getting closer to him in his head. He replaced their blue flashing lights with the flashing strobe lights of a disco. He halted the rush of feet towards him, too, and paused the moment in his imagination.

The only thing he couldn't stop was Bostridge's blood flowing towards him. It was the colour of Valberg's favourite Brunello Di Montalcino, warming the cold ground of the square. It was the red blood of a battlefield. It was weaving its way to Valberg along the golden-clay surface of the square.

But everything and everyone was coming closer by the second so he had to snap back. He was no longer dancing in Stockholm. He knew he had to move before the blood reached him.

He felt the urge to get up and keep running as far as he could until he collapsed with exhaustion, or found the edge of a cliff so he could jump into the sea. He wanted to feel himself weightless in the water, under no obligation to speak or communicate with anyone. He wanted to be lowered to the bottom of the ocean in a diving bell, on his own, to find peace and comfort. Falling to the bottom of the ocean was Valberg's sense of being saved.

CHAPTER 4

The comfortable silence in Valberg's head was replaced with pandemonium and panic. Paramedics rushed to Bostridge as Valberg pointed at him and pushed them away from himself.

'Jon, are you okay? Jon.' Kells was shouting.

Valberg looked up, slightly disorientated, and noticed that, behind everyone standing over him, the blue sky was finally breaking through. He even sensed the sun, somewhere, although he wasn't sure exactly where it was.

'The guitar solo in *Mr Blue Sky* by ELO comes really quick in the song, David – perhaps too early, don't you think?' Valberg asked, still lying on his back.

Kells was confused. 'What did he say?'

Valberg was lost in thought. 'Where did we go wrong? Then there's Mr Night. Briefly referred to in the song. But now he's coming,' Valberg said, still lost in thought.

'Get him up. For God's sake. Someone check him,' Kells demanded. He helped Valberg to his feet and gave him back his polo top and leather jacket.

'Has anyone got something to clean him with?' Kells asked.

Two paramedics were allowed through to assist Valberg, but he signalled to them that he was fine. He cleaned himself with the towels they gave him and put his top and jacket on. As he did so, he examined the buildings around the square and could see that they were beginning to clear. There was no-one left in the clock tower.

There was complete chaos around him.

Valberg began to pick up on the drama unfolding in the city centre. He could hear more police sirens from there as well. His attention became focused on what he could see of the Foyleside complex.

A massive fireball explosion and the cymbal smash of shattered glass emanated from the shopping centre. Valberg flinched. The explosion and crashes were followed by thick black smoke rising in the air.

Valberg looked at Kells and could see the despair on his face.

'X marks, or may mark, the spot of the sniper. Destroys all the evidence once again. I just hope no-one is injured, David. Jesus. City of fucking Culture. Looks like a great year ahead. Blood on the streets, rats, scum, gunfire and explosions. It's great to be back.'

Kells looked sternly at Valberg, too worried about civilian fatalities and injuries at Foyleside to have time for sarcasm. Better to be helpful.

'Can someone get me over to Foyleside? I want to see what's destroyed. Hurry. Someone ...' Valberg said looking around him. 'Or will I drive my motorbike over the Peace Bridge?'

Amid the pandemonium, Valberg was ushered away by Constable Bell and DS Wilson out of the square. It quickly became a crime scene as forensic teams swept in with tape and cameras and video equipment.

Valberg stopped in the rush and saw the body of Victor Bostridge being trundled away. He remembered the day he watched him being stretchered out of Derry Courthouse after he had personally tried to strangle the lawyer. His actions that day were futile and he regretted his behaviour.

Valberg remembered being questioned at length during Raymond Grimestone's rape trial at Derry Courthouse by Charles Creswell QC, the barrister acting for Grimestone, without Bostridge objecting or trying to help. He also recalled hearing about his mother's death that day and being driven to the City Cemetery to see her body, frozen in the snow, lying on top of the grave of his father and brother. But the desolation and futility of Bostridge's murder was consuming Valberg. Whatever he thought of the lawyer, he didn't deserve this. Bostridge seemed to have collapsed the trial of Grimes-tone for no apparent reason and Valberg was angry that day. But such anger didn't mean that he had no sympathy or compassion for the man now. How could he not?

The manner of his death was grotesque. It also reminded Valberg of Gerard O'Driscoll's killing spree in Derry in 2011. What if O'Driscoll had escaped from prison or perhaps had planned and orchestrated this whole event? Valberg felt that O'Driscoll was present in Derry or at the very least was involved in the planning and execution of what had happened at Ebrington with help from others.

Valberg's concentration was broken by Wilson.

'Bostridge's father was the trial judge—'

Valberg was still looking back at the paramedics dealing with the lawyer.

'Don't tell me – the trial judge at O'Driscoll's trial? He's already dead, I take it?'

'Yes. Suicide. A few years back. It's another old case I'm going through. Just to make sure it was suicide.'

'And his name, Linda?'

'Sir Ronald Bostridge. Ronnie, to his friends.'

Valberg, Wilson and Bell moved over to a police car waiting to take them to Foyleside. Valberg assumed command again.

'Linda, can you or Michael find out if any record is kept of every policeman and woman here today? Particularly those in the Tactical Support Unit. The armed officers who took over all the buildings. They're leaving now, but I never really recognise these people. I never pay any attention to them. Do you? Probably quite rude really and unprofessional.'

'I'm sure we can find out, some way.'

'Below the radar way, please. If you can.'

Bell was keen to help, too.

'It must be recorded somewhere, in some format.'

'Well, can one of you get on it if you don't mind?'

Linda asked, 'Is there a name in particular you're looking for?'

'Yes. Just one name. But it won't be on the list. It's impossible, the more I think about it. But check anyway. Let's go, I'll get my bike later.'

Valberg was certain Diana White had not joined the PSNI within the last year to become a member of a specialist unit trained in weaponry. That just could not be possible. O'Driscoll was messing with him yet again.

CHAPTER 5

For the duration of the short journey to Foyleside shopping centre Valberg ignored the frantic radio calls to the car, the constant ringing and beeping of police-issued Black-Berry phones, and the deafening noise of sirens blaring all around them.

He was deep in thought about Diana White and her family. Not because he was struck with emotion, thinking about their grief, but because he was playing over and over again the last telephone conversation he had with his father. He couldn't erase it from his memory. It was a telephone call he took in the presence of Diana's parents from his father in the Foyle Hospice.

Valberg could hear the weak voice in his head.

'I'm not sick. Just feeling tired.'

Valberg stared out over the top deck of Craigavon Bridge, where all the traffic was backed up. He was thinking about the number of times he was stopped with his father at police and army checkpoints on the bridge as a teenager.

He wondered if he would really like to be back in that time. Back with his father, safely in the family car and then home to his mother. But it really was a far cry from the life and stress he had inherited and lived with daily now.

Everything in his life today was rapid – constantly rushing and meeting demands. Returning telephone calls and angry emails. Back in time, life seemed slower and timeless. Life was at a more manageable and civil pace. But now, what were we all rushing towards? Demands on his time and pressures on every bone in his body. It was all stress and matters of life and death.

But no matter what, the River Foyle would keep flowing and Craigavon Bridge was as solid and permanent as ever. Concrete and metal stood strong. Immoveable in time, steady and reliable. Ever-present and a link between east and west. A link to the past, and the future.

As the traffic ground to a halt, Valberg got out of the car. He looked all around him. Even police vehicles weren't moving. Valberg wanted to walk on, on his own, but he had to stay with Wilson and Bell to get access to Foyleside. He imagined his father's car being stopped by the British Army near this spot. He could see sandbags, self-loading rifles, army berets and body armour. He felt a sense of naivety and innocence wash over him thinking about that time.

He looked back towards Spencer Road and remembered his father being animated about the bomb that had exploded in the Stairway Antique Shop. A bomb that tore the heart out of the commercial centre of the Waterside, permanently.

Valberg's father spoke constantly about that bomb. It exploded not long after he and his father had left after a browse around the shop that they visited frequently together.

'We walked past it, Josie. The bomb. It was under the stairs, I'm told. Just moments before.' Valberg recalled his father telling his mother about their escape.

The grand shop premises had been a father-and-son business that Valberg had admired, even as a young boy. It was a place of serenity and the workplace of the greatest fisherman in Derry, James Meenan, according to Valberg's father. Valberg remembered James as the politest fisherman he had ever met. He used to listen to the long conversations his father had with him about fly-fishing on the River Faughan

He could see himself waiting for his father, sensing him and James talking about him. Valberg's father was relaxed and content, full of laughter and conversation.

Those moments gone now, forever.

Valberg's patience was wearing thin and he was about to head towards Foyleside on foot when the traffic started to clear. He got back into the car and remained quiet in the back seat as it drove away, still thinking about James Meenan and the antique shop.

After a few moments, Valberg spoke.

'Michael.'

'Yes, sir?'

'Would you do something for me?'

'Anything, sir. What is it?'

'There was a bomb over in Spencer Road.'

'When was that, sir?'

'Ah. Years ago. When you were a kid.'

'Oh. I see, sir.'

'I think around the mid-eighties ...'

'Right, okay.'

'Can you see what you can hunt out about it? Anything at all. I've just remembered something. I'd like to know what happened. Don't worry now too much about it.'

'Okay, sir. Leave it with me. I'll do my best.'

'Thanks, Michael.'

Valberg recalled his father's voice again talking to his mother.

'Jimmy Meenan died today. Poor man. Never recovered from that bomb. It tore the heart out of Spencer Road, and Jimmy. I treasured taking Jon there. What a stinking war. Antique dealers as legitimate targets they said. Piffle. I must find out what happened. Well, I have to. He had three sons and four daughters. They all used to be about the shop at times. Full of life. Secure and peaceful. Jimmy loved them. That's all he talked about. Not a trouble in the world. Fishing and his children. All gone now.'

CHAPTER 6

The explosion at Foyleside was at the east car park, on the top level, facing the Foyle Embankment and Ebrington Square. By the time Valberg made it there, little was left of the burning remains of an old 4x4 Jeep Cherokee. Black, acrid smoke still smouldered from what was now wreckage.

Valberg always liked those old Jeeps. They were solid, square and totally devoid of aerodynamics. But perfect for putting a false roof on and mounting a remotely controlled rifle inside – even if it was all a decoy.

Standing at the scene of a bombsite, Valberg watched the smoke rising in the air from the vehicle and immediately realised the date – Friday 17 May and the thirty-ninth anniversary of the Dublin and Monaghan bombings of 1974. Two years also since O'Driscoll's killing spree. Every tragedy had a point in time.

What damage bombs can do. What utter carnage and wanton violence they bring – especially to innocent victims. Valberg and his father were lucky when they left the antique shop on Spencer Road. They missed the bomb, or the bomb missed them.

Tiredness was catching up on Valberg. He knew the only way to fight it was to keep focusing and thinking about the crime scene in front of him. He also knew that there was a real danger of a wave of post-traumatic stress after what he had just gone through at Ebrington.

He surveyed the scene. He watched everyone just trying to

do their fruitless best. Even with every security and CCTV camera working in Derry, the PSNI still wouldn't catch who set this up. It was too elaborate and professional.

Valberg now also discounted Bell's theory that there were two shooters from the same location. The other shooter was elsewhere. And had there been anyone here at all? He doubted that now. Was there any shooting from here at all? Were the police drawn to the dramatic explosion, to lure them away from a more logical and simple location? Valberg wished he were back over in Ebrington, studying the west bank of the city.

Valberg turned to Bell and Wilson and then looked all around him.

'They'll be looking for evidence, five or six hundred yards away. Everywhere. On rooftops and the streets. Just what whoever set this up wants. You both know the PSNI have evacuation distance protocols to follow in the wake of a bomb threat. Whoever did this knows that setting a bomb off on a rooftop is a horror story for an investigator. The evacuation distance demonstrates how far evidence can travel. The police are scurrying around like ants searching for food. With my back to the Foyle, hard as it was, I didn't sense any shooting from this location. Even less so when lying on the ground. Surely someone would have spotted shots being fired from here? This is a hoax.'

Bell and Wilson looked all around them but didn't answer Valberg.

'Then there's another problem. I've no investigative ... well, no authority or power here at all. I'm sure you've spotted Wally nosing around already. Take me away and let everyone get on with what they have to. The Serious Crime Unit will be in charge here and take over any investigation. So let's go.'

'To where, sir?' asked Bell.

'We need to find Diana White. And a better location to shoot at Ebrington Square from.'

Bell's BlackBerry rang.

'Sir, it's the Chief. He needs to talk to you, urgently.'

Valberg took Bell's phone.

'Yeah. What joy do you have for me? We're at the scene of a decoy.'

'I have the stuff of nightmares. A nightmare worse than all the nightmares you've ever had.'

'Well. What is it?'

'He's out of the Maze. O'Driscoll. Two nights ago.'

Valberg moved away and turned his back on Bell and Wilson.

'Released? Surely not?'

'No. Worse than that.'

'What could be worse than Gerard O'Driscoll released from prison?'

'Gerard O'Driscoll escaping from prison.'

'You're not serious. Jesus. That place is more secure than Fort Knox. With only one inmate … and purposely built, at a cost of millions.'

'It's such an embarrassing mess. I was told just as you stepped out towards Bostridge. But it was too late to get you back. And I didn't believe it. So I needed more information – I've just got it. I didn't want to mention it at all at Ebrington until I had the confirmation I needed, or in case someone overheard. I'm still not sure if I believe it.'

'I spoke to him on the phone. I presumed it was O'Driscoll. He called me. Are my calls still recorded? You would know. How on earth could he escape?'

'The word is he may have had inside help. Every officer is in custody under the Terrorism Act, being questioned up in Antrim and Belfast since it happened. There's a media blackout. Some journalist did get wind of it, but there's a High Court injunction in place forbidding the news being broken on any grounds. One of those "Super Injunction" things.'

'What do you mean?'

'His escape couldn't be reported. But it will now.'

'He is here, then. He's watching us. He's set this whole thing up, but with help, I suspect.'

'His entire route out of the prison has been recorded. He knew exactly where to go. He just walked up the road outside the prison and jogged away. The whole thing was filmed, but he delayed the live feed. When the actual CCTV footage was being viewed outside the prison, they were watching everything an hour late. Couldn't make it up.'

'Jesus.'

Valberg remembered how he felt when he heard his father was a jury member at O'Driscoll's trial. It had greatly disorientated him. He was still in the depths of survivor's guilt because of the murder of Detective Constable Finbar Callaghan outside the University of Ulster Magee campus, blown up in a car bomb intended for Valberg.

He had that sensation now. There was just too much to register and analyse quickly. O'Driscoll's escape had consequences for a lot of people, including Valberg.

'Like I said, Jon, the whole thing is captured on CCTV footage. Even O'Driscoll waving bye-bye to the camera in his cell, I'm told. I've also heard he ordered pizzas to the prison after he left, and it was the delivery guys who arrived first at the prison and raised the alarm. They were then followed by an army of security and sirens.'

'Like you said, David – couldn't make it up. I'll have to tell Linda and Michael here. It's only fair.'

'Well, national security is at stake, and an injunction is in place, so be careful. I'm not even supposed to know. But it'll be out soon.'

'Right. I'm off.'

'Off where?'

'To find Diana White. And a better place to shoot at Ebrington from.'

'But you're still technically suspended.'

Valberg raised his voice in anger and turned around.

'Oh. Great. And was I technically fucking suspended a while ago when you called for my help and I stepped out into a firing range? Who was my employer then? Who was I working for in that moment? You tell me. Technically unsuspend me, some bloody way. On the other hand, I can go as a citizen of the EU. Your choice. Nevertheless, I'm going. I'll make a fucking citizen's arrest if I have to. Fuck you.'

'Okay. Do it. We'll talk later. Sorry. You're right. Sorry.'

Valberg hung up and handed the phone back to Bell.

34

'Thanks, Michael. We're still looking for Diana White. We'll try her home.'

Valberg looked around him again and at the Jeep, still smouldering. It was a scene of chaos. He could sense Wilson's stare on him.

'Well, Jon, what is it now?'

'I'll fill you in on some national security on the way.'

CHAPTER 7

As the three officers got back into their car, the noise and hysteria going on around them outside was replaced by the relative quiet inside the vehicle.

Valberg said, 'Michael, would you turn off the police radio before it starts going mad again? And can both of you ignore your phones if they ring? Please. Let's get out of here, if you don't mind.'

'Where to, sir?'

'The Whites' place. Out the Mullenan Road, Michael. An old farmhouse near the border. They renovated it. The last time I was there was the night of ... well, forget that for the moment. Out the Mullenan Road anyway. Away from this.'

'Sir, I have to call it in.'

'Leave it, Michael,' said Wilson. 'Just drive.'

Silence descended inside the car. It was only when they got through the lights at the lower deck of Craigavon Bridge that Valberg cleared his throat and spoke.

'Gerard O'Driscoll has escaped from prison.'

Bell immediately turned around and nearly lost control of the car. Wilson slapped her hand on the dashboard and turned around glaring at Valberg.

'Right,' Valberg said, almost defensively. 'I have just found out, and it is all unrepeatable. There's an injunction in place and all the prison guards are in custody being questioned. So I'm told.'

'When?' asked Wilson.

'Two nights ago.'

'Well, that means ...'

'I know what it means, Linda. And wherever he was firing from, he's well gone now. If he was involved at all.'

'Do the media know?'

'Presumably. On the other hand, they're abiding by the law. But this is one story that cannot be contained. He walks into custody and walks out. Whenever it suits him.'

'Was there inside help?' Wilson queried.

'Good question. Again, presumably. That's the suspicion. The whole thing is on film – as usual. He does that to tempt us. But this time with a time delay. Therefore, those outside the prison thought they were watching the whole thing live, but they weren't. He gassed the prison. Or I presume had someone do it for him. Certainly a gas mask had to be planted. He put it on and waved to the cameras and left. So I'm reliably informed.'

'But that place cost millions. There was a huge outcry about it. He was the only inmate and ...'

'I know. I know. But it's not a PSNI fuck up, Linda. It's the Prison Service's.'

'But, Jon, it's a major security problem now for the PSNI.'

'Well, can we agree both organisations are a shambles?'

Bell looked in the rear-view mirror at Valberg, uncertainty showing in his face.

'Sir. Wasn't there some story that the prison guards ...'

'What's that, Michael?'

'That they were from the SAS or something. All brought in to look after Mr O'Driscoll. Or keep him in prison, or whatever. Special Forces. Guys finished duty from Iraq and that. They took charge of all the security. The Prison Service here couldn't handle him. Or wouldn't handle him all the time, they said. A bit crazy. That's what I heard.'

'Well, I'm told they're all in custody now being questioned under the Terrorism Act. So we shall see. I don't think the PSNI will get too much out of those guys. But expect the unexpected. Trust no-one. Believe nothing. You know. The usual in this part of the world.'

'Right, sir. I see.'

'Michael, take that turn to the left. Sharp turn to the left at Nixon's Corner and up the road. I forget the number but I know the house.'

37

Both officers' phones were constantly ringing and beeping but they ignored them as Valberg had requested. Wilson remained silent, staring seriously ahead while Valberg watched her.

'Here, Michael. Left here now, up that laneway. Don't stray beyond the border or we'll be in trouble, too. Well, you two will.'

He knew immediately when they were at the right location. The first thing Valberg noticed was a wheelchair ramp at the front of the beautiful Georgian farmhouse. The ramp looked so out of place and from an architectural point of view, awful. He could see that the house had been recently renovated and painted. Much of the area around it was pristinely cemented as well to allow easy manoeuvrability around the yard for Gareth White's wheelchair.

Valberg recalled his arrival here on an awful night years before, at a scene of bloodshed and tragedy. He remembered how dark it had been. At least he didn't need to draw his gun this time or worry about how much he'd had to drink.

He thought the White family would have moved away after all they had gone through at the evil hands of the rapist Raymond Grimestone. How could they live every day with the futility of it all?

CHAPTER 8

Felicity White came to the door. Valberg could see that she had aged rapidly. She looked smaller now as well. Shrunk into herself and half-drowned in the pool of misery so unfairly inflicted upon her and her family by Grimestone.

'Jon. You finally came. After all this time. Where have you been?'

She looked at his attire, puzzled as to why he was so informally dressed. Valberg stammered out an explanation.

'I'm here now. I'm sorry. Can I come in? Just me. I won't be long. I was called to an incident today. I was just out a spin in my new motorbike – hence the dress sense.'

'The other officers are welcome in, too, Jon. But whatever it is you want or are here about, it's good now. Gareth is asleep. The house is quiet when he's asleep.'

Felicity White turned away from the door and let Valberg follow her.

Valberg turned to Wilson and Bell.

'I'll not be long. Keep an eye on anyone coming or going.'

Wilson just nodded her head in acknowledgement.

As Valberg walked through the front door he noticed in a room to his left that Gareth White was sleeping, propped up in bed. The room was kitted out like a dimly lit hospital ward. Valberg could smell the scent of a hospital, too.

Gareth White was completely unrecognisable to Valberg. Grey, gaunt, and looking as though he had no muscle tone. He was a sorry sight. Valberg stopped and stared at him through the half-open door. His concentration was broken by Felicity.

39

'That's what Diana sees every day she comes home. Her disabled father, sleeping or just gazing at the ceiling when he's awake, making those horrible sounds. It takes me a while to calm him. He shouldn't be here. I really mean it. He should be dead. We got twice the punishment.'

Valberg remained staring at Gareth until Felicity motioned to him. 'Here, this way, Jon. I'll make a cup of tea.'

Valberg didn't answer. He walked on into the farmhouse kitchen which had views to the side and rear of the house.

On sitting down, he noticed all the ordinary things that make up a family life: photographs, paintings, postcards, plants, and clothes drying beside a Rayburn cooker. He focused and searched for photographs of Diana. There were several of her alone, smiling, but none of her with a rifle in her hands. Plenty of others with her father before his injuries adorned the kitchen.

Felicity poured the tea and Valberg asked how Diana was.

'Diana? Oh. Well, she's okay I suppose. For a child who was repeatedly raped and lost her father. And her whole life. Okay for that. No amount of therapy can save her. She even got her law degree but didn't want to be a lawyer.'

'Like me, then.'

'Well, she's doing some Master's thing now in human rights law. She doesn't talk much. I used to have an image of her in court as the non-speaking lawyer. She would just use expressions and present documents. Her face would usually tell the story. She used to wake up in the middle of the night, screaming. Then her father would do the same. I'm so helpless. Do you know what that can do to a mother? A life of innocence, pony rides and trips to the seaside. All gone in an instant.'

'I'm sorry ...'

'Sorry for what, Jon? Getting yourself on the television and your name in the paper and forgetting about us and ...'

'I've never forgotten about you. Or Diana. Never.'

'Well, once you became the Derry celebrity policeman you never came near us. Did you?'

Valberg looked around the kitchen again.

'No. You didn't.'

'I'm sorry. I'm so sorry.'

'So what brings you here now?'

'It's delicate.'

'Delicate. There's a word. Delicate. What's delicate, Jon?'

'I need to ask you a bit more about Diana.'

'Right. Study and shooting. That's all she does. No boyfriends or girlfriends. Her eyes turn in her head if you ask her. She studies so hard. For what, I don't know, as she never wants to be in a court again in her life.'

'Shooting? You said shooting.'

'She joined that club down the road. Here, I'll get you all her prizes.'

'No need. It's okay.'

'Well? So what?'

'We know she visited Gerard O'Driscoll. When he was in prison in England. Obviously you heard about O'Driscoll's killing spree some time ago?'

'I know he was responsible for Grimestone meeting his maker. The system let him off. I can only be grateful for that. O'Driscoll's back here now, Jon. Isn't he? But she didn't visit him here. Sure, no-one is allowed into that new H-Block place. There was a whole outcry about it, wasn't there?'

'Do you know if she was in contact with him in any other way?'

'Jon. For God's sake. How could that be? You police would know better than me. She's very private. We don't have a normal mother-daughter relationship. Grimestone took that, too. Another death. We don't exactly go out picking dresses together. And don't forget, he raped me, too. For a long time. I was taped to—'

'I know … I know.'

Valberg hadn't forgotten. He couldn't forget it.

'I can't cry anymore. I'm void of emotion. Just an existence. My quality time is when Gareth is sleeping. That's what my life is now. That's my expectation each day. Waiting for him to sleep so I can read a magazine or weep to myself. That's all I have. I'm not looking for sympathy or pity. But that's my lot. We never harmed anyone. We always tried to do the right thing – and look at what happened to us. There's no justice. Dead people escape it. But with no justice there is injustice. And with no afterlife, injustice has a free reign.'

Valberg allowed Felicity to continue without interruption. Eventually, she paused and gathered her emotions. She looked directly at Valberg.

'I'm told what meds to give him, and it's tempting. And who would blame me?'

'For what? What is it that's tempting?'

'Over-medicating. Who would blame me? Bet you're glad to have called now, Jon. We don't live in happy land anymore. Do we?'

Valberg thought it best to try and steer the conversation back to Diana.

'I need to talk to your daughter.'

'She'll be home soon. She went into town.'

'Have you had the news on?'

'No. Never. I don't care for it anymore. Why would I?'

The noise of a car entering the back of the yard at speed caused Felicity to rise and look out the window.

'Oh. There she is now, Jon. Driving too fast as usual.'

Valberg sprang to his feet. He saw the car hesitate momentarily then veer past the police car and screech down the laneway.

'Was that Diana?'

'Aye. What's wrong, Jon?'

Valberg recalled her hair had been brown, but it was clearly dyed blonde now.

The noise and commotion woke Gareth. Groaning and grunts could be heard from the makeshift medical bedroom.

'Jesus. That's him wakened now.'

'I have to go. We need to speak to your daughter. Can you give me a number for her?'

Felicity wrote out the number for Valberg, who was clearly now in a rush to leave. She had to raise her voice over the noises coming from the bedroom.

'Call again, Jon. Any time, even a flying visit like today.'

'We have to go. If we don't get Diana would you ask her to contact police at Strand Road?'

Felicity just looked at Valberg, expressionless. She closed the door after him as if she were putting him out of her home.

'Sir, that was her, wasn't it?' Bell asked.

'Yeah. I believe so.'

'She came in from the back of the house, she was too quick for us to stop her. We have all the details of the car. But there's a problem.'

'What's that, Michael?'

'She turned left at the bottom of the lane. I think she's headed towards the border. She'll be over it by now at the speed she's going.'

Wilson cut in.

'Jon, you have no authority here, and we've no jurisdiction to do anything in Donegal. What do we do?'

'Drive me to the border.'

CHAPTER 9

Bell drove rapidly towards the border with County Donegal. The Mullenan Road was broad and clear, with little traffic in either direction. Valberg didn't care if Bell crossed into Donegal but he didn't want him or Wilson getting into any trouble. He sensed that Bell would do whatever he asked him, nonetheless.

'Sir, in about twenty seconds or so we are over the border. The sat nav confirms it. Sir, what do we do?'

The old disused customs station was coming into view on the left-hand side of the Mullenan Road. Valberg could see Diana's red Mini Coupe with its personalised number plate, DuI LAW, parked facing away from them in an adjacent lay-by.

Bell said, 'That number plate would never pass an MOT test. But that's her car, sir. We have to stop here. We can't go on. She's across the border. What do we do?'

'You stop. Both of you, wait here. Pull in and put your emergency warning lights on but no siren. Just here on the grass verge and let me out.'

Bell pulled in and Valberg could see the road sign confirming that the speed limit was 80km per hour, marking the entry point to Donegal and the Republic of Ireland. Bell put on all the flashing lights.

'Sir. I need to radio this in.'

'Do what you have to, Michael. But I'll get out.'

'Careful, Jon,' said Wilson.

'Of course.'

44

Valberg remained focused firmly on the car. There was no crime here. Nothing to report, he thought. Just a vehicle carefully parked in a lay-by. He was still suspended from the PSNI. He wasn't officially on duty. He was offering assistance. That's all this was. But he had his usual sense of doom. His attention was distracted by Bell.

'Here, sir. Do you want my gun?' Bell offered.

Wilson stopped Bell taking his gun out by raising her arm and shaking her head. She stood on the front passenger side of the PSNI car with the door open, facing the border.

Valberg heard Wilson say, 'You can't do that, Michael. Don't even remove your weapon.'

Valberg looked back as he approached the car, signalling with his hand in the negative.

'She's right, Michael. Put it away.'

Valberg closed out everything around him. He didn't want to contemplate what would happen if the car exploded, but his past experience meant he couldn't stop the fear flooding back.

The car windows were tinted and it was hard to see in. But as Valberg got closer he could see the outline of someone in the driver's seat. He called out.

'Diana. Is that you? Diana. It's Jon. Jon Valberg of the ... of the police. I just want to talk to you. Diana, can you hear me?'

Valberg got closer and looked in through the front windscreen. Diana was slumped over. He tried to get the driver's door open. It was locked. He roared to Bell.

'Call a fucking ambulance. Do it now!'

'North or South, sir? Altnagelvin or Letterkenny?'

Valberg didn't answer. He banged on the side window but got no response. He tried to open the passenger door but it didn't budge. He was still roaring at the top of his voice for Diana. He looked around and saw some large rocks on the side of the road. He picked up the heaviest he could manage and launched it onto the front of the car to see if it would spring open the central locking system.

There was a huge crash and Valberg had to dive away from the rock bouncing back on him. The car alarm went off, the airbag engaged, and the central locking clicked open. Part of the smashed front grid fell to the ground.

Valberg rushed to the driver's door and pulled it open.

Diana was saturated in blood, made all the messier by the airbag inflating. By now, Bell was at his side, having taken off the top part of his uniform before crossing the border. He helped Valberg pull Diana out of the car and switched off the alarm.

Bell handed Valberg a first-aid kit he'd taken from the police car.

'We should get her back over the border, sir,' Bell said quietly out of earshot of Wilson, who was now on her phone.

Valberg continued to shout at Diana to bring her round as he carried her the few metres back into County Derry.

Using a small penknife, Bell shred the airbag in Diana's car and reversed the vehicle across the border and up onto the grass verge. The emergency services from both jurisdictions began arriving in a hail of sirens and flashing lights.

Valberg had cleared most of the blood now from Diana as she lay on the ground but he couldn't get her conscious. As he knelt over her he could see one deep vertical cut to her left arm. He tried his best to improvise a tourniquet, using whatever he could find in the first-aid box

'She's still alive. But I think she's taken something as well. Check the car, Michael.'

A tap on his shoulder by a green-uniformed medic from Altnagelvin Hospital, made Valberg stand up and step back. He knew now to get out of the way.

He looked around for Bell who by now had his full uniform back on.

'What a fucking day,' Valberg said to Wilson as the paramedics worked on Diana and got her ready for transportation. He felt light-headed as he looked around. It was like a standoff between North and South Korea. It was plainly ridiculous. Rules and regulations, laws and customs, stopped the lawful authorities crossing the divide to help each other, for fear of an international incident. Just stupid.

Valberg knew well what he and Bell had just done, and Wilson had witnessed. But all that mattered was Diana White's life. This stupid Korean standoff was an irrelevance.

46

His attention was drawn towards one Garda uniformed officer standing on the Donegal side of the invisible border crossing. He could see the tall officer staring at him and Valberg felt a pang of guilt. He realised that with the way he was dressed, he didn't remotely look like a police officer. Nonetheless, he decided to walk over to his colleagues, as it seemed the appropriate and proper thing to do. He wasn't on duty and still suspended but he wasn't going to get into all that.

'I think we're all okay here, gents,' Valberg said. 'Thanks for coming, but it's under control at our end.'

Even as he said it, Valberg felt his choice of words was plainly daft. He could see the Garda officer staring at Diana's car. He could also see him looking down at the smashed grid and the rock Valberg had used to activate the car alarm in the lay-by. The officer seemed to Valberg to be piecing together what had happened.

He turned away, embarrassed by what he had said, searching for Wilson.

Then it all hit Valberg hard. He felt a rush of emotion. He knew this was not the time or place for a mental breakdown, but if he didn't do something, he felt he was going to go out into the middle of the Mullenan Road and start screaming.

'Linda. Linda.'

'What is it, Jon?'

'Linda. Linda. I'm breaking. I'm not frozen anymore. I'm broken. This is it. No more. I'm going. I feel really weak. It's just come over me. When tiredness comes on me, suddenly like this, I can't control it.'

Valberg held out his left arm and turned it around, thinking about a previous failed suicide attempt he'd witnessed.

'Janice was horizontal and shallow. Diana, vertical and deep – the classic obvious sign of a real suicide attempt. We all know that.'

Wilson recalled the name of Janice Sloan, a homeless teenager Valberg had tried to help who had self-harmed and committed suicide.

Valberg made a horizontal and vertical motion with his right hand to the underside of his left arm.

'What?'

'Diana really meant to kill herself. The injury was so fucking deep. I was looking inside her arm. I could see the bone. That's not an easy cut to make.'

Suddenly Valberg stumbled forwards into Wilson's arms and went faint.

Bell and other PSNI officers hurried to help. But not before the nearby Garda officer stepped quickly over the border and got to him first. He grabbed Valberg's right hand and steadied him on his feet.

'Jon. Jon Valberg? I know who you are. Look, you'll be okay, Jon. Help is coming.'

Constable Bell and the Garda officer eased Valberg gently to the ground. A female paramedic started checking for his pulse. She had difficulty finding it and placed an oxygen mask over his face.

'We need to get him into the ambulance as well. Now!' the paramedic shouted to her colleague who was attending to Diana.

Valberg's eyes flickered and all he could see was the tall figure of a Garda officer standing over him, staring intently. Then all faded into darkness.

CHAPTER 10

Valberg was convinced he had morphed into the habitual petty criminal, Stevie McGowan. It was McGowan who had shown Valberg how to break into a car by smashing a large rock onto the bonnet to spring open the locking system.

Valberg had tried everything he could to help Stevie, but it was no use. Breaking into cars was normal for him. He couldn't drive and wasn't interested in the cars – just their contents. Crime and despair seemed to follow Stevie. Valberg had spent so much time with him and his state-benefit-reliant extended dysfunctional family, he knew them all intimately. He even fought with social services and the courts in trying to defend and support Stevie. Valberg thought there was goodness and kindness in the man somewhere. He just had to find it and show it to everyone. Valberg didn't want him getting a bullet in the leg, or the head, from a dissident IRA group.

Stevie was always late. He was even late for his appointment with Derry Action Against Drugs, the organisation that had taken on the mantle of policing the drug trade in the city. He was thirty minutes late to be exact for his pre-arranged midnight punishment shooting. Stevie had anticipated that it would be a shot to his left leg. Valberg was going to take the bullet for Stevie as his imposter. Valberg adopted Stevie's persona and was seeing everything now through Stevie's eyes.

The location for his appointment seemed appropriate – Asylum Road, Derry. Not too far from the Strand Road PSNI Station. One of the houses on the steep street was derelict.

It had a red door and was obviously abandoned. This should be a straightforward, simple matter, thought Valberg.

'You're late. You were due here last year.' Valberg was met outside the house by a man with a hoodie and a black mask covering his face. He was waiting on him. Valberg didn't recognise his voice or accent.

Valberg purposely did not reply or look at his host. This was deliberate so that he could not provide any identification evidence to the police. But he had, in his imagination, a reply to voice.

'Moron. Now I've heard your stupid voice. Stupid dickhead. Surely you boys should know to keep your stupid mouths shut.'

That was the heroin talking in Valberg's head. However, the full effects of his recent inhalation had not kicked in yet. He had not progressed to injection. Valberg hated needles and the sight of blood, even a trickle, made him nauseous.

Valberg thought he was visualising everything with laser precision. In fact, his eyes were glazed. He walked into the empty building which had its red door ajar for him. It smelled of urine and damp. Valberg made a loud sniffing noise. In the darkness he could see the outline of a handgun directing him through the house. Valberg followed it. In his hallucinogenic state he thought the gun was floating on its own. Everyone else in Derry was partying, but Valberg was turning up to be shot.

He took a deep breath and thought of his five children. They were all under six, with three different mothers and including two sets of twins. Chantelle, Mercedes, Doire, Kodi and Kash. Doire's mother, Jordyn, was by far the most reliable.

Valberg had left his Form T4 with her – 'Application for Compensation For A Personal Injury'. Valberg had studied up on the Criminal Injuries Compensation Scheme. He had his application form all filled in, expertly he believed, before he ventured out to be shot. He didn't need a solicitor and would do the entire claim himself. It was just what the government wanted. Everyone's a lawyer. No legal fees to pay.

It was better to get a bullet in his left leg. The threats against his girlfriends and children were real. He had to take his responsibilities as a father seriously. If he wanted to continue breaking into cars and stealing the contents then he had to pay the price. The anticipated shot had to be to his left leg, because that's what he had put down on the form. It was better than a bullet in the head. So best to turn up now, late as he was.

Valberg reckoned if he could only get the housing benefit sorted he could live in this house on Asylum Road with the floating handgun. Jordyn and Doire could move in. Jordyn would find the owner of the property and get it all arranged. If he could land Disability Living Allowance because of being shot, he could then get Jordyn signed up as his carer.

He just needed a grey National Health Service walking aid. One that would click on the ground to let everyone know he was nearby. Valberg would then get a set of baggy grey cotton tracksuit bottoms to match the walking aid. He would put on just enough weight to allow his belly to hang over the top of the tracksuit bottoms and cause a permanent crease on the waist band. Doire could then go to the primary school across the street. Happy days. The state would look after everyone – unless they worked for a living. Why fucking work?

Valberg would be close to his free legal-aid solicitor. And if he were facing investigation again by the PSNI, he wouldn't have far to go to sign his bail. Sweet, he thought. Happy days. Sound. Happy days.

Valberg had refrained from alcohol as directed by Lord Justice McKelvey at his last bail application. 'Not even a sherry before dinner,' as the judge had ordered. He just chased the dragon now.

But chasing the dragon resulted in dreams within dreams. Valberg was now trying to wake up and shake off Stevie Mc-Gowan.

He lay motionless waiting for someone to bring him back to reality. But not too soon. His legs felt weak now. His hands had pins and needles. His stomach was rumbling and his mouth had a metallic taste.

So perhaps it was better to continue to sleep. No-one could help Valberg and he surrendered himself. But at least there was no gunman waiting to shoot him anymore.

'I think … I think Jonny is evil. He's taking thoughts out of my head.'

'Who said that? Who's there?' Valberg shouted. 'Gerry? Gerry? Is that you? Save me. Help me. Am I evil? Do you think I'm evil, Gerry? Where are you?'

CHAPTER 11

Amanda Cleary from the *Derry Journal* took a chance. She called David Kells on his personal mobile.

'Oh, Amanda. I'm just back. I've just sat down in my office. Dear Jesus, I'm exhausted.'

'I know you won't tell me, Superintendent, but—'

'Amanda, call me David. We know each other well enough by now.'

'Well, before there's another knock on your door like the last time, can you confirm the rumour—?'

'Rumour? Derry? Rumours? Come on, Amanda.'

'Look. Is there some sort of moratorium on bad news in Derry this year, with this culture bollocks? Excuse my French.'

'The curse of the thinking class.'

'What?'

'Culture. That's what he said it was, when he was here last. And you know who I'm talking about.'

'Let's leave Jon Valberg out of this for now. I've tried hard enough on that. He's gone. Jonnie Darko. Without a trace. Head office says he's still suspended. Right? But he didn't just turn up by coincidence at Ebrington today and that border fiasco. What do you say? And this drug stuff I'm hearing about ...'

'Crime is reported as we learn about it. The public have a right to know. Justice must be public ...'

'Yeah, yeah. Blah, blah, blah. Seen to be done and all that. What's going on, David? What was all that today? It's major news all around the world. It's like a tide. Is everyone hiding in a big room somewhere? Carlin and O'Driscoll? Even Jon? Who's controlling who? What room is MI5 in there controlling the dissidents? Everything has a "Special" title. The Special Forces. Special Intelligence Wing. Special Counter Intelligence Division. A new Special Reconnaissance Regiment even. What's going on? Look. I have cast-iron sources. Something is happening. Or has happened. Or is gonna happen. Well, could it be any worse? Then there's the heroin epidemic sweeping across the estates. You know it and—'

'Amanda. Amanda. Slow down. You're going a hundred miles an hour there. There's a drug problem in this city – which I acknowledge. I have always acknowledged it.'

'Are you confirming there is a heroin problem?'

'There is a drug problem in this city, and I will leave the specifics to my officers who are investi—'

'Which officers? What are their names?'

'Hold on, my other mobile's ringing.'

'I don't hear it.'

'It's on vibrate, and it's she who must be obeyed.'

'The Chief Con? Would she talk to me?'

'No, my wife. Call me back. Bye.'

Kells hung up.

'No. No. Don't hang up. Fucker,' Amanda cursed at her mobile as she threw it down.

She was desperate to report the news and not make it. She didn't want to be a witness at Gerard O'Driscoll's upcoming criminal trial, or a witness at the much-mooted public inquiry that the British Government were content to fund – as long as legislation could be introduced to outlaw the involvement of lawyers.

Local politicians would be especially keen to know what Amanda knew. She also realised her pitch about drugs suited Kells. That was something she should have used in a longer personal conversation. It allowed Kells to get away from what Amanda was really calling him about.

'Stupid bitch,' she muttered to herself.

Amanda now, on mature reflection, had some doubts about the wisdom of her articles on O'Driscoll in the past. That was really annoying her now. She should have known better. She had become a minor celebrity as a result of her stories, but incurred the wrath of colleagues and police. Being successful in her job, she realised, was a dangerous thing in Derry. It wouldn't be long before the bile of jealously would rise and poison her.

Amanda replayed one of the messages she had recorded on her phone. She knew she was sitting on a time bomb.

'They knew he was coming and let him kill. The new PSNI. They knew. The Chief Con, Carlin – they knew. Don't tell me the holier-than-thou Saint Anna of Ardoyne didn't know. The North is in lockdown. Operation Unblinking Eye means no-one can move. They knew he was coming. And he'll go – when it suits him. A three hundred-million-pound prison and court complex won't hold him. They don't want it to. So many have helped him and supported him. And they will again.'

That was just one of a series of phone calls Amanda had recorded with an anonymous male source who phoned her constantly but she couldn't trace. She knew at some point she would give all this to Valberg.

At the moment she really wanted to ask Kells if he had any knowledge of Operation Unblinking Eye. But she never got the opportunity. That was her own fault and she knew it. She shouldn't have mentioned the heroin problem.

She tried to rationalise it all. Could she report that the PSNI had advance warning of Gerard O'Driscoll's killing spree? That the PSNI let all the innocent jurors involved in his trial die? Was it possible? Did the intelligence services know all about O'Driscoll's orchestrated activities? They would have been monitoring all calls to and from the disgraced Chief Constable, Seán Carlin. Private and personal. This wasn't the Middle East. Northern Ireland was a state, subject to the rule of law. The justice system had let a lot of people down but it wasn't corrupt. Surely not. Black Ops and Task Force Black was something for Iraq – not modern Ireland.

She knew she couldn't report on the basis of an anonymous source. A source who must know he is being recorded in all his messages. Not at the moment.

Why would the PSNI let all the jurors die? To protect what? To protect who?

Just give up, she thought. What was the point? Who cares about the truth anyway? No-one. We've all surrendered to mass consumption, she decided, and social media sites full of thoughts that should remain that way.

'I'm just another Jon Valberg cynic,' Amanda muttered again to herself.

Life is bland and soulless in Derry, Amanda mused. Like anywhere else. Mawkish tears in public and reality TV shows. No-one can afford a big house anymore, but they can afford a thousand-inch 3D Smart TV to smoke their heroin in front of on a Saturday night. Pure culture? What was going on? All this feel-good factor about Derry gave Amanda the creeps.

Amanda knew there was no point in calling Kells back on his mobile or at Strand Road station. She knew he wouldn't answer his mobile to her twice in one day. He took her calls about once a month but would never return them. Amanda realised that if she ever door-stepped him, he would never speak to her again. So in the knowledge that she would go straight to his answering service on his BlackBerry, she called him and left a mischievous message, realising it would now be a matter of record. She knew she might just be about to burn her final bridge within the PSNI. But something had to give.

The public had moved on to thoughts of the Turner Prize, Phil Coulter and Dana. All kinds of cover-up, if someone would only listen to her, thought Amanda.

Kells' mobile phone rang for a short while before it went to answering service.

'Look, David. Rumours of an intelligence scandal predating O'Driscoll. A big spook is about to be revealed. The biggest agent in recent history. Well, perhaps spook is wrong. It's an enemy within. Shite. That's wrong, too. Someone big in the PSNI. If I don't report, one of the Sundays will. Then you're in for it. Now if you give me something on the heroin, then I'll leave the other. O'Driscoll won't let us forget him. There's tension in the air and an attack is imminent. Or something. Maybe not even an attack or a spectacular, but something. It's so, so obvious. I'll get none of this printed and

I won't make the same mistakes again like last year. But someone else will. We're whores to our sources and stories. Tell me something. People can't just be killed or murdered or whatever by the state. That doesn't happen. Does it? Call me. You've got my number. Who's controlling the news this year? Who's the agent? What's breaking bad? Call me.'

It was time to look again at the memory pen of evidence O'Driscoll gave her in Foyleside car park. There has to be something here. What has she missed? Her copy was stored safely and the original was already properly delivered to the PSNI, courtesy of DCI Valberg.

She watched a shadowy video of Valberg and Chief Constable Anna Harte, with the sound switched off, having sex. All of a sudden she felt aroused in a way she had not been for some time.

'Where are you, Jon? Mentally? What are you up to? What hell have you walked into? Tell me what I've missed.'

Amanda's daughter Maya started to call her, sounding a little distressed. Amanda had made a rule she would never break. If Maya were calling for her, upset in any way, she would go to her. If any of her phones rang or an email came in, it would have to be ignored. She would not disregard her daughter. The call or email could wait. Then Amanda's mobile started to ring. She abided by her own rule and switched off the video. Her mobile went to record and Amanda attended to the love of her life. Only after ensuring Maya was asleep again did she pick up her voice message.

'Hello, Amanda. You told me to call you when ready. It's Father Doherty here. I'm a bit better. Not too sick or anything. Just a wee bit weak. I'm ready now to tell you everything. If you still want to hear it. If Jon Valberg trusted you, then so will I. But under my conditions. My confession. Will you call me, please?'

Amanda was speechless and almost afraid to call the priest back. That was the voice of a dying man, or a man who should be dead.

O'Driscoll had approached and trusted her. Valberg had trusted her and still would, thought Amanda. And now Father Doherty. Who had the most to confess of all three?

The word 'confession' confused Amanda. Why 'confession'? Or was it just a turn of phrase? It was a word that she hadn't thought of in a religious sense for some time.

'My confession.' What did it mean? Would the Derry public be ready for it? Would her editor?

CHAPTER 12

'Father Doherty. It's Amanda Cleary from the *Derry Journal*. I'm just returning your call.'

'Ah. Amanda. Thanks for calling me back. I'm a wee bit slow here on my feet. Let me get seated.'

'Take your time, Father. No rush.'

'There now. Peace at last, off my feet. I've all this stuff to take. Tablets. I never thought medication would keep me alive. Or that I would have to rely on it. Thanks be to God the main organs all remained intact after that ordeal.'

'Your health, Father, is all that matters.'

'My God. That was an awful day. I hear Jon Valberg is in hospital. I hope he's okay.'

'The hospital?'

'Aye. But knowing him, he'll be okay.'

'Right. I hope he is.'

'But, Amanda, we need to talk. I'm tired. Not long for this world. I'm a bit tortured.'

'I hope you're okay, Father. But no problem. Whatever you want and whatever way you want it.'

'I don't want to burden you. I could get some other journalist or someone else you know to—'

Amanda wasn't going to miss this opportunity and surrender it to a competitor.

'Oh. It's not a problem. You just say when you want to talk.'

'Now, then.'

'You mean right now?'

'Aye.'

'But I have my daughter here and ...'

'Tomorrow morning, then. Ten. I can do two hours. Then I will need a break for two hours. We just keep going. With God's will we can get this over in a day.'

'A day?'

'You'll need the time. Get a babysitter.'

'It's okay. My mother will help.'

'But just you. No-one else. I don't like fuss. I'm weak and don't look great. Vanity in my state and at my age. Should be the least of my problems.'

'Ah now, Father. Don't be so hard on yourself.'

'Will you come here? The parochial house, I'm on a drip and oxygen now and again.'

'Of course. I'll be there at quarter to ten. It will just be me. A recorder and a wee camera.'

Father Doherty paused.

'Hmm ... a camera?'

'If you don't ...'

'No. That's fine. I just didn't think of it. I could hear my voice in my head but I had no visual image.'

'I understand, Father.'

'Okay. I better clean up and get myself looking like that boy George Clooney.'

'That'll be easy for you, Father.'

'Ten is good.'

Amanda went to say 'Goodbye' but Father Doherty had hung up.

He had always been a tall, dark man with an athletic build – even into his eighties. He never looked like an ordinary priest to Amanda. And he certainly was a highly respected one. Amanda assumed he wanted to talk about the murderous attack on him at Long Tower Church some eighteen months before which had more than made front-page headlines. She had contributed significantly to the story. Perhaps he was going to give more information on all that. She also knew that he gave evidence at the inquest into the death of Gerard O'Driscoll's mother, Bernadette. He had discovered her body back in 1982. That, too, was all a matter of record. But what more could he add? What would be new?

She wouldn't miss the opportunity. She got her camera and digital recorder all ready and charged up for the next day. She could leave her daughter to school and go on from there. Her mother could collect Maya later.

Amanda began the process of writing out questions, even though she knew from experience that the best-laid plans usually never work out when a camera is rolling. Orders in battle rarely survive first contact. But she was a professional so spent most of the night preparing.

CHAPTER 13

At exactly 9.45am Amanda knocked on the door of Father Doherty's parochial house. An elderly woman welcomed her warmly.

'Hello. I'm Phoebe. Pleased to meet you.'

'Thank you. I'm here to see Father Doherty.'

'Oh, he's up since five this morning waiting on you. Go on in there to the living room. Straight ahead.' The housekeeper barely had the strength to keep the door open and Amanda hoped she wouldn't offer to assist her with her equipment.

Amanda loved the scent and serenity of the dated parochial house. She was apprehensive amid the religious statues and paintings and felt a ghostly pang of Catholic guilt for not believing in any of it anymore.

Father Doherty was hooked up to a drip and an oxygen bottle was connected to a mask over his mouth. He sat upright underneath a huge original oil painting of what appeared to Amanda to be the Virgin Mary with rose petals.

Amanda fixed her stare on the old man. He looked as if he had aged twenty years in one. His grey hair was now swept back, his face thin and his eyes bulging. He couldn't get to his feet but clearly had dressed himself to look like a priest as best he could. He had lost a lot of weight, even for a man in his early eighties.

After Amanda put all her equipment down she offered to shake Father Doherty's hand. He removed the oxygen mask and placed both his hands on hers in welcome.

'Thanks for coming, Amanda. Get yourself sorted. I've asked Phoebe to bring some tea before we start.'

Father Doherty's grip was cold but firm. Amanda was careful not to interfere with the drip feed to the cannula inserted into the vein on the back of his left hand.

'I could see you staring at Saint Catherine of Siena, Amanda.'

'Saint Catherine?'

'Aye. Of Siena. Not the Virgin Mary as a lot of people think. It's a beautiful painting. My favourite.'

'It is, Father. Beautiful. Absolutely stunning.'

'That woman suffered a lot. I used to pray to her quite a bit.'

'Used to, Father? I'm sure you still do.'

'Perhaps not as much as I should. Or need to,' Father Doherty joked.

The housekeeper arrived with a tray of scone bread and tea.

'Ah, thank you, Phoebe.'

Amanda could smell the freshness of the bread and expressed her appreciation to the housekeeper, too. She took a few bites of the warm scone that the butter had melted into and a sip of tea before getting her gear ready. It didn't take her long to set up the camera and digital recorder.

'Father, I will just let you speak. You say what you want.'

'Aye, but on my terms.'

'Surely. Whatever you want.'

'When I'm gone – dead. I need an assurance. This is only to be made public then. At least four weeks after I'm gone. A month. Aye, give it a month or so.'

'Father, you have it from me, but these things are never straightforward in the law.'

Amanda could see Father Doherty's discomfort when the law was mentioned. 'Well, I hope you know what I mean. But sure, not to worry for the moment, Father.'

Amanda was thinking it was better to get on with the recording.

'Aye. Not to worry, Amanda. Are you ready? I am. You'll need to think of all the questions people would have liked me to be asked. In case I miss anything, or forget.'

Amanda had a small remote control to operate the camera which was on a tripod and focused on Father Doherty. She also had a voice-activated digital recorder ready as back-up and her notepad with some questions. She believed she was as well prepared as she could be.

'Okay, Father, I'll not say much. The time and date is already recorded, so when you're ready we can begin. But ignore the camera and look at me.'

Father Doherty appeared frail but confident. Amanda was relaxed enough, thinking she had worked out the topics and the general area any discussion might lead to.

'We're recording, Father, now. On the record.'

The priest stared at Amanda. And for the first time she felt uncomfortable. It seemed to her that Father Doherty was different.

There was a pause and he took a deep breath without the aid of the oxygen mask now placed beside him. He began talking in Latin, which unnerved Amanda even more, but she recorded everything anyway.

Father Doherty paused again.

'I loved her, Amanda, but I raped her. Raped her in so many ways. Not just physically. I abused my position and I am a liar. I'm afraid I'm going to hell.'

Amanda's heart pumped hard. Even though seated, she felt dizzy. Nothing usually unsettled her on a professional basis, but this was incredible. She hid her shock well as Father Doherty continued. This was a confession. Amanda was Father Doherty's confessor. But what was he confessing to? Who had he raped?

'Don't look so shocked. The police know. Jon knows. Well, knows who my son is, not that I raped Bernadette. I hope he's okay. I've paid for it. The problem is, so have others. So many others, and I am truly sorry for that. Acts of madness. Of criminality and evil became unleashed. Cover-up and distortion. I am truly sorry. The law catches up with everyone. I may, if I am lucky, avoid its wrath and vengeance, before I die.'

'Excuse me, Father. Just for the avoidance of doubt. Who is Bernadette?'

'Bernadette O'Driscoll. Yes. I am Gerard O'Driscoll's natural, or biological, father.'

Amanda's eyes welled up. A wave of emotion ran through her as she contemplated the implications of the beginning of this remarkable confession. This was worse than the time she stood in Foyleside shopping centre believing that O'Driscoll was about to kill her.

'People are entitled to the truth, and I must unburden everything about myself and what I know, and have known, for many years. Many years. I was young. Very young. You are really only a child in your twenties. I was in love and confused. Whatever that means. Was that really so bad? That wasn't really a crime. Was it? Poor Bernadette protected me. Another secret of secrets. Paul O'Driscoll never knew. But I think he suspected. Then he was killed in that bomb. Suited me, didn't it? Terrible events. Terrible. But Gerard is my son, and I told Jon when I thought I was for hell, and lay dying in the hospital. But look at me, I'm the picture of physical and mental wellbeing.'

The last sentence was laced with sarcasm.

Amanda was quick to respond.

'Father, are you sure about this? Father. Father, please. We can leave it. Perhaps you should speak with a solicitor or something?'

'No, Amanda, I don't need the law. The law would incarcerate me and I would be a burden on the state. I think I've caused enough upheaval. Let's move on. There's a lot to get through. And ... well, I haven't long.'

'Father, I don't want to upset you doing this. It is the last thing that I would want. So please. Perhaps you should have a solicitor come here. If you confess to me then ... well, that puts me—'

'No, Amanda. No solicitor. I've heard enough confessions from solicitors alone to last an eternity. Many are tortured individuals. Let's get on with it.'

Father Doherty took a hit of oxygen from his mask before continuing.

'A solicitor would want to advise me not to confess to anything and then sign a waiver to say I didn't accept any such advice. A solicitor would know his colleagues would be wondering why he would have allowed me to confess. Lawyers hate confessions. Professionally, it never looks right. And financially, it's a disaster. Especially in these circumstances. I'm like everyone else – we all criticise the lawyers until we need one. Perhaps I need one. But I have chosen not to avail of one. So let's get on with it, Amanda.'

'Okay, Father. But we can stop any time you want. Any time at all. Just say.'

Amanda had satisfied herself professionally that she had given Father Doherty every opportunity to stop and reconsider what he was doing and to seek legal advice. She knew she was covering herself more than anything.

'Well, as I was saying. Rape. Subterfuge. Lies. Deceit. Pain. Anguish. Guilt. Responsibility. It's all there. Let's stop going around in circles. I raped her. We had an affair. I forced myself on her. More than once. And she protected me and I continued as a teacher and a priest. A fine upstanding member of the community. Sort of reminds me of the two solicitors in a way. The much-maligned Sidney Rankin and the much-respected Ian Haslette. I am much valued as I understand it. What a bloody farce. I was burning. Dying inside. Crumbling and melting, knowing my guilt. Every face, on every corner, on every street. Guilt. And the confessions I heard and presided over, when people believed in all that. A complete sham. That's all I've been. A liar and a sexual predator, perhaps. I have offended everyone. And Bernadette protected me, even when her life was taken from her. Not once. But twice. The boy became a monster. An angry monster who only recently found out the truth.'

Amanda, in a state of some shock, decided not to interrupt again unless absolutely necessary or to ask a relevant question. She took another bite of scone bread, this time a larger piece. She then took large gulps of tea, not caring that the high-quality recording equipment would pick up all the sounds of her eating and drinking.

CHAPTER 14

'I know you think less of me now and others will, too. But I'm sorry, Amanda. All these recent horrific events are the result of an act of aggression on my part. Even yesterday. It nearly all faded away. Gerard was a child who would dream at the shoreline. An altar boy who I watched over assiduously and carefully. He was magnificent, intelligent and caring. Despite all he had been through with the death of his father, even as a teenager, he was amazing. Everything caught up with him as an innocent boy who would have harmed no-one. Events outside his control ended up controlling *him*. Perhaps that's what it's like for all of us. I'd like to say it's all preordained, or there is some divine intervention. Or God's will. But that's all rubbish, isn't it? We think we control our lives. But really, our lives are in the hands of other people and circumstance.'

Amanda remained motionless and just said quietly, 'Go on, Father.'

She had learned the skill of nodding and encouraging people to speak. She even had mastered the art of the awkward silence and letting it linger. She remained in shock.

Father Doherty carefully adjusted his intravenous drip and continued.

'There's another hour or so in the bag and then it needs changed. The nurse will come. Anyway, I raped Bernadette when she tried to end our affair. I won't go into the details but I was going through what I can only describe as my personal demonic state. It was private and personal. Outwardly I was fine, but internally I was on fire and out of control. It

67

goes without question that she loved the boy. As did Paul, his real father in the eyes of so many people. What a shame . . . and a sham. I suppressed everything and moved on. It suited me. I adapted.'

Amanda was wondering if Father Doherty had raped anyone else.

'My career flourished teaching-wise and religiously. In fact, I became Ireland's only exorcist with a full papal blessing. That took me everywhere in the world. Secretly. And my own secrets came with me. I truly devoted myself to others. At times I was exorcising myself while trying to help others.'

Amanda thought that a headline outing Father Doherty as an exorcist was news enough. Now she was feeling particularly uncomfortable.

'And to this day I think I am possessed with evil and always have been. Did I pass that on to Gerard? It's fanciful stuff. Did the evil lurk inside him, then make him kill that girl? Orla Harkin. My first reaction was that he did. That the evil he had inherited from me rose and presented itself. Sometimes I wonder.'

'Well, Father, you must have been a great support to him. Especially at the time of his trial.'

'I like to think I was. And to his mother, despite what I have just told you. But I don't know. A comment from that policeman at the time. Mr Montgomery. He made some sexual comment about Gerard's mother and Gerard's likeness to me. It scared me. I think that's why I retreated from public life so much after Bernadette died.'

Father Doherty sobbed and started to lose his composure. Amanda was unsure how to react and was glad to hear a knock on the door. She left everything recording and answered it to find the nurse who had arrived early to change the drip. It gave Amanda the chance of a break and she found her way to the bathroom to compose herself.

Amanda's mind went into overdrive. Did Father Doherty help his son kill the jury members? Was he forced to, under threat of being exposed by O'Driscoll? All as incredible as an Irish exorcist with a papal blessing working in Derry. All probable. Jon Valberg would know, thought Amanda. But she would never betray a confidence or an undertaking of confidentiality. She would rather go to jail. Then she remembered the RUC's behaviour in the O'Driscoll affair. Anything was possible. She knew Valberg was a person who lived by the mantra: trust no-one and believe nothing. Amanda was starting to see the sense in that now.

She waited in the bathroom with the door ajar until she heard the nurse leave. She didn't want to talk to her or engage with her. Amanda just wasn't in the mood.

She walked nervously back into the room and immediately Father Doherty said, 'You know he is appealing the conviction?'

'I've tried to get a statement from his solicitor Christina Maguire but—'

'Watch her, Amanda. Watch her. But he has lodged an appeal.'

'With the CCRC. Criminal Cases Review Commission. Yes, I heard.'

'Well, it's true. And guess who's not standing in the way?'

'The Public Prosecution Service, no doubt.'

'Exactly. So technically he will have a clean record at that moment. And I suppose in a way his identity back. At that exact moment.'

'I suppose so, Father.'

'Sorry. I digressed there. But I'm all hooked up again. Ready to go. She's pouring this stuff into me at an extraordinary rate.'

'That's okay, Father. Can we go back a bit if you don't mind? Back to the early eighties. Nineteen eighty-two. Gerard's conviction and the period afterwards.'

Father Doherty continued.

'I was devastated when he was convicted. I held Bernadette tightly and it was all so awkward. I'd let him down, too. I'd abandoned him. Gustav Valberg in his own tormented state did his best, but it wasn't enough. He was on the jury but unfortunately wasn't the foreman. He couldn't sway the others despite all his skill and intelligence. But you see, perhaps he didn't want to. He made his own stance and that was it. Then he's haunted. A man performs his civic duty then becomes a member of the damned. But really, it was my entire fault. And to protect myself I end up as a missionary almost. But I was tormented and wracked with guilt. More so after Bernadette's death.'

'Father, I only know from paper reports what you said at the inquest. Could you tell me about all that please? If you don't mind.'

'I committed perjury as well. Swore on the bible and lied. You see, Bernadette was threatening me.'

Father Doherty shook his head.

'No. I don't like that word. It wasn't a threat. She wanted to tell the truth, as she blamed herself. She believed that her husband's murder and son's conviction were her fault, in a peculiar way. The end of their lives. That it had been all her fault. It was God's justice. God's vengeance for her love affair with me. And, Amanda, this gets worse. I'm so sorry. I was the last to see Bernadette alive and the first to see her dead.'

Father Doherty bowed his head for the first time.

'Gerard doesn't know he is the product of a violent rape. He knows I am his natural father. But what he also doesn't know is that I killed ... that I ... murdered his mother ...'

Amanda thought this couldn't get any worse.

'That female detective who worked with Jon . . . Jon . . . even he can't save me. And he's in a much more elevated position than appears. Not many know. But that young female detective ...'

'DS Linda Wilson. Father, take it easy. Please.'

'She wants to interview me. Following up a definite line of enquiry she said, into the death of Bernadette O'Driscoll. But I know what she's up to. And now there's talk of an application to the Attorney General to have a new inquest. Or if all this goes to the Public Prosecution Service I could end up charged with murder. There would be the possibility of a trial. I'll never survive that. Never.'

'Father, are you sure about all this? That may seem impertinent. Sorry. Are you sure? Really?'

'As sure as you love your daughter, Amanda. Very sure. No question about it. None.'

Amanda started to think about the quest for truth and justice. But especially the truth. What was the point here? She could see the media scrum around her about this interview . . . this confession . . . and wondered what it would achieve. The beleaguered Catholic Church was about to be hit with an atomic bomb that had the potential to wipe it out in Derry. Who else, particularly in the Church, knew about all this? There would be endless debate. Who knew what and when? And who else could be condemned over this entire affair? Then there was the move towards a public inquiry and this confession was surely relevant evidence. Everything and anything that is said or written in any format pops up somewhere. It always does. Amanda was being torn personally and professionally.

And the only policeman she trusted to help her could not be contacted.

CHAPTER 15

'Father, would you like a break?' Amanda was concerned the old priest was nearing exhaustion.

'No. It's okay. I got my bolus liquid upgrade and plenty of it. So I don't need a break now after all. Keep going. I've got more than enough fluid going into me now. At this rate I may get drowsy soon. Maybe a headache. Or both. But I want to get this over. I know the death that is coming my way – and I fully deserve it.'

'Father, that seems a bit harsh, don't you think? I'm just worried about you. I want to make sure you're okay. If I'm honest, I'm finding all this a bit upsetting.'

Father Doherty nodded in acknowledgement then stared at Amanda for thirty long seconds before speaking, his voice cracking.

'I set the whole thing up. I was strong enough then. I cut her throat and wrists with a razor blade once I got her unconscious in the bath.'

Amanda could see that this was going to get worse.

'I put her fingerprints on the blade but let it drop in the bath by accident. There was so much blood I couldn't find it. She bled to death in the lukewarm water. I searched the house for family pictures and personal items. I even found candles and lit them. Everything to try to make it look like a suicide. You know that is my main memory. I realised that even the numskull detectives in the RUC would check the candles first. To see how long they had been burning. To determine time. So I drained the bloody water now and again, my biggest mistake in fact. And I kept some hot water running to keep the body warm. To try and throw them off on the time of death. These are the little details that trip you up. If I had just cut her throat and left, that would have been better. But then it would have been a murder investigation proper. I tried, foolishly, to create some dignity, believe it or not. But there was a problem with the blood loss that eventually caused a lot of confusion. And I hadn't taken into consideration that I was under surveillance.'

'By the RUC?'

'Well, RUC or someone anyway. Perhaps Special Branch. Or someone working for the RUC in the area. It's hard to equate the description "intelligence" with the RUC and local informers. It wasn't really like the way it is today with a multitude of intelligence agencies watching each other. It was a lot simpler then. I was compromised.'

'Compromised?'

'Yes, Amanda. By someone. You see a suicide suited the RUC. It fitted all the circumstances perfectly. It especially suited the likes of Detectives Montgomery and Dickey. And, of course, our dear old friend Seán Carlin, who became the Chief Constable. And you know all about him.'

Father Doherty paused then raised his voice in anger for the first time.

'Then they all had a hold over me.'

Amanda was startled.

The old man put his head back and closed his eyes. He took a deep inhalation of air through his nose and held his breath.

The room went silent.

Father Doherty, at last, released the air from his lungs through his mouth.

'Sorry. Sorry for raising my voice ... the candles. I had to sit and wait until the candles burned out. I had even considered leaving and letting one of them start a fire. But that wasn't certain. So I sat there staring at Bernadette and looking at what I had done. I prayed for sure. But I think it was to the devil to take me. I've been doing that for decades.'

Amanda was becoming more disturbed and uncomfortable.

'I realise I've been in hell all my life, and death now might be a release for me. The easy way out. My faith is gone. This is a sham in front of you here, Amanda. And that blood. That silly mistake with the blood . . .'

'What about the blood, Father?'

'I won't dwell on it, but it was a mystery as to where a lot of her blood had gone, and again it suited the RUC not to labour over it. An assumption was made that Bernadette released the blood herself down the plughole with the water. But that would never stand up to scrutiny now. Not then, if investigated properly, and definitely not now. I was saturated in blood as well. I said it was as a result of my attempts at trying to help her. And I was commended for it. It was me who released Bernadette's blood. Into the sewer. But the candles. My God. To this day, every time I see a candle burning I'm back in that house. Raised voices and a struggle, silence, then death. Sitting with a bloody corpse in the bath waiting for the candles to burn out. Then the pretence of calling the RUC and an ambulance. I deserve what's coming to me. I always have.'

'Father, do you want a break? I know I keep asking, but are you sure you are okay to continue?'

'No. I'm fine. Press on. Get this over with please. I am to be cremated in accordance with my will, by the way. Otherwise, I am sure the righteous would dig up my grave and burn me when the truth comes out. So I'll save them all the bother.'

CHAPTER 16

Father Doherty paused again, looking at Amanda. He eventually asked her, 'Have you ever heard of Khwaja Naqib Ahmad?'

'No, Father. It's not a name I'm familiar with.'

'Ahmad is amazing. He buries the unwanted. Or parts of the unwanted . . . in Kabul. He smells of death and it lingers over him. I've read about him. If I were to be buried it would have to be by him in his graveyard. So a private cremation is best. I don't think there's a grave that can hold my body down.'

'The "unwanted", Father? What do you mean?'

'Suicide bombers. Or what's left of them. This is a suicide confession. It cuts me to pieces and will leave me in tatters.'

'Then stop now, Father, if you want.'

'No, Amanda. I must go on.'

Amanda nodded. Father Doherty's attention to detail was too perfect, she thought. Could this parochial house confession be a sham? She was beginning to doubt the authenticity of what she was hearing but thought it better to press on.

'Okay, Father. Let's go on if it suits you.'

'I've been thinking recently. Traditional authority figures. Priests, bank managers, solicitors and teachers walk in the gutter now. We receive less deferential treatment today. But I deserve what's coming to me. I walk in shadows. I live it. I always have. I have insulted everyone who placed their honest trust in me. We all have darkness beneath the surface. It rises in us eventually. Every single one of us. Those that say they don't have darkness in their being are lying.

They beguile themselves, but not others. It just depends on how you deal with it. Collectively, we are all doomed to hell. In the brightest star there is a blackness that I always see. Is there something in the air over Derry that makes this city cursed? It has cursed me. And I have cursed others and destroyed lives. I must be punished.'

Father Doherty paused and Amanda let the silence settle. She was more interested in facts and details as opposed to Father Doherty's views. Amanda could see him checking the drip feed to the cannula again before he continued.

'Jon reminded me about my many discussions in relation to the devil. About evil. It obviously made a lasting impression on him. It was in Mrs McLaughlin's house. Jon didn't know then, and I couldn't say, that I knew who was doing what. I let my guard down slightly. I think he knew that I knew more. Or suspected anyway. He sensed my emotions. How could I forget those jury members? When I heard the name William Bolton Black I realised right away what was happening and what was going to happen. If I had spoken out sooner I could have saved those other people on that jury. But I didn't . . . and just to protect myself. Then more of them were murdered. Avril Gibson and poor Paddy Sharkey. Decapitated.'

Amanda recalled the horrific deaths that had happened within hours of each other.

'You see, Jon even sensed that my faith was waning.'

'How, Father?'

'When I stood in Majella McLaughlin's living room I remember him saying that he wished he had my faith but that he sensed doubt. He was right, of course. I was a sham then and have been for a lifetime. Held up as a pillar of the community, a saint and a scholar, when I should have been castigated as a rapist and a murderer. A cheat and a liar.'

'The public don't see you that way, Father. You are highly respected.'

'Only because they do not know the reality. I can tell you, when I lay on the floor of Long Tower Church after Raymond Grimestone attacked me, I only wanted to die. I was glad he assaulted me. I deserved it. My life was flowing out of me. I was wishing death. It couldn't come quick enough. Then my own son saved me. I directed him to the sacristy and he changed his clothes into mine. My spares. And he took me to the hospital. I managed to tell him enough but I think Grimestone told him as well before he died. Grimestone had obviously got all his information from the PSNI and lured Jon to the church to try to kill him. I just gave Gerard the confirmation he needed. He asked me if I was his father. He held me tight and powdered me with morphine. He stopped the bleeding. He held my hand the whole way to the hospital dressed as a priest himself. In the blackness and seriousness of everything, I find that now risible. In a tragic way, if you can forgive me. In the chaos, no-one twigged on. How could the ambulance crew have known? And you need to check what I said there, as I have no recollection. One female paramedic went into hysterics. But that could have been Gerard's doing. Something happened, so her hysterical state caused more confusion. Was it something I said, or Gerard? The ambulance crew, unwittingly, removed two murderers from the scene to safety. I also know that I began speaking in glossolalia at the hospital. Speaking in tongues. The Bible says that would be the Holy Spirit speaking. But it wasn't. The devil inside of me was trying to escape, perhaps. I know that detective got all the video footage. Detective Wilson. She really has it in for me. Everything was filmed or videoed, on CCTV or recorded some way so I'm told.'

'Father, can I ask just one question at the moment?'

'Of course.'

'I cannot begin to understand the pain you must have been in at Long Tower. And your mental state there at that time. It seems you were in and out of consciousness. So how ... I am not being disrespectful ...'

'You are being a lawyer, then.'

'God no, Father.'

'I understand. Go on. Ask your question.'

'In a way, Father. It is meant respectfully, and I suppose I have a duty to ask, but how do you know these details about what happened at the church? I mean, your transfer and that to the hospital, the paramedic breaking down and the CCTV footage. How do you know these details? Who told you?'

'Gerard. Gerard told me everything. We have spoken a lot since.'

Amanda realised she should have kept her mouth firmly shut. How many times had she heard solicitors, barristers and police officers say 'never ask a question unless you know the answer'? Amanda realised she had made the mistake of wearing a pretend modern-day Clarence Darrow or Atticus Finch hat. Shut up, sit up and listen, she thought.

CHAPTER 17

'Can we go back to Bernadette, Amanda? If you don't mind?'

'Yes. Of course, Father. Whatever you want.'

'Everyone assumed it was suicide. It seemed obvious.'

Father Doherty looked away and shook his head.

'Her husband blown to bits and her son a child murderer. It was inevitable almost. Not much thought went into it. And such a cruel thing then for Gerard not to be allowed to go to his own mother's funeral. The seeds of evil and anger were firmly planted in Gerard. He became emotionless. There was a complete metamorphosis in his being. In his soul and in his mind. He wasn't the boy he used to be. I think part of me invaded him. The evil in me grew in him. He became detached, like me, from everything and everyone. But he was also fearless. I was always a coward. I couldn't face up to what I had become. What I had done. Until now. But he did. He still fears no-one. But you know what, Amanda?'

'Yes, Father. What is it?'

'Enough is enough. There comes a time for everyone. I apologise to you for unburdening my guilt in this way. We won't get through everything and I have a headache coming on. I'm getting a bit dizzy. Just mildly at this point. Anyway, can I talk about Ian Haslette?'

'The solicitor?'

'Aye. Ian confided in me and confessed in a way.'

'But as far as I know he wasn't Catholic. Do you mean a general confession?'

'Most strangely in a confessional box. A long time ago. Before the police discovered what they showed you from Clarendon Street and all of Gerard's research material. Long before that. Many years in fact.'

'Okay, Father, go on.'

'Well, as another tormented individual, the truth hit hard. For him. For Gustav Valberg, his dear friend, and for so many others. Tragic beyond belief.'

Father Doherty paused again.

'Ian killed Orla Harkin. If his confession to me is to be believed. That innocent girl. Full of life. Of hope. Of expectation. But the circumstances remain unclear. Untested and vague I must say. It is that concern, among many other things, that has driven me to this moment. I must say I'm not sure if Orla's death was by accident or design. All I can say is that Ian confessed to me that he killed her and sobbed uncontrollably in a Catholic confessional box.'

Father Doherty let out a sigh.

'And his wife.'

'His wife?'

'Lily. Again the circumstances remain unclear. Perhaps typical of the confession of a lawyer. Creating some doubt. But Detective Wilson is examining all that, too. Or perhaps re-examining it all.'

'Why? What's the point?'

'The truth, Amanda. Society is obsessed with it. The world is. No matter who it hurts or what devastation it causes. The truth. That's what she is pursuing.'

'I thought Lily Haslette fell down the stairs at home.'

'Well, I think she had a little nudge from Ian.'

Father Doherty hesitated, a look of self-disgust in his face.

'I apologise. A terrible and disrespectful choice of words. Nonetheless, Ian was another fine upstanding member of the community. Highly respected and regarded. But a killer for all that. A murderer . . .? I'm not sure about that. Lawyers tell us we can't libel the dead. So your colleagues in the journalistic world will have a field day with all of this. They can say whatever they want about him.'

'Father, this is an extreme amount of . . . information.'

Amanda did not want to say 'allegations'. But the phrase was in her mind. She knew a natural break in the interview would come soon, but perhaps she should ask the priest to continue. Or would it be best to stop now and schedule another session? But this really wasn't an interview, she realised. It really was a confession by Father Doherty. She wanted him to stick to what he knew as fact. What he witnessed and carried out himself as a matter of reality. He was claiming that Ian Haslette confessed to him that he had killed Orla Harkin and his wife. But Amanda wanted to hear Father Doherty's first-hand account of his own participation in what appeared to be a great degree of unlawfulness. She knew that his terms for the meeting dictated this was always meant to be the confession of a dead man with no cross-examination allowed.

Amanda's thoughts were disturbed once again by Father Doherty.

'It's often said that the past is always present.'

Amanda nodded in agreement.

'It is, Father. It is. You said you were talking to Gerard. How is that?'

'By phone, mainly. He is in the best place he can be now. By consent, really. He could break out, or be broken out, any time he wants. They paid millions to house him and keep the public safe from him. Millions. For a prison and court. The first of its kind. And like me, his health is not good. He hasn't long at all.'

Father Doherty pressed on, despite his growing tiredness.

'A few more things. I visited Gerard at Carstairs prison as well. When he was housed there. Along with his daughter.'

Amanda was even more perplexed and amazed now.

'Gerard. Your son? He has a daughter?'

'Matida Jawara. She's Angolan. Well, American now. And a beautiful girl she is. Gerard saved her from rape and certain death in Angola, years ago. She's twenty now or so. Gerard adopted her. Well, in his own way. He loves that girl as his daughter with all his heart and soul. And she loves him. That's obvious to me now. She is very well looked after by him and financially secure for the rest of her life. But she wants to be a lawyer. Gerard laughed at that and encouraged her to be an artist. But he failed. Everyone wants to be a lawyer. Why is that, Amanda?'

81

Amanda had no interest in the question or any answer.

'Father, is this okay to record? I mean, are you sure your son ... Gerard . . . is okay with you saying this? I mean, about his daughter.'

'Aye. Aye. He has no problem. But he did say that he would leave that judgement call to you and perhaps Jon Valberg. Gerard said to me he was certain that the only person you would speak to about all of this would be Jon. Is that right?'

'If I could reach him. Or if he would return my calls. He's not exactly the sort of person with a social media account.'

Father Doherty laughed for the first time, but clearly in some discomfort. He touched the saline drip again.

'I don't think Gerard is that sort of person either. Gerard once said to me that it was the people who had no online or social networking profile that the so-called security services had the most interest in. I remember him joking about that with me and his daughter.'

Father Doherty shook his head and Amanda stared again at the painting of Saint Catherine. She had eaten all the scone bread.

CHAPTER 18

'Amanda, just one final thing – or person – I would like to talk about.'

'Yes, Father.'

'Sidney Rankin. The solicitor who died at the Emerald Bank. Another poor unfortunate soul who took secrets to the grave.'

Amanda remained silent.

'I had a difficult relationship with Sidney. I think of his wife and his son and grandchildren. Of course, there is great tragedy in his background, too. Very, very sad. Truly awful. He lost two daughters when they were very young. Most horrific. Did you know that?'

'Not the precise details, Father. But in all that has gone on in the last two years here I've been hearing bits and pieces about so many people. So many rumours and allegations.'

Amanda realised she had stressed the term 'allegations'.

Father Doherty didn't pick up on it.

'I was too hard on Sidney. I want to apologise for that now. I'm very sorry. We all were too hard on him. Too critical. Too judgemental. All of us. I am truly sorry for that. Deeply sorry and ashamed. I had no idea what the police were doing to him.'

'What do you mean, Father?'

'He had two daughters and they vanished into thin air. The day of that bombing up the coast near Coleraine. A number of police officers were killed, including Detective Wilson's father. I remember it well. Years ago. Do you?'

'It's more that I learned about it from press coverage. A huge landmine explosion on the coast. The footage always showed such a beautiful day. And Mr Rankin's children vanished? But I was only a young thing then as well, Father.'

'Vanished. That's right.'

'Were they caught up in the bomb?'

'That's a very perceptive question, Amanda. Another parked car was destroyed in that bomb.'

'No-one inside?'

'Well, not the owner.'

'Who was the owner?'

'It was an old Jag.'

'Right. But did the police trace the owner?'

'I'm sure they did.'

'Forgive me, Father, but what's the problem? I'm sorry, but do you doubt this?'

'No. No. No doubt at all. My mind is drifting. Sorry. Forgive me.'

'The car, then. Who owned the car?'

'Ian Haslette. The other dead solicitor. Orla's killer. Lily's killer and ...'

Father Doherty shook his head and dropped it.

'He may have had Sidney Rankin's girls in the car ... abducted and locked in it.'

'In the car, Father? Surely not.'

'Yes. Then the car, perhaps unwittingly, was parked by Ian near this monstrous landmine and was obliterated with the children inside. That's the best interpretation I can put on this. Even the kindest – horrific as it is.'

'My God, Father.'

'They ceased to exist. It was a huge explosion and I've heard the car was full of petrol. They were reduced to ash in moments. No bodies. No funerals. No goodbyes. Not knowing what way they died. What their last words were. Awful.'

'Father. The implications of this ... well, it's most serious. The police must have known ...'

'They did. And fed Sidney scraps over the years. Scraps of information that were useless to him. But they used him. You must remember, Amanda. Those dark days of the RUC and Special Branch. They got away with so much. When you thought they couldn't go any lower … well, they usually did. Ian was going to confess all. Ian Haslette told Jon's mother. I'm sure of it. He was always saying to me he would and I discouraged him. When he did, I think she snapped. That's what made her go to the cemetery where she was caught in that awful snow storm. She died at the grave of her husband and son.'

'Does Mrs Rankin know any of this? I've heard she's unwell but still alive, I understand. I mean, Father, I know the times we are living in, but there could be an innocent explanation. He could have discovered the girls lost or something and was just helping them. Would that not be a kinder and more humane explanation? The days before mobile phones and that. But anyway, does Mrs Rankin know any of this?'

'No. Her husband never told her as far as I know. He was totally compromised by the whole thing. Totally. The search for the truth destroyed him. The search for his truth. A number of police officers, including Chief Constable Carlin at the time, said they would help him and had definite leads as to the whereabouts of his daughters, if he would help them.'

'Help them?'

'Sidney got the call every time someone was arrested without a solicitor. He sat in on interviews for years doing nothing for anyone. Little he could do, of course, on many occasions, but he was reliable for the police. Other solicitors were jealous of the amount of work he got and rumours circulated. And you know what Derry is like when a rumour starts. This even carried on well after Gerard was convicted. Gerard has all this recorded and I've heard and seen it. I had no inclination of any of this at the time of Gerard's sham trial. But I knew something wasn't right. It was more than a lazy solicitor making his money easy. It was deeper than that.'

'I'm not sure I understand this, Father.'

'Then I was compromised as well. I was just as bad so I left. We abandoned Gerard. He has certainly wrung the truth from all of us now. And I have often wondered, in this country plagued by deceit and lies, how many other lawyers were compromised in such a way as well. Another fanciful notion, yes. But I wonder.'

Amanda remained in deep shock. There was so much to

check out and verify. Months of work. She found it all hard to believe.

'Amanda. I'm tired now. That's enough. Turn everything off. Please.'

Amanda didn't flinch. She was glad to stop the recording. She was suffering from information overload. Or, as she viewed it, allegation overload. She also had banner headline overload. She had so many to choose from. For some reason, the fact that Father Doherty was an exorcist seemed like a good credible story. Was all the rest worth the trauma it inevitably would cause? She wanted to talk to Valberg about this, and only him.

'Well, Amanda. Is it all off?'

'Yes, Father. All of it. Are you okay?'

'Not really. How could I be?'

'Sorry, Father. I understand.'

'No you don't. And that is a compliment. You haven't faced the devil. You haven't done the devil's work. You haven't murdered. You haven't lied and misled people. You do what you want with the recording when I'm dead and cremated. Leave it at least a month then do as you please when I'm gone. There will be no rising on the third day and sitting at the right hand of the lord for me, I am afraid. So it's good-bye, Amanda, and thank you.'

Amanda nervously put out her hand to shake Father Doherty's for what she believed would be the last time. She glanced up at the magnificent oil painting of Saint Catherine as she made to leave.

There is often that moment at the end of an interview, Amanda realised, with all recording devices switched off, when the relaxed interviewee makes a monumental revelation that should have been recorded, but is lost.

The old priest cleared his throat and spoke again.

'Amanda, would you check something for me? Well, for you.'

'Of course, Father. What is it?'

'Saint Catherine. I see you're taken by her since you came in here. Check her out. Her life and how she died. Her legacy. Do that some day. Would you do that?'

'Yes, Father. I will. I definitely will. I promise.'

'Go home to your daughter. These events are only start-ing. The whole affair is chaos theory personified. One simple thing. A child going for a pint of milk sets off a chain reac-tion that must now be stopped. Or perhaps, Amanda, my rape of Bernadette. That is the first event. Not an innocent child complying dutifully with the request of her mother. I apologise again. Look at what has been missed, not discov-ered. Do you know who said that to me last?'

'No, Father.'

'Jon Valberg. Speak to him. And you may discover who really killed all those innocent people.'

Now Amanda most definitely wished all her recording de-vices were on.

'Sorry, Father. But what do you mean by that? You mean Gerard is not the killer?'

'He is not well. Or has not been well. He has mood swings and anger outbursts that no-one can control. A split person-ality disorder. And he will not medicate for that. I wanted to say to Jon in Majella McLaughlin's house that Gerard hadn't killed her—'

'But, Father, he is implicated for certain by the police. The expertise and military precision of all the murders is obvious for all to see.'

'Presume nothing, Amanda. Police sometimes jump to conclusions and then get forensic people to support them. Lazy investigation. Jon would never let that happen. But Gerard is most unwell. He is dying, Amanda. He'll either lose it again or hopefully calm down. He just needs to shift his anger.'

Amanda could not accept O'Driscoll's innocence now. No-one would, she thought. The problem with this contention by Father Doherty is that it had the possibility of negating any truth in his confession.

'We are all compromised in this awful mess – including police officers, who tried to be honest,' continued Father Do-herty. 'Derry, like everywhere in Ireland, has recently had an outpouring of family secrets. It all gets to boiling point and must escape. Perhaps a weakness in the human condition and the times that we are in. No-one seems to be content unless they are blubbering about their personal life on the television or the internet. Who cares? Why can't people keep their counsel? I repeat, I deserve what's coming to me. I deserve it and the public should know all about me, despite what I've just said.'

'I understand, Father.'

'Contact Jon and pray to Saint Catherine.'

'I will try hard on both, but the praying might be easier.'

'Amanda, that's a magnificent response. You have brought me some relief today. Thank you and goodbye.'

'Bye, Father. I hope I see you again soon.'

Father Doherty didn't respond. He shook Amanda's hand again, smiled thinly at her, and closed his eyes with a deep sigh.

CHAPTER 19

Amanda was full of emotion and confusion. Was Father Doherty speaking the truth? His confession had the deception of Gerard O'Driscoll written all over it, she thought.

If what she was told was the truth, then so what? A great story, yes, but what would it achieve now? She realised that Father Doherty had placed great trust in her and she must respect that. But on her journey home, she didn't know whether to burst out crying or vomit. Or was she obliged to report all this at once to the police? If only she could contact Valberg. She knew she'd never get near him at the hospital. He always seemed to be protected by more than just the police. Valberg, she realised, only really presented himself to her when it suited him.

As she continued her journey she became agitated and annoyed. She knew she would pour over the recorded material endlessly but she needed to make copies of everything first to hide away, just to be safe and protect herself.

How long would Father Doherty last? A week? A month? He didn't look well, but his mind was sharp. Amanda remembered the tone of Gerard O'Driscoll's voice when she encountered him at the car park. She thought she could hear that same commanding and confident tone in Father Doherty as well. Weak, elderly and sick as he was.

What was the truth? Was she safe to libel the dead and utilise that neat posthumous legal technicality? What damage would it do? What pressures would it put her under, and her daughter? Was this all worth it? Was the revelation of the truth, according to Father Doherty, worth it?

These questions and issues were professional for Amanda. However, the personal and emotive element of everything started to flood her as she thought of Valberg and his deceased family. She could see him agitated and annoyed, brave and perplexed. She could see him covered in blood and doing his best. She had portrayed him as some sort of hero in previous articles and she felt embarrassed about all that – even ashamed. She remembered his father's court notes that Valberg had entrusted her with. She felt somehow she had let him down and betrayed him.

Most of all, she remembered the young policeman fighting for the truth and for justice in relation to Janice Sloan after she died in prison. She could also see Valberg, in the witness box at Derry Magistrates Court, talking about salt from the Dead Sea. Was his noble corruption worth it? She had found it hard to accept the evidence he had given. Amanda depressingly realised that O'Driscoll had used Valberg. Was O'Driscoll's father now using her, she wondered?

There was so much to take in. Perhaps the best thing to do was to put the recordings away and look at them in a week or two, or even longer. Now was not the time for reaction and print. It was time for mature reflection. A good night's sleep and some distancing from everything, perhaps even for a few weeks, was the best thing to do at the moment. That was what Amanda determined to do. Get home, have a bath, relax and sleep.

Think about it all tomorrow. Everything would be clearer in the morning in a much more relaxed and safe environment.

CHAPTER 20

Amanda had her old digital radio alarm set for 7.00am the next day. She preferred waking up to the news on BBC Radio Foyle each weekday morning. Despite all she had heard the day before, she had no recollection of any bad dreams or nightmares. She slept soundly and fully. She was refreshed and ready to face the day and enjoy some time with her daughter. That is until she heard Katherine Ferguson announce that Father James Doherty had died peacefully in his sleep overnight. Ferguson delivered the story slowly and deliberately.

'Radio Foyle has learnt of the sad death of Father James Doherty, just moments before we came on air this morning. Already the tributes are flowing in to us and there is a sense of shock, despite his age, that Father Doherty is gone. We have heard from so many people already, nationally and internationally, and we will try to bring all those tributes to you. We expect it will be a busy schedule this morning, as the news is dominated here with the passing of a brave priest who meant so much to so many people in this community. Text, email or call us with your stories and experiences of Father James Doherty and we will get through as many of them as we can ...'

Amanda said, 'Jesus. Holy fuck,' as she sat up in bed.

She imagined Gerard O'Driscoll in his prison cell getting the news. His acting father was blown to bits and the news of that would have been horrific. His mother had committed suicide in the bath, so he must have been told, and he was not allowed to go to her funeral. He would have got that news in a prison cell as well. His biological father, whose life he had once saved, was now dead. And most definitely, O'Driscoll would not be allowed to go to his funeral. There would be no compassionate bail application by his solicitor Christina Maguire, flying in from London with her red-soled Christian Louboutin shoes in order to bring chaos and glamour to the High Court.

Amanda suddenly realised the danger of the astonishing information she now possessed.

There would be a controversial funeral service, as Father Doherty had said he wanted to be privately cremated. But for the moment, the tributes were flowing into Radio Foyle for the deceased priest. Not a bad word was uttered. Amanda knew she had the potential to stop all that faultless praise in its tracks. There was nothing like a Derry rumour to destroy someone – even when they are dead.

Derry people, thought Amanda, had a knack of creating their own laws and assumptions as it suited them. That stretched to defaming the dead.

However, as news of Father Doherty's death hit the media, another story was breaking with the daylight.

Radio Foyle was reporting emerging news about an incident at the Maze where the spree killer Gerard O'Driscoll was incarcerated. Details were 'sketchy', but as soon as the station had any more details they would update the story.

CHAPTER 21

Valberg woke quietly. He didn't feel agitated or confused. He remembered what had happened to him and where he was. Altnagelvin Hospital smelt like it always did.

David Kells stood over Valberg's bed.

'Is Diana White okay? Is she alive?' Valberg asked.

'She's alive, in a coma,' replied Kells. 'But ...'

'But what? What is it, David?'

'Father Doherty has died. Peacefully, in his sleep.'

'Peacefully. That's good. At least he had that. In his sleep, too. A great way to go. Sad all the same.'

'I know. Very sad all the same.'

'I'm surprised he lasted this long, David. Poor man.'

'Very sad.'

'Obviously, he wasn't well on many fronts. Physically and mentally, as far as I could tell, David. His injuries were awful. I'll never forget that night I came on him at Long Tower Church, and the next day. When I hear his name now, I think of that early morning discovery of Majella McLaughlin's body and his arrival at the scene. I had a strange conversation with him and he struck me as someone who had lost faith – in everything. I'll never forget him. He was very helpful to a lot of people and highly regarded.'

'His funeral service is to be private and out of the country somewhere. That's all I can find out at the moment.'

'It would be a big funeral here.'

'It would. But the details of his service remain strictly confidential, including where he is to be buried. But there is to be a memorial service at some point in the city.'

'When, I suppose, the great unwashed can turn up in tears. Someone, somewhere, will trace his funeral service no doubt.'

'No doubt, Jon.'

'Maybe he's to be interred at the Vatican or Rome or something like that in accordance with the terms of his will. Perhaps there is a special exorcists' funeral service and burial conducted only in secret.'

'That sounds credible, I suppose.'

'You know what, David?'

'What?'

'I wish I could wake up somewhere, someday ... or lift the phone to answer and not to be told someone I know is dead, murdered or has committed suicide. I'd even take a nuisance call selling me life assurance for a change. Even conduct a civil conversation with the sad bastard on the other end of the phone.'

'Father Doherty's gone. With his secrets, Jon.'

'Perhaps for the best. Let them rest with him I say.'

'Agreed. A funeral we are able to avoid.'

'Yes.'

'Well, better you know now.'

'Thanks, David. Anyway, did anyone tell you about my hypotension?'

'Low blood pressure?'

'It was the shock of the cut. I was looking inside her arm after I momentarily got the blood wiped away from it. It set me back a bit. I was also exhausted. That's the way it hits me. Suddenly. I get no warning. But I suppose by now I should feel it coming. Perhaps I'm narcoleptic as well. I'm getting tests done for all sorts of things.'

'You saved Diana White's life.'

Valberg shook his head.

'Nightmare.'

'You'd have to have low blood pressure, Jon. You couldn't be like the rest of us. Not high, but low ... but I'm glad you're okay. And whatever you do, don't get up too fast. You'll be okay, though, they said.'

Valberg slowly got out of his bed and slumped down onto a large leather chair in the room. He was wearing an unfashionable green hospital-supplied robe.

He put his head back and closed his eyes.

'My favourite headache time again.'

Kells waited for Valberg to relax.

'We have to send you to a medical. Some psychological examination or appraisal thing. This suspension sham needs rectified. It's turned into a not-so-credible shambles I fear.'

'David, don't bullshit me. I know what this is.'

'Well, need I say any more? We need to make sure our set-up appears right or I am in the Twilight Zone. A bit like you.'

'Am I not beyond psychoanalysis?'

'The Irish are. But you're a sort of Swede, as they say.'

'You mean a fucking turnip.'

'Will you do it?'

'What have I got to lose? Apart from my dignity. Yeah. Do it. Make the time. Make this bullshit all seem normal.'

'It's already made. Tomorrow at three? It's a private clinic with a Doctor Susannah Crawford.'

'A cop shrink?'

'Jon. Go bloody easy on her. For God's sake. Please. For me. Let me form-fill and get you through the evaluation and have you classed as fit for work again. If you want back, that is. You do, don't you? We have to formally get you back to work. I think it's expected of us.'

Valberg remained motionless, his eyes closed, head back. He dropped his arms to his side carelessly.

'Is this the same room I was in the last time? Don't think so. The Valberg Ward?'

'Let's get this suspension lifted and move on. I mean, your behaviour at Ebrington was as bizarre as it gets – even for you. Say nothing of the border.'

'Say fucking nothing then, David.'

'Okay. For now.'

Valberg knew that Kells was getting impatient with him.

'I have no fear, David. Why is that? I used to have fear. Fear of failure, fate, tragedy. But it's all gone. I feel better now, believe it or not. All the shit we worry about. Fear. That's all it is. Well, the fear is gone, but the mood dives are never-ending. They're getting deeper, too.'

'It's like you want to be killed. And that ... well, you're wishing someone would do it. But the problem with that is

95

that it puts everyone in danger. Jon, you can't just take your clothes off in public and walk towards ... well, a shooting range.'

'I stopped it, didn't I? You asked for my help. You called me. And at last we might have some evidence. A melted rifle and a remote control system. Perhaps something might come from it. From the Foyleside scene. And if Diana White recovers she'll have to be interviewed.'

'Yes, Jon. But the real person we need the evidence against has just escaped from prison. In case you've forgotten. There's still no announcement. But it's coming.'

'His prints, in a way, are all over what happened yesterday. He's directed it or maybe ... and a nightmare for you, David ... maybe he's put someone, or more than one person, up to this. That mounted gun in the Jeep at Foyleside was a dummy. We all fell for it. All resources and attention were focused there. He caught us again.'

'Jon, you know what is being said?'

'David. For fuck's sake. You think I even care?'

'Well, you had your hands around Bostridge's neck a while ago.'

'How could I forget? Fat—'

'Hopefully that won't be in your statement.'

'That he was a fat shit? Or that I had my hands around his neck?'

Kells didn't answer.

Valberg lifted his hands to his head and continued with some annoyance.

'David, the barrister was targeted and picked for a reason. It was convenient he was a third-rate lawyer living off his father's reputation – and who deliberately fucked up that Grimestone trial. Is he dead because of that or his father? Or both? My sense is that there is more to come. And we know, I suppose, what the real reason is. Linda told me his father, Sir Ronnie Bostridge, was O'Driscoll's trial judge who did everything he could to sway O'Driscoll's jury to conviction.'

'Successfully. Apart from your father.'

'Successfully enough to secure a majority verdict.'

'Okay, Jon.'

'This has, yet again, O'Driscoll written all over it. How many times do we say or think that? Or what's worse ...'

'What's worse?'

'A copycat killer, David?'

'I don't think so. But maybe it is.'

'We've had years of that in this town in real terms. And it's still going on. Perhaps all the killings in this place are copycat killings. On both sides.'

'Maybe.'

Valberg was a bit calmer now and spoke slower.

'Anyway. Keep it simple, stupid. Look at what we've missed. Strip it down. Can we get the names of every person who visited O'Driscoll since he was put in custody?'

'Everyone?'

'Let's start with the general public. There will be a record. What's wrong with basic police investigation in the normal, logical and simple way? Have we forgotten how to do that, David?'

Kells shook his head.

'Jesus, Jon. Did we ever know?'

'Okay. Let's start with that. There'll be CCTV footage as well. ID cards I assume. The whole works, just to get in there. To Carstairs first, then Long Kesh.'

'You mean the Maze.'

'Long Kesh sounds better. Yeah. I like the sound of Long Kesh better.'

'Perhaps you should have gone to visit him?'

'Part of the arrangement I had with O'Driscoll's solicitor was to stay away from him.'

'Professionally I can see that. But personally?'

Valberg sensed Kells was hiding something. He had never seen him so serious.

'Maybe don't bother with having the suspension lifted, Jon. Maybe we'll leave that.'

'It wouldn't look right, would it? If we don't. I can't be un-official anymore. If anyone can see through the sham we've created it's O'Driscoll. He's no-one's fool. I think he knows more about me than we know about him.'

'Well, perhaps we cancel the appointment with Doctor Crawford for tomorrow and put it off for a few days.'

'Is that official, unofficial or extremely unofficial, David? Where are you going with all this? You're all over the fucking place. Not like you.'

'It's our only chance at the moment while Headquarters goes nuts, Anna threatens to resign again, and the copycat war, as your conjecture goes, continues. As predictable as the rain in Derry. It's meltdown. The nuclear reactor is about to blow.'

'Okay. Jesus. Calm down, David. Leave me swinging my lead again and put my great medical evaluation off? Seriously? I think I should do it. I'll have to make my own arrangements, though.'

'If you don't mind me asking, how's the insomnia, Jon?'

'Still three days at a time. There's nothing I can do. In hotels I black out the windows. I carry black bin liners and Sellotape everywhere I go. I make it clear at hotel receptions I am not to be disturbed. I'm getting blackout blinds that you can stick to the windows to save me carrying around the liners. Some hotels are okay though with good curtains. It's the first thing I examine in a room when I enter. The fucking curtains. Eh, what a guy I am.'

'But, Jon, you can't go on like this. You can't just collapse the way you did at the border.'

'I know. It becomes all-consuming. I'll work on it. I promise.'

'I hope so. For your own good, Jon.'

'I understand. I am. I will. God, sure I'm going to a cop shrink now.'

CHAPTER 22

Kells glared at his mobile phone as it rang and he sighed. He took the call and Valberg could hear him say very little apart from, 'Yes' and 'Okay'.

Valberg watched the serious demeanour of Kells worsen, becoming low and depressed. He wondered if there were more shootings, bombings, murder and death. He had in his mind O'Driscoll's claims that he could be dying. But nothing that came out of O'Driscoll's mouth was ever straightforward.

Then Kells looked at Valberg, took a deep breath and shrugged his shoulders.

'You're all over the news and the internet again. Naked from the waist up. Someone even filmed you undressing and walking over to Bostridge with your hands up. And stretched out. Why did you do that? Anyway, the copycat rumour has started. You'll be all over the press again.'

'Run with it. Better a copycat killer at the moment than O'Driscoll escaped from prison and directing everything.'

'Jon, you're still suspended pending resolution of that whole issue of your weapon and Mr Haslette. You'll have to go through the motions of some further hearings and a proper medical at some point. But soon. Procedure and all that.'

'Procedure, David. Give them what they want. Yeah. Murder on the streets, exploding cars with weaponry mounted inside firing at police and civilians. International incidents and the chief suspect, who attempted suicide, in a coma. Yeah. Fucking send me to a shrink for an evaluation ... *blodigit helvete ...*'

'We're agreed, then?'

'A-fucking-greed,' Valberg replied sarcastically while rolling his eyes. 'Set up the appointment for tomorrow with the shrink and I'll go as soon as I'm out of here.'

'Right. Okay. Here, you'll need this.'

Kells gave Valberg a new mobile phone.

'Another BlackBerry burner phone, David?'

'It's all charged up and ready to go. We must be in contact at all times. And you have your own weapon.'

'Built in tracer device in the phone no doubt, to keep tabs on me and the battery keeps it bugged?'

Kells didn't answer.

'Don't worry, David. I'll get cleaned up and ready to go in no time ... and back to my normal safe and sane self.'

Kells was leaving and Valberg stopped him.

'Sorry. Sorry. David. Hold on. There's one visit I want to do that I haven't and should have.'

'Where's that?'

'Orla Harkin's mother. It's a visit I've always been meaning to do.'

'You know she still lives in the same house. That poor woman.'

'I know.'

'I'll not ask why, but let her know in advance. Or get someone to let her know. Jesus, don't just turn up unannounced.'

'Everything goes back to the beginning. Everything. I feel the need to talk to her. I want to strip everything down, like I said. For my own sake, too, as all this stuff about my father and Ian Haslette has fried my brains. Anyway, is that okay?'

'Just as long as she knows in advance. I don't want you turning up with blue lights flashing and sirens blaring on the Lecky Road and a whole situation. Not another one. Do it through her solicitor or something like that. Keep it calm and dignified.'

'Okay. Thanks, David. Calm and dignified. Bye.'

'I'll get you the details, or someone will, for your appointment with Doctor Crawford I told you about earlier. I'll arrange for you to be telephoned or we will get a text sent to you.'

'Can't wait.'

CHAPTER 23

Valberg decided not to go through the predictable ordeal of turning up at a psychiatrist's private office and starting a debate that would lead to a row about whether he should go through with the session at all. He was determined not to have a Tony Soprano moment and all that might lead to and the mind games involved. He would do the session as requested by Kells and get it over with.

This was just something he had to do, as he was convinced he wouldn't open up that much and reveal his innermost thoughts anyway.

Valberg never told anyone what he was really thinking on a personal level – and he had to protect himself professionally as well. However, if he had to give the appearance of at least wanting back in the PSNI formally, and his suspension lifted, then he was going to have to go through this charade. So he decided to get on with it.

Doctor Susannah Crawford's private clinic, thankfully, thought Valberg, wasn't in the grounds of Gransha Hospital. He had too many bad memories of visits there in the past on a professional basis. The one thing that always struck him about visiting Gransha was the number of people he knew who were patients in the place. They seemed so normal out of the precincts of the hospital. And why wouldn't they?

So with some trepidation, Valberg entered the well-laid-out and comfortable Georgian offices of Doctor Susannah Crawford in Queen Street.

Valberg was glad the doctor had not chosen Asylum Road as a base from which to work. What an address that would be, he thought.

The receptionist took him straight through to Doctor Crawford.

Valberg dispensed with pleasantries and introductions and got straight to it once settled. He thought by getting going himself he'd be in more control of the conversation.

'Look, the main problem is my sleep patterns, Doctor. That's why I'm here really. Isn't it? I never thought it would cause so much chaos in my head. Or in my life generally. I need you to know that I suffer from murophobia, I'm an alcoholic and I have hypotension. I say alcoholic but I'm in recovery mode. I recall seeing a note on the front of my GP's file that there's a risk I'm bipolar as well. But sleep. That's my main problem as I see it. Then I think I'm sort of narco-leptic as well. You see I just collapse into sleep.'

'Sorry, Mr Valberg. It's great that you share this now but slow down. I won't get all this into my notes if you keep on at that rate.'

Valberg realised he was, despite what he had attempted to avoid, now going to have a Tony Soprano moment and the 'ground rules' explained.

'No, Doctor. Sorry. I'm sorry for going on.'

Valberg looked around the room which was quite spartan. He was searching for a painting to look at but there were none. He'd been through many intense psychological tests and examinations before, but this one seemed different.

He didn't like chairs without arm rests and he was sitting in one trying to avoid folding his arms. He felt like smoking a cigar and asking for a glass of whiskey but knew it wouldn't be permitted or appropriate.

Doctor Crawford was glancing over some notes and then confirmed the confidentiality of the consultation. That got Valberg going again.

'Confidentiality? There's no such thing anymore. It doesn't exist. It's just a well-meaning concept in law and medicine. Everything pops up somewhere. Eventually. Nothing is private. People have surrendered their most private and unnecessary thought processes to the internet and social websites.

Even someone's most inner thoughts are not confidential anymore. They become public and permanent. People don't stop to think. I know that from my work. The permanent nature, and the damage it can do, of a silly or stupid thought can't be cured.'

'Well, I have a professional obligation to—'

'I understand. But that well-intentioned professional obligation can be negated by a court anytime … with embarrassing effects for a lot of people.'

'Well …'

'Sorry, Doctor. I remember a case once when I was a junior officer in CID. It was a road traffic accident scam involving a lot of money. Well, anyway, one of the alleged victims of one alleged road traffic accident had her GP notes produced for the case. Her entire life was in the GP's file in a brown manila envelope. In court, sitting carelessly on a bench between solicitors and barristers. As she lied through her teeth in the witness box about the fake road traffic accident, she forgot the truth she told to her GP about her mental state over many years. All of it dutifully written down and recorded in confidence by the GP. I don't think I need to …'

'No. I understand. I've seen that happen.'

'It wasn't her lies that really tripped her up. It was the truth. She thought she was safe and secure talking in confidence to her GP, and then her own counsellor, but everything was written down and put back at her.'

'Yes. That's troubling.'

'And the other thing I remember about that case is that at lunchtime, her GP file with her life and her secret of secrets all in there was lying open on the court benches for all to see. Because there were multiple copies made of the notes, too. They were everywhere.'

'I see. Perhaps the lawyers and the court should be more discreet.'

'Confidentiality? Doesn't exist.'

'Nonetheless, I am duty bound, I must repeat, to confirm to you the confidential nature of this consultation. Well, unless you confess to any illegality.'

'Great advice, Doctor.'

'Can we get on with it, then? I already have all your personal details, so we don't need to go over all that. I've just been checking them while you were speaking.'

'Okay.'

'Your sleep patterns, you were saying. Or lack of them.'

'Yes. My sleep.'

'It's understandable. Sleep deprivation is very common. But let's ease into this. Take your time.'

Valberg ignored the request.

'So you think my condition is common?'

'In modern life, many people suffer from many sleep disorders.'

'Modern-day life; whatever that means. Okay. I can buy that. I understand.'

'What do you do to try to get to sleep?'

'You mean like counting sheep?'

'Well, if it works, would you care?'

'My mind is a bit more complex than that, Doctor.'

'Call me, Susannah. Tell me, then. What do you usually think about before sleeping?'

Valberg remained silent and Doctor Crawford let the silence linger. Valberg couldn't say what he believed he would be thinking about tonight before he tried to get to sleep, as it now would involve Doctor Crawford tied to his bed and saying 'no'. He had been rude to her on arrival and realised he should have demonstrated a few more pleasantries to her. That would have been more professional. But tonight, Doctor Crawford was going to be tied to his bed in his thoughts. Valberg then began the process of changing that image and decided he wanted to be tied to the bed instead. By Doctor Crawford.

Valberg, giving every appearance of being genuine, began to speak much more slowly and seriously.

'I'm running in the open towards a cliff. Or just running for the sake of it. To tire myself out. Then I feel myself falling into the water from a height. A great height. Or perhaps falling to a great depth. Sinking slowly. But it feels more like falling. I feel, or see myself, looking up at my physical body falling in. I'm looking up to my left. Northwest. I can't see my face, though. But I see my body. I'm fully clothed at this point.'

Valberg paused, but Doctor Crawford didn't interject.

'The disturbance of the water. I see that. I am silent. I am still. I am dropping to the bottom of the ocean. I am peaceful and into the arms of Christ of the Abyss.'

'Christ of the what?'

'The Abyss. But you'd need diving gear to reach it. And I'm not wearing any diving gear.'

'And where is this abyss?'

'At the bottom of the ocean. Drop me to the bottom of the ocean. Well, the Med. The Mediterranean Sea. On the Italian Riviera. Between Camogli and Portofino. Haven't you heard of it?'

'No. Sorry.'

'That's what I want. What I deserve. The bottom. My body to rot in the salt water. That's how I feel. Every night or every time I try to sleep. Weightless. Formless. Like water itself. I've adapted and saved myself. I've become the water. Mad. Isn't it?'

'But surely, Jon, you would die. Would you not?'

'No, I don't die. I see everyone who has died, though. They still don't see me.'

'How come?'

'They are blinded and I am ashamed. They choose not to see me. I'm an outcast. A leper. An unclean Gentile. But I am peaceful and alone. Completely mad. Insane. I know.'

'Objectively or subjectively?'

Valberg shook his head and paused again.

'I've never told anyone that. Ever. What does it mean?'

'How often do you sense this?'

'Quite a lot now. As each day goes by, the details are becoming clearer. The cliff seems nearer. It's not just a falling asleep thing. I see myself falling to the bottom of the ocean all the time. But I am really at peace when I watch myself. The images are sharper now. Getting clearer by the day. There are some people I want to see and they're not there. Then, just last night, I was talking to Orla.'

'Orla?'

'Orla Harkin. She's nine. The child who was killed years ago. I'm sure you've heard about her. Haven't you?'

'Yes. I have.'

'I only see her in her First Communion dress, when she would have been younger than nine. White gloves, rosary beads and a prayer book. Like the beads Majella McLaughlin tried to reach as she was dying. She was a murder victim. A more recent one. You do know all about the murder spree in Derry?'

'Yes. I've heard about it, obviously. But I wouldn't know the details. The image of a woman, for example, reaching for a pair of rosary beads. I didn't know that.'

'Anyway, Orla's okay. She really is. Really. She's okay.'

'In your hallucination she is okay?'

'You call it what you want, Susannah. But she is okay.'

Valberg sighed and went silent again for a short while.

He joined his hands and put his head back on the chair.

'How do I know that, you wonder? That Orla's okay. I don't know that as a fact. But my senses say she is okay. At peace. My senses and gut instinct work well in my professional life. Such as it was.'

CHAPTER 24

Doctor Crawford tried to draw Valberg out some more as he sat quietly in front of her.

'What else happens when you swim with Jesus at the bottom of the sea, Jon?'

'I just dive down. Sometimes, but not all the time, in a diving bell. I see everyone, and I look back up and I think I see myself again, being raised up or pushed up by Jesus. Then it stops and I approach falling asleep. But the one constant is that Orla is okay. I've seen her. Orla is okay.'

'Is this a religious experience for you?'

'I don't think so. Perhaps blasphemous.'

'Blasphemous? Why, Jon?'

'Because I've gone even deeper recently, and slightly surreal with it all. If that's indeed possible.'

'Yes. Go on.'

'I change into Christ of the Abyss.'

'Valberg of the Abyss?'

Valberg laughed.

'Yes. That's it. But just for seconds. I reach the bottom. I am steady. Relaxed and sure. I have become Valberg of the Abyss. Just for a moment. A brief moment. Then everything changes suddenly. But I don't know what to do. It's blurred then. All the images to that point are crystal clear. Then it fades to haze. Unclear. The red gurnard appears and I can't move.'

'The red gurnard?'

'Chelidonichthys cuculus. I'm at the bottom then. With a bottom feeder I can't get past. At the depths. Can't go any lower. Then I will sleep. It just takes a while to get there. That's all.'

'And do you feel relaxed then? And able to sleep?'

'Yes. Relaxed physically but not mentally. Relaxed enough to sleep, though.'

'Is that progress then for you, do you feel?'

Valberg shook his head.

'I'm not sure. I'm still bothered. And I sense I'm standing in front of a giant red gurnard and can't get past it. When I try, it opens out its tentacles and fins. There's no way past. But I sleep all the same. Sometimes standing up or floating in the water.'

'Well, that's positive. At least you get to sleep. It's a long journey, but you get there.'

Valberg thought for a moment then nodded in agreement.

'I do. I suppose so. Although the type of sleep can vary. Sometimes deep, but most times shallow.'

'Do you dream?'

'Not often. I hallucinate more when I am awake. I don't dream like normal people. Well, I rarely do anything like a normal person, but dreaming? No. I don't see it as dreaming.'

'Okay.'

Valberg paused again then smiled.

'But I can dream of my perfect day.'

'What's that?'

Valberg stayed silent.

He sipped some water that Doctor Crawford had poured for him.

'A year or two ago I'd have said fishing with my father. But there's an annoyance in me that moves me away from that image.'

'Why, Jon?'

'I've too many questions for him but I don't want to hear the answers.'

'About what?'

'Family and business. His family. His business. My brother. My mother. I suppose a lot about his work. What he really did. He was a man with many secrets, too. His real work ...'

Valberg paused. He didn't want to get into too much about his father.

'He was an expert tax consultant with a very private clientele.'

'Okay, Jon. Well, what is your perfect day now, then?'

Valberg was glad to get off the subject of his father and answered quickly.

'I love the Palio.'

'The horse race? In Italy?'

'Yeah. I'd like to go to the Palio in July. Then swim with Christ of the Abyss the same day, in the evening. Or perhaps the other way around. Swim in the morning and head for the Palio in the evening. I'd just about make it to Siena. With a beautiful woman as a companion all day.'

'Sounds wonderful, Jon.'

'Beautiful. A perfect, beautiful day. I'd actually get even more pleasure out of watching this beautiful woman enjoying the day. The swim, then the horse race. I'd love watching her. Really. I'd get so much satisfaction out of that. Then some Brunello red wine into the early hours of the morning. Life is so short for all of us. So we have to grab the joy whenever we can.'

CHAPTER 25

Valberg was wondering if he had done enough to avoid talking about his father.

'How do you feel about your father now, Jon?'

Valberg sighed in abject failure.

'Sometimes when I think of him I think of the worst fishing knot ever.'

'What do you mean?'

'Have you ever fished?'

'No.'

'Well, the knot or tangle can be horrendous. And the circumstances that you are in, or the place, can be even worse. Standing in the river with your waders on, or out on the sea with the boat rocking. You look at the mess and your initial thought is that this puzzle, this tangled web, will never undo itself. Or that you can't figure it out. But you do. Eventually. You take your time. You steady yourself and become patient.'

'I can understand that.'

'I've no doubt he cared for me. Well, loved me. I never doubted that.'

'But you doubt something?'

'There are so many conversations in my head that I wished I had with him. I dream that I am dreaming about him, asking him questions but ... but so many things are better left unsaid. People can't do that now. They don't keep their counsel. They do all their thinking with the brain cells in their thumbs. On Shitter or Fuckbook. Perhaps I should just try to feel the way he would about things and let it be.'

110

'Are you angry?'

'I was. Not now, though. But I can be. Sometimes.'

'Does it affect your work?'

'Well, I haven't been working for the police lately. I'm sure you know. I've been working privately. For a big law firm. From London and elsewhere. Over quite a few months now. I came back here for a break, would you believe it? To see a bit of the City of Culture and all that, and to test my new motorbike skills.'

'That must have been interesting. Working for the law firm.'

'It is. Or it was. Scary as well, though. You wouldn't believe what goes on and what people will pay to find out. About the ones they love the most, usually.'

Valberg went silent. Once again he wanted to get on to a new topic. To get away from talking about his father.

'The last case involved a young boy and an attempted abduction. A revenge thing really, as the father got his son back. Morocco. On a day trip from the south of Spain. They were in a medina. One parent thought the other had the child's hand.'

Valberg stopped again.

'Never let a child's hand go, Doctor. Sorry. Susannah. Never.'

'Good advice, Jon. What happened in Morocco?'

'Oh. Sorry. The boy. Well, he vanished. You can imagine the scene. You see there was a mock funeral that took everyone by surprise. No dead body at all. But they came rushing through these narrow streets with a body held high and in grief, chanting in Arabic. Naturally, your attention would be drawn away towards that. But the father had sense. Amid the screaming and the panic he had the intelligence and wit to jump up on a table and look all around him. And there the boy was being led away in the searing heat, his blonde hair distinctive, held by the hand of a woman with a black burka on in the distance, walking up a dusty hill. No-one could stop that man then getting to his child. No-one.'

'What happened?'

'He got his child back safely into the hands of his wife and away.'

'And they left?'

'Yeah. Left okay and calmed the kid down.'

'That's a relief.'

'It was. But something stirred in the man. He became possessed with revenge. His wife told me everything. She couldn't stop him. The red mist descended and the next day he got the boat back to Morocco. Despite the pleas of his distraught wife, more than content that they had got their son back.'

'Oh no. To get the woman?'

'To get the woman. Correct. No doubt. But now he's missing. So he didn't lose his son. But the son has lost his father. I'm supposed to go back and tidy all that up. Investigate and see if I can find the father.'

'I hope you find him.'

'So do I.'

'Why did the family go to a law firm? Why not the lawful authorities?'

'Because they have deep pockets. So they can. And there's the lawless element of it. A perfect case for me, they said. I will get back on to searching for him, though my Arabic always fails me. I just about get by with my vulgar Spanish. But Arabic? No.'

Valberg went quiet again for a while. It was a long stillness.

'Can I go back to my fantasy perfect day? Or I suppose night. Away from the Palio and the red wine this time.'

'Sure, Jon. What is it?'

'I'm in Ronnie Scott's in London with my own jazz band. I'm the drummer. Thrashing out my own compositions together with a bit of Dave Brubeck. Really swinging. Playing with an unorthodox style. I'm no style but all styles. Even a bit of rock in there. But technically, I'm a wizard. The audience are bewildered and I am lost in the music. But not in the technical side. I'm lost in the emotive, passionate side that I can only get to because I'm so technically ... well, brilliant. This is what makes me an enigma in the jazz world. And I'm only twenty-three. A kid. But the music is flowing out of my veins and I'm touching and connecting with everyone in the room.'

'That sounds great.'

'Yeah. But it's not the best bit.'

'What's that?'

'When it's over, this tall Canadian wants to shake my hand. He starts talking to me about time signatures. We are in the comfort of strangers' zone. He's really comfortable with me, and the conversation flows like the drumming before. He wants to shake my hand.'

'Who is he?'

'Neil Peart.'

'Who's Neil Peart?'

Valberg wanted to roll his eyes and shake his head. But he had been rude enough so far.

Valberg just imagined hearing Miles Davis in his head.

'I'm finished now, Doctor. That's enough. I'm going.'

Valberg got up to walk out.

Doctor Crawford spoke. 'Perhaps you will tell me about your worst nightmare, if you would please sit down again. Now that you have told me about your perfect day.'

'Nightmares, Susannah. Nightmares. Everything becomes a nightmare when you live the way I do all the time. Some people are afraid of everything. If you have fear that is. Again, that's a problem for me in the opposite sort of way. I'm mostly fearless. Anyway, no, next time. I'm going. You fill out your report whatever way you want. Was that enough?'

'Enough? But I need more time, Jon. Come on. We've just met. Just started. One session isn't enough.'

Valberg had to decide to play the game or have the Tony Soprano row now with the doctor. Sex with her was also an option in his mind. But his libido was low.

He had the door opened to leave but closed it and sat back down again.

'Okay, Doctor. Nightmares. You want to hear about my nightmares? My worst fears?'

'Yes. Please.'

Valberg sat down.

113

CHAPTER 26

'I just want to keep running. Just gather my breath and wind myself up, ready to launch. Wound up like a coil or a spring. Without stopping I run to the cliff I mentioned. And fall over. I just keep falling. I've no energy. I'm trying to grab hold of everyone and everything. But it's no use. No-one will hold out their hand to help me anymore. I'm just falling all the time. I have to decide to be deaf or blind. I can't make up my mind. But someone is telling me, if I choose blindness or deafness, I will survive. So which is it, Doctor? Susannah, what shall it be?'

'It's your choice, Jon.'

'No choice really.'

Valberg closed his eyes.

'I choose blindness. The dark. The bleak, emptiness of nothing visual anymore. What if a child, who could once see, is blinded by someone else? Blindness. Just looking further into the dark. So I have to use my imagination more than ever. And what's wrong with that?'

Valberg opened his eyes.

'I do that a lot by the way. Use my imagination.'

'Is that it, Jon? Falling and choosing between blindness and deafness? Your worst nightmare?'

'Do you need more?'

'I need to know exactly how you feel.'

'Oh. The fall into blindness and deafness is the easy part.'

'What's the difficult part?'

Valberg remained silent again. He sighed.

'The dead. And time is running out for me. I see the dead

114

all the time. I don't mean in images, like ghosts. I actually believe I'm talking to them. Even when I'm blind. I still see them; touch, feel and smell them. In a strange way the dead give me confidence or blight me with a recklessness that is dangerous.'

'Do you mean in reference to the safety of others? Or a death wish?'

'That's another reason why I'm here, Susannah. Isn't it? The PSNI are worried I'm a threat not only to myself but to others. This whole thing is a sham and the more I reveal myself to you, well, the less likely I'll have my suspension lifted. And what's more, if I really tell you what I'm thinking, you might have me locked up.'

'I'm not sure about that, Jon. Try me. I've heard a lot in here. We will proceed on the basis that you want your suspension lifted. You do, don't you?'

Valberg went silent again for a short while. He knew he was opening up more than he had ever before, to anyone.

'What I am about to tell you, I have never told anyone. It is the mother of all revelations as far as I'm concerned, and something I have to live with every day of my life. No matter how well things are going for me, this nightmare haunts me. It's like a claw in my back. The nails of the claw are firmly embedded in me. If I move too fast, or have any enjoyment in any situation, the claw will tug at me, to remind me of what I've done.'

'Go on, Jon. What have you done? Tell me everything.'

Valberg paused yet again for a short while.

'I'm at an AA meeting, making a confession. "Hello. My name is Jon." "Hi, Jon." What a fucking nightmare for me. I'm making my confession to my fellow alcoholics. I have a sponsor, too. Let's call him Nigel. I tell them what led to my drinking problems. I was caught with the body of a dead child. Orla Harkin. The girl I mentioned earlier to you, Susannah. The one I said was okay. She's only nine. And all along it was me. I murdered her. I framed a friend from school. I'm a real devious and secretive bastard. Just like my father. I agreed to meet – well, I wouldn't say his name to the group – out the line, along the Letterkenny Road, and I tricked him. I didn't turn up. I tricked my friend.'

'Your friend?'

'A stranger who helped me at school when I dropped my books one day. He told me *Death of a Naturalist* was his favourite poetry book as well when he saw mine.'

'The Seamus Heaney publication?'

'Yes. It still remains my favourite as well. Forget all that Chaucer bollocks. The stranger helped pick my stuff up and studied the book. We were just teenagers. Kids. He was waiting for me out the line. As arranged. We had agreed a spot to meet that we both knew. I was aware the dead body was there from the night before. But he won't squeal on me, no matter what I do. I tell the group that I have this burden of responsibility hanging over me. No matter how hard I try, I can't own up to the truth. To this terrible thing that I've done. What good would it do anyway? A good man has done a bad thing, I tell them. Because I think I'm good.'

'In that imaginary situation you believe you are good?'

'That's a difficult question. Perhaps it's more of a case of I'd like to think I'm a good man. Doesn't every man think that way?'

'Okay. Go on.'

'So, ultimately, what use is the truth? I ask everyone this. We created this elaborate secret plan that has existed for years. That's why I joined the police. Part of my cover-up and subterfuge. An act of insanity. I was untouchable then. He couldn't get me. At least that's what I thought. But he has. And others. In his way. We've fooled everyone in law enforcement and the media so far. But it was me all along. I deserve what's coming to me. I'm guilty. The law catches all of us in the end. I'm a fraud. I've just confessed to murder to the group, Susannah. My new best friends. What do I do now? Are you bound by confidentiality? I am totally exposed. Laid bare like an open wound. My worst nightmare. What do I do? What do we do now?'

'Well, if you speak the truth then you have just confessed, potentially I suppose, to some part in a murder and I would have to report it to the police. That's what would happen if this were reality.'

'I had that nightmare a while ago but it has turned into reality for me in my consciousness. I add bits on every time

I think about it. It gets more real every time. Not a sleeping nightmare anymore. What do we do here, Susannah?'

'We keep talking. You keep talking. How did you kill her, Jon? Where do you want to take this, or go further? What happened? Do you tell the group?'

'It's all mixed up. Orla ran out the line to get away from a male family member, maybe an uncle. No-one would believe her. I calmed her down. Sat her down. She told me everything. She said she wanted to die. Have you ever had a nine-year-old child in your presence talking about wanting to die? That's horrific. Moving and completely sad. Awful. I was just helping her. That's all. It's shaped the man I am. The person I've become. The girl was abused in life and worse than that ...'

'What's worse, Jon?'

'Abused in death also. By all of us. I think my employers know. They don't want me back and I'm not going back. I'm not really on suspension. That was a hoax, too. Don't you know that? I was sort of ... undercover. I'm slowly dying all the same. I've let everyone down. So, as I continue to fall, Susannah, I still have this choice. Blindness or deafness.'

'Go on.'

'I choose blindness because I am ashamed of myself and what I've done. Now the group know. I don't want to ever have to look at myself in the mirror again. Doctor, I'm really fucked up. I've also fucked up a lot of lives. That's my nightmare getting worse. That's my confession. But I don't have to be sleeping to think that. It's something in my daily consciousness. It's a sense that is growing stronger by the day. Especially since he came back. The boy I double-crossed and who has really remained loyal to me by sparing my life. Maybe he enjoys the pain I'm in. That's why he has spared me. To ensure I suffer. Am I chronically stressed and depressed? The books I read tell me I am. And the fucking internet. Sorry. I don't think I'm risk-bipolar anymore. I'm the full monty now. Totally bipolar. Sometimes I believe people take thoughts out of my head. I keep telling junior officers to never tell anyone what they're thinking.'

'You really want to feel like a child killer? Is that it?'

'I don't have a choice in the nightmare. I am a child killer.'

'Do you go there to try to understand the mind of someone who would harm a child? To make it real? To think the way they would, perhaps?'

'Well, the one thing that's definitely true is that it isn't a nightmare. I mean in the real sense of the term. I have these elaborate thoughts all the time. It's a total scene played out in my head. These thoughts never leave me. I can't shake them off. My mind is mashed, but it works for me. I think in strange ways. Very few people can tolerate me, or me them. I don't suffer fools gladly. I don't have the patience my father had. But I'm getting there. Will my honesty now land me in even more trouble?'

'If that truly is your worst nightmare, then I'm glad you told me.'

'It's made even worse by revealing it at an AA meeting. I'd never go to one of those things in real life. But it doesn't end there. Due process then kicks in.'

'What do you mean?'

'You see, I have this image that someone from the group pretends to go to the toilet but really goes off and phones the police. The police come then and arrest me for murder. I go through a tedious legal circus, but what makes things worse is that when I am in court, it is not a court of law or justice.'

'What is it then, Jon?'

'Everyone's nightmare. The court of public opinion. There are no rules of evidence, or steps of procedural propriety. No judge to control when everyone speaks. It's just a free for all. Nothing. When I speak to try and defend myself, I'm cut across and shouted down by politicians. It's their chaotic rules. The law of petty committees and groups. My real worst nightmare. It just gets worse and all descends into anarchy. Fucking mad, isn't it, Susannah?'

'You seem to tolerate the comfort of strangers all the same, Jon. Me, for example, and your participants at an AA meeting – to a degree anyway – in your imagination. That would be some confession to make.'

'The bigger the lie, the easier it is to believe. Everyone in Derry can relate to that.'

Valberg stopped speaking and remained silent again, realising he had been talking too much for his liking.

'I've had enough now, Susannah. That's enough. Believe it or not, I'm tired and feel like sleeping. But I wonder if your patients really tell you truthfully what they are thinking. Or do they make it all up?'

'Everyone is different, Jon. If this works for you, then it works for me.'

'Sorry if I digress a lot.'

'It's okay. I'll do my report for now unless there's anything else? Perhaps that's enough for today. Especially if you're tired. But we may have to meet again.'

'No. No. No disrespect. But I don't think so.'

'I'll give you my card with my personal number. Call it anytime you want. If I can ever help you or if you just want to talk.'

'I will. Thank you. I really appreciate that. But you might regret it.'

Valberg got up and left without saying goodbye. He had a sudden urge to visit Orla Harkin's mother. He wanted to get arrangements in place as soon as possible. It was something he must do. His only other thought on leaving was the possibility that what he had just confessed in therapy being known by his father. The chance that it could have easily been Valberg himself who was discovered beside the dead body of Orla Harkin instead of O'Driscoll. He mused over that notion and the consequences that would have developed.

CHAPTER 27

Dottie Harkin's television was so loud it could be heard outside her front door on Lecky Road. She had it permanently on a cycle of news channels. It was currently resting on Sky News.

She still heard her doorbell ring all the same. Oxygen was free-flowing into her through tubes strapped to her face from a small bottle fixed with motorised wheels that she rolled in front of her everywhere she went.

'Come on in, Mr Valberg. Thanks for letting me know you were coming. The police rang me and told me. You're a wee bit early. Get a seat there. Tea?'

'Thank you. No sugar and a little milk.'

Mrs Harkin gestured towards the living-room sofa. The room was filled with framed pictures of her dead daughter, and a fifty-inch, flat-screen television and sound system loomed over the mantelpiece.

'You sit there, love. There's a rumour about the town about some big announcement about the inquiry. My solicitor says I shouldn't talk to you unless he's here. I told him you were coming. He's just a young fella. Alex Devine. He's really taken Orla's case to heart. I had so many solicitors knocking on my door after there was an announcement about a public inquiry. He must have been the only one who didn't knock.'

'Is he coming here now, Mrs Harkin?'

'Naw. Not at all, Mr Valberg.'

'That's good, then.'

'He always calls me before he comes to visit. I told him you were coming and he said he might phone you. Did he?

120

I think he worries about me too much. And you know I just let him get on with it. He wouldn't have caused any trouble for you. I think he probably just wanted to fill you in on my medical condition and all. A courtesy sort of thing. So did he call?'

'No. Not that I know of. But I'm a bit hard to get at the moment. I haven't been at the station recently.'

'Doesn't matter. Jesus, son, I've had more people through this house in the last year than I've had in the last thirty. I'm gonna put the snib on the door, too, so that no-one can get in. Sometimes my nosey brother can't help himself. Always walking over here once he gets the sniff of a stranger in the house asking questions again about Orla. He sees a strange car parked outside and he's over like a moth to a flame.'

'I see. And what's his name?'

'Thomas. He used to be a second-hand car salesman.'

'Okay.'

'But you're not really a stranger. You know all about Orla's case I'm told, but we've never met. I went looking for you one day. But I've read all about you and that, although I didn't see you on the mad day in court. I heard you in the witness box, but I wasn't myself that day. Full of nerve tablets and really not looking at anyone. You know. Did you see me?'

'Yes. For sure I did. I understand how you feel. There's no need to explain.'

'I knew you'd call someday. With everyone running away from that O'Driscoll boy, the wee young solicitor was the only one to help me up and out of the courthouse. He didn't even know who I was.'

'Some compassion from a lawyer. A brave one, too. A remarkable thing, Mrs Harkin.'

'Well, you're here now, Mr Valberg. I did try to go and see you at Strand Road over a year ago now I think. I was in an awful state then that day, too. Some stranger saved my life outside the police station.'

'I'm sorry it's taken so long, Mrs Harkin. I'm glad the stranger saved you as well.'

'Ah. Don't worry about that and here ... have a look at

this. It's a picture of Orla in her First Communion dress. Everyone says she looks like me. What do you think? I talk as if she were still here.'

'It's beautiful, Mrs Harkin. She is beautiful. An angel. You both wear your hair the same. She was . . . well . . . is such a bright-looking child in the photograph.'

'She was my angel from heaven. Here, I better get the tea. No sugar and just some milk did you say?'

'Yes. A little milk.'

'I can move about the house easier than a courtroom. My oxygen bottle has new wheels now, with a wee battery-oper-ated motor. Great job, isn't it? Can you keep the TV on there. I'm afraid in case I miss the news. I've the radio on low in the kitchen as well. Just in case the news comes through.'

The television was still blaring in the living room. Inter-est rates were to rise, a car bomb in Baghdad killed 113 people so far, including women and children, and trade re-lations between America and China were at an all-time low. The price of a barrel of oil was increasing.

Mrs Harkin reappeared with the tea and biscuits and had a seat.

'I suppose you want to ask me about that day. The day that she went missing, Mr Valberg?'

'We can get to that eventually as needs be. But I'd really like to hear about Orla. I want to know everything you can tell me. If you don't mind. Tell me about your daughter.'

'We never left this house and we never changed her room. I know you find that hard to believe. But we kept all her stuff. I can talk about all this easier now without breaking down. I've done it so much. But I must say, son, no-one, not any other police officer, journalist, politician or anyone else asked me about Orla the way you have. Not one person has asked me to tell them about Orla. My child.'

'It's okay, Mrs Harkin. I didn't mean to intrude.'

'When I see you now in the flesh, Mr Valberg, you look a bit different. I've all the press clippings from the past year or so. I had a picture of you somewhere. It's ages since I looked at it. Will I get it? The picture I have of you and show you it?'

'Don't worry about that now, Mrs Harkin.'

'No matter. You're right. The door is locked and I'll just rest here now with the tea, but keep the news on. I'll lower it a little so we're not shouting at each other. God knows, there's been enough shouting and crying in this house over the years. Too much. It has to stop.'

Mrs Harkin went silent staring at the photographs of her daughter.

'Okay, Mrs Harkin. When you're ready. Tell me about your daughter.'

'It's all I have. The photographs. The hope. I keep thinking she's going to walk through the door. You see, any parent of a dead child would. It's the way we are conditioned. Why would we not think that way? So what? I've watched so many things on the TV about missing children and their parents. We're a sort of colony. A leper colony. If someone is looking for something from us, well, they'll find us. Find me. But there's times when most people just walk to the other side of the street and avoid me. They don't want to talk about Orla.'

'I'm sorry to hear that.'

'Ah. That's okay. Human nature I expect. The only place I go to is chapel anyway. But my faith is on the wane. I have even thought of killing myself, many times. The public eventually find people like me too much to handle. I know. We get the pity vote every now and then. It makes people feel good about themselves. Giving us a bit of sympathy. But no-one really sticks with us. Or can stick us for long. The death of a child can cause so much trouble in a family and beyond. God, I should know that. So much family resentment and blame. Awful. Things that are unimaginable.'

Mrs Harkin paused.

'But if she comes back, does she walk through the door as a nine-year-old child? Returned from the dead? Is that right? The way I remember her? But we are all older now. And her father is gone. He never survived. Never could. You reach the lowest point of despair when you actually surrender to the fact that your child is now better off dead and gone.'

'That's very harsh on yourself, Mrs Harkin. Undeserving in many ways.'

'What I really want, and what is just as impossible, is to turn back time. Not to have had my last conversation with her from the kitchen with no eye contact. I was shouting for her to take the change from the mantelpiece and go and get a pint of milk. Such a normal thing. "I'm away now, Mammy." That's the last words she spoke to me. "All right, love," I said. The door shut. She was gone. No return, Mr Valberg. I sent her out into a thunderstorm. She was never to see the light of day again. I have to live with that every day.'

Mrs Harkin sighed.

'I hear all these people on the TV searching for truth and justice. Justice this and justice that. But what does it mean? It's so shallow. The only thing I know as a definite fact, Mr Valberg, about Orla's case, is that I never made eye contact with her before she left. That's all I know. I'm so confused now. And my solicitor has told me he knows that Mr O'Driscoll's case – or his conviction – will be thrown out. What's the point of it all? I wish I could speak to that boy. Face-to-face. Just call him by his name. Gerard.'

'What would you like to ask him, Mrs Harkin?'

'Sorry, Mr Valberg. You asked me about Orla and I've been jabbering on about myself.'

'It's okay. What would you like to ask Gerard?'

Mrs Harkin rubbed her eyes and then looked at her hands.

'I'd like to be as close to him as I am to you. And look at him, the way I'm looking at you, and tell him I'm so sorry for all the pain that he, his mother and father went through in their lives. I'd tell him that I never felt comfortable with his conviction. Something wasn't right. I always knew it. I'd try and hold his hand. Tell him I'm not long for this life. But that he should not have suffered the way he did. I don't want to ask him about all the recent stuff in Derry. I can only see Orla. Everything goes back to the beginning. It always does.'

'I'm sure he'd like to hear all that. Especially from you. And you really mean it. Your apology. It is so obviously from the heart.'

Mrs Harkin's stare was even more intense now.

'It is. And it's funny. But I had been angry for over thirty years. Angry at everyone and everything. I'm still confused and saddened. Obviously. But the anger has gone. I've let it go. I don't react to loud voices and shouting anymore. I've stopped making demands. Stopped complaining. I've mellowed in my old age. I just think the truth might walk through my door one day. Peace. I'd just like peace. It's a very cynical world now. Isn't it, Mr Valberg? Since my faith left me I'm a bit more relaxed about dying. I sort of convince myself I have faith and I'll see Orla again but that's all rubbish. Isn't it? I know that now. I'm just cynical now. That's all.'

'I understand, Mrs Harkin. But don't underestimate your apology to Gerard. Especially from you. There's no need for you to apologise to anyone, for anything.'

'An apology may not do much good. But at least I'd get saying it. If I could meet with him, perhaps I'd like to ask him if he noticed anything about Orla when he stumbled over her. Anything at all? Any memory of anything? I know now there wasn't a mark on her body. Back in nineteen eighty-two you just accepted what you were told by anyone in any sort of authority. Today no-one accepts anything, especially when it is from someone who is supposed to be in authority. We question everything and respect nothing. I try. But I've lost all faith in the justice system, too. Not just religion. It's so desolate.'

'Don't be so hard on yourself, Mrs Harkin.'

'I know. I know. But those two policemen.'

'Dickey and Montgomery?'

'Aye, them two. Then they were murdered over at the hospital. Awful. They told me that Orla had been interfered with. I didn't know what they meant then. I know now. But it was best that I didn't know the details, they said. I never told her father. So I took their word. But that young solicitor has since found out that that was all rubbish, and Orla died of a broken neck only. There wasn't a bruise or a mark on her body. She wouldn't have suffered or anything, I'm told. Not like she was buried in a hole or a cave or something in the dark. She wouldn't have been screaming or anything like that. Well, that's what I tell myself. But all I know as a fact is that when Orla left this house, I spoke to her from the kitchen. No eye contact. That's always haunted me.'

'From what I know, Mrs Harkin, your daughter did not suffer.'

'At least I have that, then.'

'Can you tell me more about Orla?'

CHAPTER 28

Mrs Harkin looked around her living room and sighed softly before she spoke.

'Orla had beautiful eyes. Really blue. A bit of a tomboy in many ways. But such a beautiful little girl. She was talented at art and writing. Loved reading, too. She said from a very early age that she wanted to be an art teacher. First it was an artist, but then an art teacher. Typical of her. Always wanting to help others. She would have been a great art teacher. I've kept all her paintings and stories up in her room. Nothing is changed. Nothing. I won't let anyone else clean the room. I keep it as it was and I haven't thrown out anything. We couldn't afford frames or anything. Orla kept everything so neat in scrapbooks. Some of them made by herself.'

'Mrs Harkin, she sounds like a great girl.'

'She was. Very creative and secretive in her own way, too. A wise head for a nine-year-old, which made what happened to her even more confusing for me. If I could just find out how it came to be that she walks out of here and ends up out the line, lying on her back dead the next day with a broken neck, maybe I could die in peace. Sorry, Mr Valberg.'

'It's quite all right. Go on. Tell me more about her.'

'Some of her stories and pictures were scary, but I only found those ones after the funeral. They were stuffed down the side of her bed.'

Mrs Harkin sighed once more then continued.

'She did that thing, preserving insects in the books. Like butterflies and even one with a big moth. Then she had her

127

wee stories written around them. Around the dead insects. She had an old jar. A big fat one, where she collected all the insects. She had two of them, in fact. God, just when I say that now I can see her face lighting up from one day when an old jam jar was finished. She really wanted it. The jars are still in her room. Two of them anyway. She had the insects in self-made paper books and jars.'

'How creative.'

'I know. I put them all in her scrapbooks. Some of her stories I just didn't understand. I still don't. But mostly, everything was typical of a young innocent child full of life, without a worry in the world.'

'Nothing or no-one bothered her, then?'

'Not that I know of. And she certainly wasn't spoilt. Well, not the way children are today. Her daddy spoilt her to bits with love all the same. They loved each other so much. It was really touching to witness. All gone now.'

'He's passed away?'

'He was heartbroken. Never could recover. Anyway, art, writing and reading was all she ever done. And that collecting the insects thing. In her own world. Orla's world. We got a sign made – 'Orla's World'. It's still on her door. She had her wee friends and it was so sad watching them all crying and confused when she died. Orla's white coffin was in here. Just where you are sitting, Mr Valberg. The queue to get in was all the way down the Lecky Road to Free Derry Corner almost. It stretched for ages.'

'That's a lot of people.'

'I think no-one could believe she was dead and wanted to see the body just to convince themselves. Everyone left the house in tears after seeing her in the wee coffin. Some broke down in the house. Strangers even. People I never knew. And didn't know Orla. Me and her father were out of it over those days of the wake and funeral. We couldn't cope or understand what was happening.'

'Who could blame you, Mrs Harkin?'

'Ah. Terrible. What's to be done?'

'Can I ask you something, Mrs Harkin?'

'Aye. What is it?'

'Can I go up and look at her room? I promise I won't ...'

'Of course you can. By all means do.'

'You wouldn't mind? I don't want to hold you back too much longer. And the tea was delicious. Thank you.'

'You go on now. Give me your cup there. Go on ahead. It's the first door facing you at the top of the stairs. Her sign is on the door. Go on. If it helps you and can do anything at all to help Orla's case ... well, go on. No problem. Take your time and I'll listen to the news. It'll not take our Thomas long anyway before he shows up.'

'Mrs Harkin, why don't you imagine your last conversation with Orla, perhaps here in this room? Together. And you give her a hug and a kiss before she ...'

'Before she leaves?'

'Why not?'

'I'm ahead of you there, son. I do that all the time. Why, if I didn't do that I'd be dead long ago.'

The telephone rang in the living room. Mrs Harkin turned the television down and answered it. 'It's my solicitor here,' she confirmed.

'Go on, Mrs Harkin.'

'Any news, then? The policeman's with me now. Mr Valberg. We've had a lovely chat and he's going up to look at Orla's room now. He's just finished his tea. He's going up now. He's a lovely man. Lovely. It was great to finally talk to him and get some things off my chest.'

CHAPTER 29

Gerard O'Driscoll stood in the small hallway of Orla's home. He looked at himself in the circular mirror that hung on one of the faux wood-panelled walls. He didn't think he looked like a policeman at all, never mind Jon Valberg. He even wondered if Mrs Harkin had just been playing along with him. He scratched at the cake on his face he used to hide his scar and pulled off the wig he was wearing.

It was a similar hallway to his own childhood home. He remembered it so well. And recalled arriving home from school to find his own mother, crippled in anguish, wailing uncontrollably as she stood in the tight passageway. She had just heard the news of her husband's murder, blown up in an IRA bomb that allegedly exploded prematurely. That scene was seared into his mind. He had collapsed in heartache into his mother's weak and lifeless arms. The image was very strong in his head now and made him falter slightly.

A loud banging on the front door focused him again. Someone was calling, 'Dottie. Dottie. Are you in there? Bloody snib is on the door. It's Thomas. What's going on in there? Dottie. Dottie. Can you hear me?'

O'Driscoll stared with disdain at the door and said quietly, 'The moth has arrived. But there's no bright light for him here anymore.'

O'Driscoll moved quietly towards the stairs. He heard Mrs Harkin answer her solicitor.

'But that can't be right. Sure he's here now. I hear him going up the stairs. I'm not getting out of me own house. Don't be daft, Alex, Mr Valberg can't be with you. He's here now. In my house. The snib is on the door and no-one can get in. For God's sake, Alex, calm down, son. You'll give yourself a heart attack or a stroke.'

O'Driscoll knew he didn't have long.

With a few strides, O'Driscoll was at 'Orla's World'. He opened the door carefully. Mrs Harkin was now calling him and her brother was banging on the door even more loudly. It was not the peaceful and graceful moment O'Driscoll thought he would have in Orla's bedroom. It wasn't the way he imagined it in his head as he sipped his tea downstairs. Nothing much was now.

Mrs Harkin started shouting from the bottom of the stairs.

'Hi, you up there. Who are you? Go away, Thomas. I'm not answering the door. I'm not taking the snib off. Go away. I've no fear in me anymore.'

O'Driscoll could also hear sirens in the distance. Were they for him? He wasn't sure, but the solicitor must have contacted all the emergency services. He thought of lying down on Orla's bed. Just to relax. He briefly imagined being arrested without any struggle.

It was a small single bed facing the window against the wall to his immediate right as he entered the room. Orla was certainly not spoilt the way children are today. The room wasn't strewn with disused toys. Pictures of princesses and angels covered the walls and scrapbooks were piled high on the floor by the window and on a small dresser table. O'Driscoll wished he had time to read them. He dared not remove or disturb anything. The room was simple, neat and small. But all a young girl needed, thought O'Driscoll. A cabbage patch doll lay on Orla's bed. The pastel colours of the curtains and duvet didn't match the dark pattern colours of the carpet. O'Driscoll took in what he could. Especially the brash 1980s colours.

There was a large portrait photograph of Orla hanging on the wall above the bed. The image immediately burned deep into O'Driscoll's mind as he looked at Orla's mouth and her smiling white teeth.

'Speak, speak softly to me, Orla,' he whispered above the noise from below.

The sirens outside were getting louder and O'Driscoll could see a bit of the bottom of the City Cemetery from the window facing him. Time to turn and leave. No dramatic jump out the back window. He did not want to disturb the room.

Just before he turned to leave he noticed the tools of the amateur entomologist; a killing jar and a relaxing jar. O'Driscoll could see that Orla had some expertise in her hobby. One of the jars – the larger one – must have been the killing jar, O'Driscoll thought, which still had the outline of some darkened tape around its lower half to prolong its potency and protect it from sunlight. The other jar, used to relax the trapped insects, would then help to soften them. O'Driscoll knew that insects were normally then 'pinned' and collected for preservation. He concluded that the ones Orla did not successfully pin and collect from the relaxing jar were still preserved by her in her homemade books, directly from the killing jar. Nothing was wasted. What a clever girl. Like him, she must have spent a lot of time on her own.

O'Driscoll turned and went back down the stairs. He immediately looked at Mrs Harkin, still standing in the hallway and still shouting at her nosey brother to go away.

'It's okay, son. I won't let Thomas in, and I'll let you leave. Go out the back door. That way. No-one will notice. Were you let out of prison or what happened? My solicitor says it could be you. Is it you? Gerard?'

O'Driscoll didn't speak but took Mrs Harkin's offer and hurried past her. He was at the back door in no time and about to run when he stopped and turned around.

'Mrs Harkin.'

She just about made it to the door behind him, wheeling her oxygen tank in front of her.

'What is it, son? You better go on.'

'Orla. I just realised from the big photograph in her room. I remembered.'

'What is it?'

'I tried ...'

O'Driscoll was breaking. His voice shook.

'I tried to wake her up. That's all I did. I couldn't believe she was dead. I didn't touch or harm her. I promise you. I slipped and fell on her but didn't harm her.'

O'Driscoll shook his head in distress.

'I cried into her. I remember my tears falling on her face, on her mouth, her lips, but ...'

'Tell me.'

'She was content, Mrs Harkin. Peaceful. It was as if she didn't want to be disturbed. Or awakened. I know that's strange. But that's what I thought. She was calm. She is with the angels, Mrs Harkin. You must believe that. Don't believe what they say about me. Your daughter is safe. That's all that matters. You must be at peace. Of everyone in this mess you deserve the most. Peace.'

Mrs Harkin stumbled as if to faint, falling forwards, but O'Driscoll steadied her and held her.

'Go, son. Go. Thank you.'

O'Driscoll looked at the old woman one last time and left, leaping over the wooden fence to dogs barking and sirens blaring and hurried away through the Brandywell towards the City Cemetery.

CHAPTER 30

A cacophony of police sirens in the Brandywell was going to be a recipe for disaster. Valberg knew he was liable to get pelted by bricks just for stepping out of a police vehicle in the area. Or even a bullet in his brain. Nothing much had changed in the last twenty years.

His pre-arranged visit had certainly not gone to plan. He had been calmly sitting in Alex Devine's office having a cup of coffee when Alex rang Mrs Harkin to confirm he and Valberg would be dropping round soon for a friendly chat. Now he couldn't believe he was arriving at Mrs Harkin's house for the first time in a blaze of drama and sirens – exactly what Chief Superintendent Kells didn't want.

'Jesus Christ,' Valberg muttered to himself.

The simultaneous arrival of hordes of the media just added to the hysteria. Valberg was sure they couldn't know that O'Driscoll was here. But he immediately realised the media knew something was going to break and they were there for Mrs Harkin's reaction.

As he hurried out of the police car driven by Constable Bell, Valberg noticed Mrs Harkin's front door was already open. As he entered the hallway and looked in to his right, he could see Mrs Harkin sitting with an oxygen mask on, clutching a photograph that he assumed featured Orla. She was fixated with the television. Was this her last hope for truth and justice?

The news channel was flashing the breaking news.

'We're going live now to Derry to our reporter, Terry McBride, who has the story on the dramatic developments

134

we have just been telling you about. Can you bring us up to date, Terry?'

Valberg could hear McBride being interviewed. He could see that everyone was absorbed with his responses while the police quickly swarmed over the premises and surrounding area.

'What we know now is that Mr Gerard O'Driscoll has escaped from the Maze prison. The story has been circulating within news media here in the last couple of hours. But it is now officially confirmed.'

There were gasps from everyone around Valberg, including some police officers.

'He is at large and the police have just issued a statement via PSNI Headquarters in Belfast just moments ago to say, in effect, that no-one is to approach Mr O'Driscoll in any shape or fashion. Understandably so.'

'Has he escaped from the purpose-built prison, Terry, we've heard so much about?'

'Yes, Jeremy. It appears he was able to escape with no damage caused or injuries to any prison staff.'

'And this specially constructed complex was designed with the sole purpose of holding Mr O'Driscoll, with its own courtroom and security so that he never had to leave when he was to go on trial?'

'Yes. That's exactly right. A public inquiry was supposed to be held there as well.'

'What is to happen now, Terry?'

'We understand the Secretary of State for Northern Ireland is due to make a statement about the inquiry shortly. In respect of the court complex, everything was to be self-contained within it. The first of its kind.'

'At a cost of millions, that many critics say could have been used for health or education instead of lawyers.'

'That is correct. Three hundred million is the figure quoted. Many say it cost hundreds of millions more. Especially with the court they added on and the facilities for the lawyers.'

'Did that drive the costs up?'

'That apparently did inflate the price extraordinarily and caused further outrage.'

'So what else has happened there today?'

'The other piece of fascinating news here, Jeremy, is that the Public Prosecution Service have also issued a statement just moments ago to say a number of extremely important things. Firstly, there will be no charges proceeded with in relation to the ex-Chief Constable Seán Carlin. Nor will criminal charges of any sort be proceeded with in relation to Mr O'Driscoll either. It's understood all these decisions have been taken at the highest level on the grounds of national security. That line won't come as much of a surprise to many sceptics here.'

'What have the families of Mr O'Driscoll's alleged victims been saying about all this? This all seems somewhat orchestrated, don't you think?'

'Yes. I can certainly see that. But there's nothing yet from the families of O'Driscoll's alleged victims, as this news is just breaking.'

'And you would think they will be very upset by all of this.'

'I am sure they, and lots of politicians and lawyers, will have much to say soon. With so many lawyers representing so many interested parties at potential trials, and the inquiry, I am sure there will be much disquiet in the legal world particularly. The number of legal cases and settings – inquiries and trials and so forth – would have been massive and the number of solicitors and barristers involved, well, colossal. An army of lawyers were due to set up camp at the Maze complex.'

'Yes, I can see there will be some disquiet in the legal profession for sure there, Terry.'

'What's more, Jeremy, is that we also understand the Public Prosecution Service will not be making any submissions to the court when Mr O'Driscoll's appeal against conviction and his sentence for the murder of nine-year-old Orla Harkin comes before the Court of Appeal in the near future. It's thought that the death of this child, in nineteen eighty-two, was the catalyst for recent unfortunate events here.'

'So it is likely Mr O'Driscoll's conviction will be quashed then, Terry? Is that right? Another legal avenue effectively over?'

'Yes, Jeremy. That seems to be the logic of it.'

Mrs Harkin sobbed into the photograph she was grasping.

The truth and justice world was in free fall.

'But let's go back to this escape. It's hard to believe, isn't it? He was the most closely guarded prisoner, and perhaps the most dangerous one, ever to be in custody in the United Kingdom or Ireland.'

'Yes. That's correct.'

'His alleged offences in Derry alone made worldwide headlines.'

'O'Driscoll's story did indeed travel far and wide.'

'And the rows that the politicians had about the use of the Maze as essentially a secure legal factory with a prison, to deal with all the matters arising from the O'Driscoll affair, were bloody. If you excuse the language. This will cause outrage, surely? You had a multi-million-pound high-security prison for one inmate, on remand no less, and he has escaped. Not something you want in your culture year either in Londonderry, surely?'

'Yes, Jeremy. Outrage and fear in this community. Remember, this man instilled a level of fear in this city not even experienced in over thirty years of intense violence. We understand Special Forces are to be drafted in to track him down. There are unconfirmed reports that there will be international input into the hunt for O'Driscoll.'

'What are the public advised to do, Terry?'

'At this moment, the advice seems to be sensible. Stay indoors and do not in any circumstances approach Mr O'Driscoll if he is spotted. We further understand the police here will set up a special emergency line to call if the fugitive is seen anywhere.'

'Thank you, Terry. There's certainly a lot to take in and contemplate. Please do keep us up to date. Let's turn now to our resident legal expert, Leslie Goodfellow, to discuss the ramifications and implications of these dramatic developments ...'

Valberg caught a better glimpse now of the television from the hallway as he moved a little closer in. He looked on in disbelief.

'Fuck me,' he said, shaking his head.

Police continued to flood the area and a helicopter was buzzing overhead. He would get no sense out of Mrs Harkin at the moment, concluded Valberg. The scene was chaotic. The police were trying to hold the media back, while at the same time searching for O'Driscoll and securing an appropriate boundary to ensure their own safety in an area in which they were still despised.

Fully armed police were moving in significant numbers through the Harkin house and beyond, scouring back lanes and alleyways. In the street, several youths were calling them 'scumbags' and spat in their direction.

Valberg's phone rang and his immediate thought was that it was Amanda Cleary requesting to get past police lines. He knew he had been extra careful with his new number and burner phone and wondered how she had reached him. But the caller's identification was withheld.

'Hello.'

'Thus hath the candle singd the moath.'

'What? Gerry. Where are you?'

'A bit breathless again. But safe now.'

'Where are you? Tell me. And how did you get this new number?'

'Did anyone do basic police investigation? Anyone?'

'Gerry. End this now. Today.'

'Check Thomas, the dirty rat. A car salesman. Thomas King. King fucking rat. Mrs Harkin's brother. I pretended I didn't know about him when she mentioned him. He's there now, in consoling mode. He'll be with the solicitor drawing up a statement next. He'll have something in there about compensation I'd bet. While it's all going on would you do something for me?'

'What's that, Gerry? Are you going to send me on another one of your wild goose chases again? Another red herring? Another false cryptic lead is it, with Thomas the rat? What do you want?'

'The room at the top of the stairs. Orla's room. Her mother never changed it. Now's your best chance. Go and have a look. For both of us. Tell me what you see when we next talk. Go on. I had no time to check it as that bloody merchant of venom was banging on the front door.'

'Where are you? I've heard the news. You're an innocent man, Gerry. Officially innocent. Come forward. Meet me somewhere. Anywhere. You name it. I'm sure being unlaw-fully at large is the least of your worries.'

'It all goes back to the beginning, Jon. The battle lines are drawn away from culture city. There'll be no inquiry either, by the way. The legal process is void. So hell will be un-leashed. On me that is. You see, I had a moment sitting in Orla's house. I'm in mercy mode. I'm not long for this world. My body and mind are abandoning me. The moth Mrs Har-kin mentioned to me made me think about mercy. Hath not an innocent man eyes? Mercy, Jon. Mercy.'

'Where, Gerry? Where can we meet? I've no time for this. I never do.'

'Check her room. Like I said, I'd no time. Well, I've got even less time now. But you have all the time in the world, Jon. Orla was an apprentice entomologist no less. You'll find a killing jar and a relaxing jar.'

The line went dead. There was still pandemonium going on around Valberg. He felt he was back at the beginning. Back staring at Billy Black hanging from Craigavon Bridge and at the angry scene at Paddy Sharkey's blood-soaked house from two years ago. He felt he was back in the bow-els of an investigation into O'Driscoll's murder spree that was going nowhere. The investigation was a shambles until O'Driscoll handed himself in to the police. It got even more shambolic after that.

Valberg went through the unnecessary mechanics in his head of asking Mrs Harkin for permission to visit her daugh-ter's room but decided against it. Her GP had now arrived and was dealing with her in the living room. DS Wilson and Constables Bell and Hastings were now helping to secure the area. Alex Devine had appeared and was scribbling out some notes in the crowded hallway.

Police let Valberg past and he walked directly up the stairs. He felt as though everyone else was high on drugs, operating at a million miles an hour, while he was in delib-erate slow motion mode.

In a state of quiet calm, Valberg arrived at Orla's World.

CHAPTER 31

Valberg, like O'Driscoll, first noticed the cabbage patch doll on the bed and the large printed photograph of Orla on the wall. Both were hard to miss. He also saw the two glass jars O'Driscoll told him about sitting on a small table.

The noise of the television downstairs was booming and loud. Valberg decided to ignore it. His eyes were drawn to the scrapbooks and Beatrix Potter books in tidy bundles.

Valberg thought of his own 1982 bedroom. Orla's room had defeated the brutal dictator: time. It stood still. The moment was frozen. The sensation was strong and alive. Valberg had stepped back in time. He was in his own room as a teenager. He was thinner. His hair was longer. He couldn't decide if the guitar solo in *The Analog Kid*, or *Chemistry* was his favourite from Rush's 1982 album, *Signals*. It was a fantastic problem to have. He even felt taller. He stood straight and put his shoulders back. He was waiting on the World Cup in Spain and looking forward to seeing Brazil.

The old coloured Hitachi television in the living room was transported to Valberg's bedroom. It was to make way for a new model with 'deluxe' colour. The ancient TV was so thick its wooden frame also acted as an excellent bookshelf for all those unnecessary A-level books. Once Valberg and his father navigated the heavy device up the stairs, he remembered his father saying, 'I wonder if we will ever see you again, Jon?' The television found pride of place at the bottom of Valberg's bed. BBC1, BBC2, and ITV were clear enough, but what a hassle it was trying to get RTÉ, Valberg remembered.

Valberg could smell and see his own room as he stood in Orla's. Time meant nothing now. Surely Gerry would have had a similar room, thought Valberg. Why wouldn't he? He didn't have a father to help him carry up an old TV. But his bedroom must have been peaceful and private enough to be able to study and do homework.

With his own TV, Valberg could now watch *Blackadder*. He also kept a close lookout for when the film *Don't Look Now* was to be on, as he was mesmerised with the beauty of Julie Christie. He hadn't thought about her in years. Standing in Orla's bedroom, he was flooded with thoughts of the actress. What a beautiful woman. What a brilliant actress.

All good memories, thought Valberg. And getting better in his head. If he were to go downstairs, his mother would be cooking dinner. His father would be tying flies. He would see the dinner table laid out for three people. A father, a mother and their son. They would eat quietly together. They wouldn't say much. But all three loved each other deeply, always and forever. Eventually time would end this.

Orla's World, for the moment, had the effect of taking Valberg back to a better time in his life. He just wished he had spoken more at dinner. He wished he had spoken more to his parents in general, about anything and everything. He wished that he hadn't rushed his meals so much, anxious to get back upstairs and study or listen to music. Or hope that *Don't Look Now* would be on. He reached out to touch his father, but a young girl's voice startled him.

'Hi. Who are you, mister? What are yee doing in there?'

Valberg saw Orla's photograph on turning around and the sight of the girl startled him even more. Momentarily, he thought it was Orla, or that he was hallucinating.

Valberg was muffled and unclear in his answer.

'I'm ... was ... I'm a member of ... I'm a policeman.'

'You don't look like a cop to me. I'm gett'n me da.'

'No. Wait. Wait. What's your name?'

'What's my name? What's *your* name?'

'Jon.'

'Are you that Jon Valberg boy? I've heard your bangers have gone and you're bonkers.'

'Is that so?'

141

'Aye.'

'It's probably true, then. I like that word. Bonkers. Haven't heard it in years.'

Valberg smiled.

'Are you bonkers then, Mr Valberg?'

Valberg didn't reply.

The girl continued.

'I came up here to get away from the noise downstairs. Me ma lets me come up here when I'm sad.'

'Only when you're sad?'

'That's not right. Just whenever I want. I made the sad bit up.'

Valberg smiled.

'Can you tell me your name?'

'Me da says never tell a cop anything.'

'So, are you related to Orla?'

'Mister, you ask a whole lot of questions. Anyway, aye. Me ma is a cousin or something. I'm not too sure about all that family stuff. I never met her. Just hear all about her. We're the same age now. Nine.'

'It's a beautiful age.'

'It's mental down the stairs. It always is when something starts. It's a bit of a creep show. I don't think it's helping old Dottie at all. But I don't understand everything. Anyway. Were you up here reading her stuff coz if you were I'm calling—'

Valberg politely cut in.

'I haven't touched anything. Not a thing. I thought about it, though. But I've decided not to. Not without Orla's mother's permission. Is that okay?'

'Well, you're a cop, so I don't believe a word you say as me da says you're all scumbags.'

'Is that so?'

'Aye. But I don't have to agree with him. Do I?'

Valberg smiled again.

'Anyway. Your bangers have gone they said, but I read all about yee in the *Journal*. You're not a real mad person, are you?'

Valberg didn't have to reply as a female voice was calling;

'Amelia. Amelia. Are you up there?'

Valberg was quick to interject and smiled.

'What a name! Amelia. What a beautiful name.'

Amelia shouted back.

'It's okay, Ma. I'm up here with that crazy cop you all talk about. Mr Valberg. But, Ma, he's not mad or anything. I was just showing him Orla's room. He asked me first yee know. Definitely not mad, so I'm okay.'

Valberg smiled again and sighed. Being in Orla's room had taken him to a place and time he wished he could go back to. But that's all it was. A wish. He felt positive and relaxed and ready to talk to Mrs Harkin when she was ready, despite the commotion down the stairs.

'I was just doing what you were doing, Mr Valberg,' said Amelia.

'What's that?'

'Coming up here for some peace. And if you want to know what's in Orla's stuff you don't need to read it.'

'Why not, Amelia?'

'Just ask me. I've read it all. I know everything. The lot. I've read that stuff for years. I didn't understand the words at first. But then when I understood the words I didn't understand what she was saying. But I can now and ...'

'Perhaps you can tell me someday. If your daddy allows you.'

Amelia smiled. 'I made that up, too. He'll not mind.'

'Okay.'

'But I didn't make up the part about you, or everyone saying you were a bit bonkers.'

'There's that word again, Amelia. Well, it was nice to meet you.'

'You, too. I suppose. I never talked to a cop before.'

'Thank you. And what a beautiful name.'

'It was Orla's, too.'

'Orla's?'

'Her middle name. Orla Amelia Harkin.'

'Right. I see.'

'She flew a plane from America to here. On her own. Not our Orla . . .'

'Oh ...' Valberg laughed.

'Amelia Earhart. Here to Derry. Did you know that, Mr

Valberg? I did a project for it at school and I got a prize. I made up a story that she never left here and lived in Derry for the rest of her life. She was here all the time. You see, I could do a whole pile of stuff about Derry and have Amelia Earhart in the middle of it all. Because she never left. That's really bonkers.'

'Can I see it sometime? That's a great idea. The thought of Amelia Earhart living in Derry all this time after all. Fantastic. Brilliant. Well done.'

'It's up in the Assembly Hall. I put pictures and diagrams and everything on it. My photo was in the *Journal*. I made up the story that she never left Derry and told her story for the last eighty years. I had to check a lot on the internet. And books.'

'Congratulations, Amelia. Well done.'

'I carried around a notebook since I was four or five and used to write wee stories. I'd make things up in my imagination, like Orla. I just drew wee pictures and put some words to them. I've still got them, too. I still do it. I think my stories, or things that happen to me, help me write. I'm just trying to be like Orla.'

'Brilliant, Amelia. Your mum and dad must be so proud of you.'

Amelia stared at Valberg.

Reluctantly, Valberg knew his time in 1982 had to come to an end and his discussion about Amelia Earhart was also going to finish. It was a topic Valberg's father was animated about and Valberg recalled his father having never understood why more wasn't made of the queen of aviation in Derry.

He closed Orla's door. He hadn't felt in such a good mood for some time.

Amelia said, 'Bye,' and disappeared down the stairs as quickly has she had appeared.

CHAPTER 32

The noise had calmed a little in Mrs Harkin's house and the television had mercifully been switched to mute. Wilson was standing at the bottom of the stairs waiting on Valberg. She pulled the living-room door closed.

'She'll only talk to you. And on your own. She doesn't even want the solicitor present. She's under a lot of pressure but strangely ...'

'Strangely what, Linda?'

'Very calm. Peaceful. She's not too worried about O'Driscoll at large, or the end of the legal process. The Secretary of State was on and ...'

'No public inquiry either?'

'That's right. National security. Calls for resignations everywhere.'

'Security of the truth, Linda. Keeping justice secure and safe enough so no-one gets any experience of it. Put truth and justice in a sealed box somewhere in a government office. Far too much at stake. I could be the only person in court and without a job when all this is over. I was the only one with a criminal conviction after the attacks by Raymond the Reaper as a result of too much alcohol in my system.'

'You don't seem too worried all the same.'

'I never relish the thought of a witness box. No-one does. Even when they're speaking the truth.'

'Well, Mrs Harkin and her solicitor are going out to give something to the press outside. Then it's agreed we are all leaving. Just as orchestrated as all that bullshit on the TV we've just watched down here. You'd think Headquarters could have let us know.'

'Headquarters isn't running this show, Linda. This is all being driven from elsewhere. Anyway, I'm staying to talk with Mrs Harkin. If that is what she wants?'

'Yes.'

'We are to all start leaving now ...'

The living-room door opened and out came Mrs Harkin with Alex Devine and her brother Thomas. The solicitor nodded at Valberg and gestured to him to wait in the living room.

Valberg focused on Mrs Harkin's battery-operated oxygen tank with wheels.

All the other people in the house left, including Amelia with her mother. Mrs Harkin, her solicitor and her brother gathered together outside the front door. Valberg went in and sat in the living room on his own, staring at the muted television, with images of dead Iraqi women and children, torn to pieces, in the latest bomb blast that day in Baghdad. The camera crews had arrived early at the bomb scene and Valberg thought Sky were broadcasting too soon. He stared at the silent television. The despair on the faces of those not killed in the bomb blast was agonising for Valberg to watch; utter futility and desolation. Always desolation. But he didn't want to change the channel. The bomb had been massive and the death toll had now risen to 207. It looked as if the world was ending to Valberg, starting in the Middle East.

Valberg believed the images on the television would be an assault on the viewers watching them. The scene was devastating and bloody. But all too often, such images were also as quickly forgotten as viewed. The media would move on to another atrocity. Or another plane crash or natural disaster. The death toll always needed increasing to make headline news.

Valberg was totally focussed on the television until he heard Devine clearing his throat outside. He peered out of the living-room window and thought the young solicitor looked very nervous in front of the jostling media.

'I'll just read a prepared statement here on behalf of my client, Mrs Dottie Harkin ... if you all give me a moment ...'

Valberg momentarily caught the eye of Mrs Harkin who appeared bewildered. He slumped back again and continued to watch the TV while straining slightly to listen to Devine.

'My client has listened carefully to all the developments today, which seem to bring the legal process, in some areas, to an end. Subject, of course, to challenge by any interested party wishing to do so. But it shouldn't bring to an end the PSNI investigation into the murder of Mrs Harkin's daughter, Orla, and the tracking down of her killer ...'

Thomas King broke in, nodding his head saying, 'Hear, hear!'

'That investigation should be renewed with vigour. There must be some degree of accountability in these matters. No stone should be left unturned in the quest for truth and justice. And justice delayed is justice denied ...'

Thomas King broke in a second time. 'And we want compensation for my ... my, ah ... my sister. Aye, we want compensation for our family.' With his hands shaking, King then lit a cigarette.

What a fucking disaster this was turning into for the solicitor, Valberg thought. Alex Devine wasn't long qualified and this was his big chance at Derry stardom and celebrity status. It was all going terribly wrong. His predictable and clichéd statement made all the more nauseous by the interruptions of a moron.

The dead bodies were still piling up in Iraq according to reports on the television. The death toll was still rising. A camera team were now at the crater left by the bomb. It was like a bloodied Grand Canyon.

Then the television screen suddenly switched to a live close-up of Mrs Harkin.

But poor Alex never made it to the big time. Valberg grabbed the remote and unmuted the sound. All that could be heard from the solicitor was, 'Thank you.'

Then Amanda Cleary's unmistakeable voice could be heard asking, 'Mrs Harkin, what have you got to say to Gerard O'Driscoll?'

A simple and direct question. That was why everyone had really gathered outside Mrs Harkin's house. She seemed to take ages to acknowledge the question, let alone answer it.

Valberg smiled. 'Take your time, Mrs Harkin. Make them wait,' he said to himself.

'You know what, love? I'm tired but content today. A lot more content than many of you here. And a lot more content than I was yesterday. I want for nothing. Really. I don't. Not now. Not from today. Orla's not coming back. She can't. She's not nine anymore either. But that's the way I'll remember her. I'd call that boy by his first name. Gerard. He had a mother. And a father. He was from this city, too, you know. He had his father taken away from him. Like many sons. Was anyone ever brought to justice for that? Naw. He didn't live that far away from here either. Who are we to judge anyone? Let the police do their job and find out who killed Orla or ... or perhaps let it go ...'

The press gathering all moved in their positions. Alex Devine was in shock. Thomas King started coughing then lit another cigarette.

'I've found out today, from praying to God, that Orla was at peace when she died. I really feel that. That she was content and settled. That she wasn't in pain. Hadn't suffered. That someone cared for her when she lay on the riverbank of the Foyle, so much that he cried for her, that he tried to wake her. So I'm okay. I'd say sorry to Gerard. Sorry to him sincerely for the murder of his father and the sad death of his mother. I'm sorry his tears of anguish didn't wake up my daughter.'

There was total silence. Mrs Harkin captivated everyone. She cleared her throat and continued.

'I've heard the news. My solicitor told me Gerard escaped from this billion-pound prison and court we've all heard about. I've heard all the rows about money. Look at me. Look at my house. You're all here now, but you'll be gone in five minutes. Back to your own families. Your own sons and daughters.'

Mrs Harkin paused again. No-one moved or spoke.

'I'll still be here. If Gerard wants to come and see me, then he's more than welcome. And one last thing, everyone. You have all fed on my grief and that of others for a long time. It's not a criticism of you all here today. I can only thank you for your support in keeping Orla's case alive. But I'd like to say to everyone who has suffered the way I have – for whatever reason – don't let your grief turn to bitterness. If you do, then you become another victim. There has to be something better ahead for all of us. That's all I've got to say. I have to go now because I need to change my oxygen tank.'

Mrs Harkin became emotional for the first time and with her voice breaking she said, 'Cheerio.'

The press were more than respectful towards Mrs Harkin as she turned to go back into her home, her motorised oxygen tank helping to steady her.

Valberg stood up and watched the press leaving. The moment Amanda Cleary spotted him he decided it was time to slip out the back door. He instinctively knew Mrs Harkin had had enough of talking for one day. He had imagined a quiet and undisturbed conversation with her. But that was now impossible. He left just before they all returned inside.

Valberg decided he would call Alex Devine later and explain his hasty exit.

CHAPTER 33

Seán Carlin paused and looked around the bunker at all those present.

'We have to get him. Before he gets us. Is that clear?'

No-one answered.

'You have all been carefully selected for an operation that has full "JAG" approval. For the uninitiated, that means we have full legal authority to deal with O'Driscoll from a Judge Advocate General. A military lawyer, who has already ruled on the legality of the proposed operation.'

'Sorry, sir, what does "deal with O'Driscoll" mean?' asked Mike. 'Does it mean dead or alive? Do we shoot to maim? We've been trained to shoot to kill. What's expected of us? I mean, sir, we don't want a grey area, do we?'

'No. We don't, Mike. I don't anyway.'

'We don't want to be stuck in a witness box, behind a curtain like a coward, being referred to as witness-fucking-X with voice distortion and sunglasses. A load of fucking bollocks. Questioned by some overfed fat bastard barrister about whether I shot to kill or maim.'

'Okay, Mike, I hear you.'

'Or if I could have apprehended him. Then bundled into a car with a blanket over my head like a sex offender. Then my brief from the Treasury Solicitors Office dragged in and out of court the same way. Fucking abysmal.'

'The positive side about your query, Mike, is that if it becomes a reality it will mean that you are still alive after the operation. And a lot richer.'

150

There was mild laughter in the room.

'Look, all six of you have been chosen for this operation and all of you will be handsomely paid, if you are successful. Failure is not an option. In fact, let me be clear, if any of you die it will be in combat in Afghanistan.'

'Or a plane or helicopter accident over Iraq usually does the trick,' one of the other soldiers said from the back of the room. He was sitting on his own and had an American accent.

Mike spoke up again.

'We're the Dysfunctional Half-Dozen for fuck sake. Look at us. A bunch of misfits and renegades, working on our own, with our two new crazy Bosnian-Serb friends.'

Mike looked around at the two Serbs in the room. He knew of the gossip and suspicion that followed them. He wasn't sure of all the details but the strong rumour was that O'Driscoll had killed their father and had been paid to do it. Perhaps they were even financing this whole operation, Mike considered. But whoever was paying, Mike didn't care.

'And we all know this is personal for them. They're on a revenge mission, avoiding the court in The Hague,' Mike said.

The two Serbs remained motionless. Their stare fixed firmly on Carlin.

Carlin lost his temper.

'Now listen. All of you. Do you want to be briefed or not? Leave now if you want no more part in this.'

The room remained silent.

'Okay. So you're a mixture of ex-British soldiers and other military experts from further afield. You make up the Dysfunctional Half-Dozen, as Mike so aptly calls you. I've gathered all of you here in Lisburn for a reason. You are accountable to no-one but me.'

'And who are you accountable to, sir?' Mike asked.

'Don't you worry about that. I wouldn't be giving you orders and instructions unless I could. Take it that you don't exist.'

'With respect, sir, so what? How does that help us? Mike asked.

'Look,' continued Carlin. 'We control this place. Don't doubt it. This operations room was assembled at even more expense than the Maze prison complex after the ceasefires of nineteen ninety-four. Since most of the work to kit out the intelligence unit here was deep underground, the public and very few politicians know anything about its very existence. We've spent the last twenty years making what we already controlled from London even stronger here now. On British soil in Ireland. What do you think we were doing all this time? Dealing with parades and Policing Board showcases in hotels? Get real. You will all have the full backing of the British Army. They haven't gone away either. They're everywhere. We've melted into so-called "Northern Irish" society in a way we couldn't before nineteen ninety-four. Our intelligence here is supreme. The envy of the world. Okay, ultimately I answer to Whitehall. But who the fuck doesn't? This operation to neutralise O'Driscoll is legal and will remain legal. So if you make it to a witness box you have succeeded. When you leave the witness box you will be two million pounds richer. Each of you.'

The room continued to remain silent.

'The operation has to be below the radar. It will not be reported. It can't be reported. I repeat, you don't exist. Why do you think you are in such a place as this? You are in intelligence heaven. Eventually, intelligence will be evidence. Wait and see. But there always has to be plausible deniability, all the way to the top of the political ladder. That's democracy at its best. Our American friend at the back of the room is correct. Make no doubt about that either. If O'Driscoll kills all of you, your bodies will be put into a helicopter or plane and crashed into a mountain in Afghanistan or Iraq, with pilot error to blame. Or shot down by enemy combatants. You'll be praised posthumously and anonymously. That's the reality of this operation. The reality of the life you have chosen. So I ask again, does anyone want to leave before I continue?'

No-one answered. Carlin looked directly at Mike and spoke more calmly now.

'I know you are playing devil's advocate with me. That's okay. I know you're just saying what the rest of the men are thinking. I also know you can't help yourself, Mike, and out pops what you're thinking. That's you and you're well known for it. I accept that. Remember you are dealing with one man. And as dysfunctional as you would like to call yourselves, remember, you're not like a bunch of pensioners who were on jury duty thirty years ago. I will be honest with you.'

Carlin paused.

'Captured alive is best.'

Carlin deliberately paused again looking around the room at everyone in it.

'But not essential. Alive is preferable but not a prerequisite for collecting your two million.'

'Can I speak again, sir?' asked Mike.

'Go on.'

'Like you said, perhaps I am just articulating what everyone else is thinking.'

Mike looked around the room at the men, most of whom he knew.

'But if intelligence is as good as you say in this bogland of lunatics. If there is a Joint Operations Centre of some sort between here and London or Derry, why can't O'Driscoll be neutralised and we can watch it all on Kill TV? If you know where he is, with the flick of a switch he is dead meat. Perhaps even vaporised. We've all spent hours, fucking weeks and months, wiping out people in Iraq and Afghanistan and watching it eating greasy fish and chips. Why throw twelve million of Her Majesty's UK sterling pounds at a bunch of has-beens? Or in my cynical mind, are we being set up here to be neutralised ourselves? O'Driscoll is known to most of us in this room. Perhaps not personally, but by reputation. Did he really kill those jury members? What the fuck is going on? And with respect, sir, I've heard all this stuff about intelligence before. It is a never-ending story. Some other intelligence crew will be watching you, sir, and us, and then someone watching them. The Brits have practised this for centuries. They created and perfected the system. Why don't we just flick a switch and kill him?'

Carlin ignored the tone of Mike's attitude towards him.

'Mike, Kill TV may not be legal in this instance. The preference is he is taken alive anyway. But only a preference.

And I stress again, not a prerequisite for this mission. I can't emphasise that enough. To all of you.'

'That sounds a bit personal, sir. Capture him alive for what? To humiliate him? He's had enough of that as a teenager for a lifetime. You don't capture a man like O'Driscoll to humiliate him. It's kill or be killed.'

Carlin stared hard at the operative.

'That's for others to decide, Mike. And it's way beyond your pay grade for you to be consulted.'

CHAPTER 34

'Well, where is O'Driscoll now?' Mike asked. 'If your intelligence is that good, surely you must know.'

Carlin paused before he answered, which allowed Mike to continue.

'We seem to be back to a good old basic seek-and-find mission, despite all the great intelligence you talk about, sir.'

'He has used a number of locations, but we need him in one of the remotest, and away from Derry.'

'And where would that be, sir?'

'Our information is that he is in Glenshane Forest. Special Forces have confirmed that.'

'Special Forces? A forest, sir?'

'Yes. And you are to move on him under cover of darkness within the next twenty-four hours.'

'If he's at that location already he has the advantage. Why hit him there?'

'Away from the cultural celebrations, Mike. It's better for us. The PSNI will get a pat on the back when it's all over. Okay, there was that problem in Ebrington Square recently, but wait and see. When this year's over the PSNI will come out of it smelling like roses.'

'I've no doubt about that, sir. But nonetheless, the events in Ebrington nearly caused a train wreck PR-wise. That fucking crazy cop that had you by the balls ... but no matter. Not my problem. None of my business. I want the fucking money.'

Carlin didn't rise to the attack on him and remained calm.

'So, O'Driscoll's in the forest. We go into the forest. He's waiting on us.'

'Yes, Mike. That's the long and short of it.'

'Why not send in a pack of dogs, sir? Or why not draw him out?'

'We need a bit more subtlety than that, Mike. And because we want you to go in and bring him out. Dead or alive.'

'O'Driscoll – with his training and survival skills – could last at least two weeks in there, if not longer. And we're expected to go in and get him out in the dark. In a few hours. He'll be well bunkered down, camouflaged bivouac shelters, high ground, traps even. Happy as a coyote hiding from a hunter.'

Carlin looked around at the other men. Mike continued.

'You'll need the whole of the British Army to surround that forest. I know it well. It covers thousands of acres. It's as wild and unwelcoming as the cold, damp air that surrounds it. Even in the summer. If we get out alive, the British Army then, for Queen and country, would be better to burn the place down. Or spray it all with white phosphorous. Then you might get him. I've been in that forest many times. It's humongous. The Provisional IRA used it over the years. We all know that. Our Serb friends may not. But most of us do.'

'Well, you tell us what else you know about the place, Mike,' Carlin requested.

'It's perfect for O'Driscoll. You're like Cromwell, sir, sending the Red Coats in for a priest. Do you think dear old Gerard will be sitting at the Priest's Chair beside the Mass Rock waiting for us with altar wine to replenish our thirst? Will he keep the grotto there ready for us to pray at first, like the Templars before the Crusades? Or better still, why don't we all agree to meet up afterwards at the Ponderosa for refreshments, some hearty chat and welcoming humour with the locals. By the way, if any of us make it alive as far as the Mass Rock, we should thank God. What's the name of this operation, sir? Operation Lying Boy?'

'As good as any, Mike. I had another in mind, but that will do. We have to bring the battle to O'Driscoll. The legal process as far as he is concerned, is dead.'

'Like your own, sir?'

Carlin continued to remain calm and didn't react with anger. There could be no delay.

'Yes, Mike. Like my own charade. I was never in any doubt it was going nowhere. Sometimes at this level you have to make sacrifices. I've done that many times. I've known a lot of you for over twenty-five years. I was involved in the recruitment of many in this room. This is what you have been trained for. This is your bonus plan at the end of your careers. None of you, like me, are getting any younger. This is your chance for one final operation that will justify all the shit you have been through for years. So, when the time comes, is there anyone in this room who doesn't want to be involved? There's still time to leave.'

No-one answered.

'I shall take your silence as consent. You'll have a more detailed briefing within the next few hours. I have calls to make and people to see. I'm really just the messenger in all of this. That's all.'

Mike responded quickly for the final time.

'Distancing yourself already before we all get wiped out, or become pawns in the political mire that will erupt if this all goes pear-shaped? Very good, sir. Very British. A great demonstration of English intelligence core principles at their fucking devious and stinking best. Nice one.'

Carlin looked around one last time. 'No more questions, then?'

The room remained silent. Carlin left and the American spoke.

'What's the reference to this Lying Boy, Mike?'

'Many years ago during what was known as the Penal Laws—'

'I know about the Penal Laws, Mike.'

'Well, when Catholic Mass wasn't allowed to be said, Cromwell sent the Red Coats into Glenshane Forest in the hunt for a priest.'

'One priest? He sent the Red Coats in for one priest?'

'I know. I know. Urban legend or whatever. But it does sound familiar, does it not, after what we've just heard?'

'It does.'

'Anyway. Cromwell's men assembled at the forest. If I'm right, at the top of the mountain there, named Lying Boy. There's an Irish name for it, but fuck knows, I don't know it.'

'And you're telling me this priest was in the forest? On his own?'

'Yeah. Sure. That's the story.'

'And did they get him?'

'No. They didn't.'

'That doesn't augur well, then. The Red Coats couldn't find one priest. Jesus.'

'The place is wild. It's like a small atomic bomb dropped on it and the trees just grew then whatever way they wanted very fast. All affected by radiation.'

'Sorry, what's Lying Boy, then?'

'It's the name given to a young boy the Red Coats met up with who gave them false information as to where the priest was. They perished trying to find him. Their bodies were never recovered. Some shit then about stories of the Red Ghosts of Glenshane. Bollocks obviously. They are supposed to have been captured by the priest and converted to Catholicism and now, well ... they protect the forest and anyone who seeks shelter there.'

'Are you making this crap up? Come on.'

'No. I'm not. Someone else might have, though. I'm just telling you. I've been at the Priest's Chair and the Mass Rock. They really do exist, so does the grotto. That's the area the priest is supposed to have hid out at.'

'Right. Sure.'

'You just need a little credibility to a story. Then it takes on a life of its own.'

The other men in the room remained silent.

'We should get a good night's kip,' said Mike. 'I have a feeling we'll be sent in there tomorrow. But first, we need to make sure that Carlin pays us the five hundred grand advance he promised us all if we signed up for this shit op. So are we all in? If so, let's have your bank details for these fuckers.'

The Dysfunctional Half-Dozen nodded in agreement.

CHAPTER 35

Valberg hadn't been to his parents' home for some time. He never even organised a cleaner to look after the old house, but had sensibly left the heating system on a timer.

He pushed back the front door and immediately could smell and feel the comfort of the past. He could also hear the faint rumble of the oil-fired boiler. It was just after nine in the morning and the house was peaceful and warm.

Valberg stared at a bundle of unopened embossed envelopes that he had thrown on the hall table from previous visits. They were from Mains, Graham and Jobbing Solicitors, and some were more bulky than others. He surmised the correspondence was all to do with the estates of his mother and father. He couldn't bring himself to open any of them.

More letters had arrived since his last visit and he put them all together.

Valberg knew from his own investigations that Mains & Co were the same solicitors appointed by the Law Society to take over the running of Ian Haslette's lucrative probate practice. Nice work if you can get it, he thought, poring over the files of dead lawyers and their clients.

Valberg's disdain for the very existence of such a law firm, landing such lucrative work, made him reluctant to engage with them. But he concluded someone had to do it. No doubt they would be picking over the bones of Sidney Rankin and Son Solicitors as well.

Valberg arranged the envelopes in date sequence as best he could tell from the postmarks. He picked out the earliest letter, the middle one and the most recent. He knew the law firm would charge up every letter to him and deduct the cost from any monies left in the estates of his deceased parents, Valberg being the sole beneficiary. Every letter sent to him, Valberg assumed, was most likely seeking some sort of co-operation on his part. So Valberg pragmatically decided to stop his foolish behaviour and engage with Mains, Graham and Jobbing. Once again he had to be professional when he least wanted to be.

Valberg dropped the rest of the envelopes carelessly on the hallway floor, kicked them into a corner, and took the three chosen to the kitchen table.

Valberg opened the earliest envelope but felt a wave of disdain come over him at having to read it. After condolences and sympathy, he had the terms of business of Mains, Graham and Jobbing inflicted upon him, and he had no choice but to agree to it. He was now the only executor and beneficiary alive of the estates of each parent and could take the business elsewhere he knew, but that would be a whole hassle in itself. Better the devil you don't even know at this stage. Because the devil will always take care of its own anyway.

'Fuck me sideways,' Valberg muttered. 'Fucking useless solicitors.'

The estate now to be administered was essentially his mother's, as all that his father had owned was, by law and in accordance with his father's will, devolved to her.

The solicitors asked that Valberg make contact with them immediately to arrange an appointment to have his mother's estate valued so that an Inland Revenue account could be prepared. This would determine the amount of Inheritance Tax that would have to be paid. Valberg was advised this was urgent.

It was urgent over six months ago so it would be really urgent now.

Valberg thought of Mrs Rankin, desperately begging him to hide the War of Independence medal from the Emerald Bank and the Inland Revenue. He gladly and gleefully helped her. He recalled her debt-ridden, soon to be repossessed home and all her belongings in boxes waiting to be taken away, just like her. The poor woman was penniless.

160

Her two daughters had disappeared and her son had a mental breakdown. Her husband had died in Valberg's arms and was then obliterated with explosives at the Emerald Bank siege less than two years before.

He knew he was going to inherit something now, but the amount meant nothing to him. He would prefer it if Mrs Rankin had at least enough to survive more than him. A few life assurance policies belonging to his parents no doubt might have some value, and the family home could be sold. More than enough to do him, Valberg thought.

The second letter from the law firm was not so polite and a bit more hysterical. It was also full of 'disappointment' that Valberg had not contacted them. There was even a hint of anger in the letter. He threw it where he felt it belonged – in the bin.

The third and latest letter was not so hysterical or aggressive, more calm and reasoned. The beauty of some distancing from a fraught legal issue was working. The firm had now estimated the value of the estate of Valberg's mother and the likely Inheritance Tax payable. However, in the absence of any co-operation from Valberg, the firm said they would have no choice other than to apply to the court to have Mr Trevor Mains, their senior partner, appointed as a substituted executor 'forthwith' in order to distribute the assets of the deceased in a 'timely fashion' and more importantly, in accordance with the wishes of the testatrix, Valberg's mother.

Valberg, at that moment, became the mad, demanding, impatient and ungrateful client wanting everything done yesterday, despite the fact he had not responded to all the letters sent from the solicitors, or engaged with them in any way at all to date. All the delay here, he knew, was entirely his own fault.

He called the law firm with some annoyance, but this was immediately soothed by the calm, confident voice of the receptionist.

'Mains, Graham and Jobbing Solicitors. How can I help you?'

Fuck, what a voice. It was whispering to him.

'Hello. Hello. Can I help you?'

'Yes. Sorry. My name is Jon Valberg. Could I speak with Mr Mains please?'

'Yes. Just hold on a second and I will see if he is available.'

Valberg knew to interpret that to mean Mr Mains would decide if he would take the call or not.

He really liked the voice of the receptionist.

Valberg's libido rush was slightly dampened by the sound of a cheesy instrumental version of *The Girl From Ipanema* played over the telephone while he was on hold.

The song took Valberg back to his first meeting with Inspector Antonio Domingo in Malaga. He recalled the Frank Sinatra version being played in the background while they drank a few bottles of Brunello at the café in Malaga. There had been many such meetings since, but Valberg always remembered that day fondly.

'Putting you through now, Mr Valberg.'

'Thank you.'

Valberg was well calmed down by this stage. The receptionist's voice and *The Girl From Ipanema* had worked wonders.

'Jon? Mr Valberg?'

'Yes.'

'You're a hard man to get. We tried every avenue, even through the police service.'

'I'm sorry. The fault is all mine. I've opened a few of your letters only today and again, sorry. You've got me now.'

Always deflect the annoyance of an opponent, thought Valberg. 'You've got me now' hid a litany of rudeness in not replying to any of the letters from the law firm.

'Ah. That's okay. We got cracking on, but I would need to see you. And, of course, I'm sorry about the death of your parents. Please accept my late condolences. Please also, if I may mention, Mr Haslette. Ian. He didn't deserve to die the way he did.'

'No-one would.'

'I did know him a bit, and your father. But look, it's better you know now so we can sort everything out. You realise we were appointed by the Law Society ...'

'I know. That's okay. You don't need to go into all that. I understand.'

'Right. Thanks. So, the estate of your parents ... well, your mother's now, is quite sizeable. Inheritance Tax wasn't an issue between your father and mother. It's not payable in that circumstance as you probably know. And your father planned everything with the exactitude and precision that you would expect of him, I'm sure.'

'He was a very detailed man. In many ways, Mr Mains.'

'Oh. I know. He used every legal remedy he could, but ultimately death and taxes and that's it. The death tax follows all of us to the grave.'

'I agree.'

'Are you sitting down, Jon?'

'No.'

'Well, anyway ... I'll leave the gross figures out and just skip to the bottom line. The net value of your mother's estate is around one point five million pounds.'

'What?'

'Well, all largely from your father, but she was well covered, too, with many policies. They all added up. They both had death benefits on their policies of around five hundred thousand each. So it all adds up.'

'You're fucking kidding me. Jesus.'

'No, Jon. No. Don't be surprised. Your dad and Mr Haslette were very close and a great team. Your father had many investments in the Far East, too, sheltered from the recession. He seems to have been the Warren Buffett of China. He had many government bonds, shares and investments, and it's all yours now.'

'Holy sweet fuck. Seriously? They paid him that much?'

'They?'

'Sorry. Well, his investments.'

'Yes. All legal and above board.'

'Jesus. On that amount, forty per cent to the scum doesn't mean anything really, Mr Mains. Does it? Forty per cent Inheritance Tax. Is it still that rate?'

'I assume you mean our friends in the Revenue?'

Valberg stared at the notepaper of Mains, Graham and Jobbing and the small print at the bottom that read, 'All telephone calls to this office will be recorded for lawful business purposes.'

'Yes, Mr Mains. Our dear beloved friends at Her Majesty's Revenue and Customs. Well, I suppose the tax on one million ...'

'Sorry, Jon. Just to clarify. The figure I gave you is *net* one point five million. That's after all taxes are deducted.'

'My God. I didn't expect that. I knew he and Ian Haslette were tight and he kept all his stuff there. But, Jesus, one point five million net. My God. It's like winning the lotto.'

'Jon, I know you are a busy man. I can come and meet you if that helps.'

'No. No. We'll sort something. Perhaps meet in Derry somewhere, yes. But not at my parents' home.'

'I'll go to the police station there.'

'No. Not there either. We'll sort something. I'll call you again in a while. As soon as I can. I promise.'

'Okay.'

'Right. Okay. I'll be in touch.'

'Sorry, Jon. Just so you know. I knew your father a bit, and Ian, as I said. I remember the legendary stories about their fishing exploits. Sorry, do you have time? I don't want to delay you.'

'Right. Go ahead. It's okay.'

'You see, they had a thing going over the years about the biggest salmon caught between them and Ian won. Great story. They recorded all their catches in some sort of notebook. I'm sure you have heard all about it. It just all came to me when I heard you were on the phone. Look, I'm really sorry for going on about this. Have you heard it? The story about the salmon?'

Valberg paused, not sure if he was interested in the story. He was only thinking of the one and a half million pounds. But he thought he may as well give the man who told him he was to inherit so much money a bit of civility.

'Not that I can recall.'

'Your father never surpassed Ian. Never caught a bigger salmon. Back in nineteen eighty-two, I think it was.'

'Nineteen eighty-two?'

'Yes, Jon. Ian caught this monster of a salmon on the Foyle. The story goes, it was so big, he put it in the boot of his car and drove straight to your dad's house, opened the boot, showed it to your dad, said nothing and your dad was flummoxed. There were all sorts of rumours about the size of this monster salmon but the truth is in the notebook. I always wondered if I'd ever find out. I'm a fisherman myself, you see. They kept that competition going for years and Ian told me all about it.'

'Right. Okay.'

'You see he teased me. Apparently it was lashing with rain the night he caught it. And your dad, according to Ian, stood in your driveway in a trance, soaked in the rain. In disbelief that Ian had caught such a big salmon and beat him. He made your father come out of the house and stare at this thing in the boot of his car. Not like today where someone would just take a photo and text it or whatever. The deal between them was that the evidence had to be produced to each other no matter what the circumstance. Just friendly competition between them. Great story, isn't it?'

'Did you say a book? They kept a book?'

'Yeah. Just an old diary with a record of all the fish they caught. Date, weight, size and so forth.'

'This book has all those details?'

'Yes. Meaningless to everyone else but your dad and Ian.'

'Have you got the book?'

'It's in Ian's stuff somewhere. He made all the entries. It was him that said your dad was "flummoxed" when he viewed the fish in his car. "Gustav flummoxed ... June 1982", if I recall the entry correctly. It's about somewhere.'

'And you found out the truth, then?'

'The truth?'

'The actual weight of the salmon. What was it?'

'My goodness. A monster. Thirty-five pounds and seven ounces is the entry. I'll never forget the day I came on that going through Ian's stuff. A salmon that size. What a monster.'

'Keep it for me. The notebook. I'd love to see it.'

'Okay, Jon. And you will call?'

'Yes. I will.'

'Do you think you ... or the police, if you forgive me for asking, will ever get Ian's killer?'

'I think the team dealing with that are pursuing a definite line of enquiry, Mr Mains.'

165

'Let's hope so. Ian was a good man.'

'Okay, Mr Mains. Bye for now.'

'Grand, Jon. Speak again soon. And thanks for calling.'

Valberg hung up and said out loud to himself, 'Flummoxed. *I'm* fucking flummoxed to the tune of one and a half million. Jesus.'

The amount of money he was to inherit pleased him considerably. He was leaving the PSNI anyway, but now this made his fate certain.

Valberg searched YouTube on his mobile for *The Girl From Ipanema* and found the original version by Astrud Gilberto. It was a mixture of Portuguese and English.

It was time for a glass of wine.

Valberg sat and drank, staring straight in front of him, listening to the song and thinking about what he had just been told. He knew that a salmon weighing over thirty-five pounds was a fish to be proud of and show off.

He knew the story he had just been told was probably by this stage embellished out of all proportion. But after all he had heard and thought about, after all his anger towards his father, did he only witness the idiosyncratic terms of a personal fishing competition between two middle-aged men when he watched his father stare into the boot of Ian Haslette's car all those years ago? He wanted to believe the story and fit it to the sequence of events. He could hear again Ian Haslette's car crunching to a halt in the Valberg family driveway. He could hear the boot slamming and the car speeding away. Anything was possible. It was a nicer image to think about than the image of his father staring into the boot of a car with the body of a dead child in it and doing nothing about it at the time. If only after all this time the salmon story could be exchanged for the reality of what actually happened and what he personally witnessed.

Over the next month or longer, Valberg knew he had to get his parents' home sold and deal with the administration of both of their estates. This meant complete co-operation with Mains, Graham and Jobbing. Four to five weeks of boring hell awaited him.

CHAPTER 36

Glenshane Forest was desolate and intimidating as darkness took its full grip.

'I don't see this ending good,' said Mike as he and five other members of Task Force Supreme were about to be deposited by an RAF Puma helicopter near the vast woodland for the commencement of Operation Lying Boy. The others ignored him.

The team had received their briefing from Carlin two hours earlier in the intelligence bunker at MI5 Headquarters in Lisburn. And confirmation that their advance payment was already deposited in a bank account of their choosing.

The team were assured by Carlin that O'Driscoll was definitely using Glenshane Forest as a hideout. Intelligence confirmed it, backed up by sightings from Special Forces.

'Yeah,' Mike had said to Carlin. 'And I bet our friend has weapons of mass destruction that can obliterate Derry in forty-five minutes, too! Heard enough of that shit.'

It was an unusual operation for the operatives in that they had never been on such an urgent action before to 'deal with' one man. The team had only been assembled the previous day and had been given only four hours to complete the mission. Normally, operations into forests could last days.

It was clear to Mike they were playing straight into O'Driscoll's hands. And the helicopter didn't help maintain secrecy. If he hadn't known they were coming before, then he would now. More planning and preparation would have been preferable.

Glenshane Forest could have been anywhere. Had it not been for the shortness of the journey, the men could have been transported to some coniferous landscape in Scandinavia or Scotland. The area was vast and, although supposed to be working as a team, Mike knew it really was a case of every man for himself. That perhaps signalled their defeat already.

Mike was worried about the two Serbs, now called Radovan and Ratko by the team. Rad and Rat for short. Mike knew the one American on the team, Skip, and the other two English ex-SAS soldiers, Doug and Gary. They were all veterans of escapades in various guises in the Middle East, mainly over the last fifteen years – apart from Rad and Rat. Their expertise in murder was instilled in them in the Balkans.

Skip was particularly well known as 'Forest' or 'Jungle' Skip. He was an ex-American Marine instructor who had written *Don't Die, Won't Die*, a manual about survival in the wilderness, especially forests.

Mike was confident that he could lead most of the men as a secure team and they would follow all his orders, but he wasn't sure about the Serbs. How Carlin and the intelligence services came to have them involved in such an operation was a mystery to Mike. He was wary of them and knew their modus operandi was personal and not professional.

But he conveniently overlooked all that with the thought of a substantial amount of money eventually resting in his bank account. Perhaps the Serbs were contributing to the cost.

At this point he wasn't worried about appearing in a witness box anymore either, looking like an alleged sex offender. He was content to proceed. He also wasn't concerned about what anyone would think or say to him as long as he could find a way to survive the operation. He made sure he was partnered with Skip.

This wasn't personal for Mike in the way he knew it was for Rad and Rat. It was business with a fine payday at the end. Mike knew it was believed that O'Driscoll killed the father of the two Serbs and they were determined to kill O'Driscoll in revenge. Mike and the others had no interest in revenge. Just the money.

Mike considered it might be best to send the two Serbs into the forest first to see how long they would survive. So they were dropped off at the top of the Glenshane Road for entry to the forest from there.

Thankfully, there was no traffic about. Mike had asked Carlin to get the PSNI to set up some sham checkpoints on either side of the Glenshane Road to allow them all to get into position.

Mike and the rest of the team watched Rad and Rat through night-vision scopes and binoculars. The Serbs melted into the green dark wilderness of the forest, the first combatants ready for action.

Mike watched and said, 'They've just passed the point of vanishing.'

Once they were out of sight, Mike wanted the others to gain entry at two different locations maintaining full radio silence.

The agreed rendezvous after the first sweep of the forest on foot would be at the Priest's Chair. Time wasn't on their side. But the Chair wasn't too far into the forest and was a perfect meeting point.

The next pairing was the two ex-SAS men, Doug and Gary, who were dropped in a more central location at what Mike called the 'Belfast side' of Glenshane Forest.

Mike and Skip would enter the forest near the top of Lying Boy Mountain itself. They had the most ground to cover on foot to make it to the Priest's Chair. This would allow them to meet whatever came their way, as Mike believed that O'Driscoll was likely to try to escape in their direction.

Mike looked down from the helicopter.

'Skip, I don't think we have realised the vastness of this place. Fucking hell. Look at it. Even in the dark. It's bigger than I remember, although I notice a lot of it is cleared. But let's see if we make it to the Priest's Chair or the Mass Rock for a prayer ... or the Ponderosa for a drink.'

Skip didn't answer.

The two men jumped out of the Puma helicopter with all their gear, landing safely.

CHAPTER 37

The first thing Mike noticed, after the noise of the departing helicopter evaporated, was the stillness and quiet of the forest followed thereafter by the sound of a squealing animal.

'Fucking hell. What's that, Skip?'

'Probably just a rabbit, Mike, caught by another animal. Or a wild fox.'

'A fox makes that noise?'

'It does.'

'I've been in some shitholes before, including this one, but that noise is weird.'

Mike never imagined a fox screeching in such a way. He still thought it was something else. But he was not too worried at this stage. He believed he was strapped with enough ammunition, guns and explosives to destroy the forest if required. And anything or anyone who came his way.

The two men knew the direction in which they were going and proceeded carefully; initially, slowly and deliberately on foot. They had to move in the direction of the top of the Glenshane Road. It was the area in which Rad and Rat had previously been dropped off at. Both men got their bearings quickly enough.

They picked up the pace through and downwards into the middle of the forest. It got darker the further they went.

All the soldiers had silent handheld transponder locators. They could attach them to their black protective clothing for use as needs be. By now they had all picked up a signal

170

and location for each other. Mike was content that everyone would know where each other would be.

All was going to plan so far.

Still, Mike and Skip had the most distance to cover to get to the meeting point at the Priest's Chair.

Mike was taken again by the vastness of the forest and the size of the trees. It was a huge landscape for sure, but as he looked up through the canopy he felt tiny and insignificant. The only things higher than the trees were the flickering stars. Up there as well, somewhere, among hundreds of satellites in geostationary orbit around the globe, one in particular would be picking up the location of all the men in the forest. Mike was hoping that particular satellite would never break down.

The lure of the bonus plan money, Mike now began to think, had stilted his judgement. This was a survival mission in reality. Sending six special operatives into Glenshane Forest who were past their best was perhaps reckless and suicidal, even with all the advanced equipment and technology at their disposal. But press on, he thought. So far so good. A walk through the deep dark wood with the smell of fresh air and the pine thick and pleasant as it was, and those beautiful stars and satellites in the sky lighting the way.

Mike was very conscious of animal sounds and smells. He watched Skip closely as they continued to move swiftly without any difficulty to the meeting point.

They worked in patterns of movement. One of them would move ahead of the other, stop, allow his partner to pass and move on, and then he would stop again. They stayed a reasonable distance from each other as well and didn't falter in their precise and professional advance downwards through the forest.

Every time they stopped to check their positions and that of the others, Mike thought the squealing noise was getting louder and closer.

He whispered to Skip, 'What the fuck is that? Is there a bloody fox following us?'

'Ignore it. It could be a trapped animal. It's just echoing round the forest. That's the sort of thing that can drive you crazy in a place like this on your own. Ignore it. Shut it out. Suppress it. Keep cool and keep your eyes open. The night-vision goggles are your saving grace. Don't ever take them off in this terrain.'

Mike found it hard to ignore the pitch of the squealing. When he thought of a fox or a pack of foxes, he imagined howling, not high-pitched squealing. The sound was getting louder and seemed to echo all around the forest as it cut sharply through the trees. There didn't seem to be any escaping from it.

Mike advised Skip that Rad and Rat had made it to the Priest's Chair. The transponder locators were working. The other two members of the team were close to it. Mike could see Skip checking his own transponder and they both nodded in the affirmative to each other and kept moving.

Nothing had come their way so far and nothing obstructed their progress either. Everything was still going according to plan.

CHAPTER 38

'That fucking noise is driving me crackers, Skip. But we better keep moving.'

Mike turned to look for Skip, but he had disappeared. 'Skip. Skip.'

Mike got down on his hunkers and looked all around him. No movement. The night was still. Skip had vanished into the darkness. Mike looked at his transponder and could immediately see that it had been deactivated. The satellite had crashed or there had been interference with the transmitter. He feared O'Driscoll was close enough to allow him to disable the equipment.

Mike had no idea exactly where he or anyone else was without the aid of the transponder as a GPS locator system. He dared not call out for Skip too loudly or turn on a flashlight. He could only hear what he believed to be an animal in distress.

His night-vision goggles were still operating. Everything was green. He remained motionless and controlled his breathing as best he could.

He moved to his left, and slightly back, towards where he last believed Skip had been. But there was nothing there. No equipment or anything left behind at all. He decided to try radio contact. But as soon as he switched it on all he could hear was the dreaded screeching and squealing. It was even louder now. His position was compromised at this point, he realised, and it appeared obvious to him that at least one of the other radios, or men, was lying beside a dying animal.

Mike had plenty of equipment but decided only to carry a number of handguns for protection. All the other men had packed enough heavier equipment he felt no need for. He now regretted that. Still, it allowed him some freedom of movement not to be walking with a rifle stuck to his face.

It suddenly became very quiet. The squealing and the screeching stopped. That noise was replaced by the soft ping and light of his handheld transponder coming back on and getting a signal.

He got down on one knee to take a breath and examined the transponder. It revealed that everyone had made it to the Priest's Chair and he was getting closer. It was less than five hundred yards in front of him. He and Skip had covered more ground than he thought they had.

Mike was sweating and continued as carefully as he could forwards. He did not see any evidence of anyone living in the forest. He knew it was vast. But there was no sense of any human habitation, no trace of any type of shelter, or even a fire or rubbish. Perhaps O'Driscoll was not here at all. Perhaps their employers had lured him and the other soldiers to their death, Mike pondered, not for the first time.

Suddenly there was a splash of liquid over Mike and he was as good as blinded. He pulled off his goggles and was in total blackness. He knew his eyes would take a while to adapt. He searched for his flashlight. That, too, had got splattered but he flicked it on for a second to make sure he wasn't physically blinded. He was glad he could still see. He turned the flashlight off immediately and got down on his hunkers again. His transponder locator cut out once more and the squealing and screeching started again.

He was now in the nightmare position. He had no vision and the horrendous noise was back.

Mike decided to continue forward as his vision started to adjust to the dark. He looked up again and could see the stars. But the trees were so huge. They seemed to go on forever. They were like the multiple lanes of a motorway to the stars. There was no communication with the outside world and every device he had was blocked. O'Driscoll, or someone else, was definitely close.

Mike moved forward a few trees at a time and began to sense he was getting closer to the Priest's Chair and the grotto. As his breathing got heavier the tension in his body increased.

He began pushing fiercely with his tongue at an orthodontist's plate he had in his upper pallet. It was uncomfortable and was disturbing his breathing. Mike realised he should have taken it out before the operation. He had been too vain and Operation Lying Boy was arranged too hastily. He pushed so hard with his tongue on the plate that it popped out. He bent down and found it and got it into his jacket pocket. He would clean it later.

Now toothless to the front of his mouth, Mike felt liberated. The tension in his head lifted. He even felt lighter and more agile. He let out a sigh of relief. Just then he realised he could make out the Priest's Chair not far in front of him.

Someone was sitting on the chair. It looked like they were smoking a cigar.

Mike heard animals in a frenzy eating at something, tearing flesh. It was only as he got closer to the chair that he could see a small pack of foxes eating the remains of two human bodies.

The person on the chair got up and walked towards the bodies and the foxes. The foxes scattered.

'Mike. I've been waiting on you. Would you like a cigar? Dead giveaway in a forest – the scent of cigar smoke. You didn't smell it? Awful fire hazard as well. Here, have a seat.'

CHAPTER 39

Mike raised his gun. O'Driscoll was standing in front of him beside the Priest's Chair.

Here he was, the twelve-million-pound man who couldn't be secured in a three hundred-million-pound prison.

'On your knees. Do it now,' demanded Mike, more in hope than expectation.

'No, Mike. I must respectfully decline. Come closer. I won't bite. I'll let our friends take care of Rad and Rat later. I just gave them an appetiser. I'll bury what is left of them. Although I know a good pig farmer. You see, pigs will eat the bones, too. You know that. This guy, up the country, has two monster pigs that will eat anything. Great business. He's got so many customers. Cash jobs only, mind you. Every trace of evidence and DNA gone forever.'

Mike moved closer with more force and determination.

'Shut it. Shut it. Shut the fuck up. Get the fuck down on your knees now or I will shoot.'

'No you won't. Anyway, with those few steps you have just taken, you're mine now. I've just activated all the trip wires around the site here. You are surrounded by booby traps. One step the wrong way and *boom*. You become a liquid mass. It's a very quick death. You won't feel a thing. A slight gasp on your part, but your body will just sort of dissolve and scatter. So let's talk, Mike. Have a seat, my friend. Neither of us has much time. I certainly don't. And time is money. You can keep your gun and whatever else you have there. I don't mind. A bit easier to talk all the same without one of us pointing a weapon at the other, don't you think?'

O'Driscoll gestured with his left hand at the Priest's Chair.

'Take a seat my friend. Let's talk. You're a man known for speaking his mind openly and frankly – some would say inappropriately, too – but I like that. So, come on. You can do it. Have a seat and we can discuss this.'

Mike hesitated.

'What about the wire traps?'

O'Driscoll clicked something attached to his belt.

'All safe now, Mike. Come ahead.'

Mike lowered his gun, moved forward carefully, and sat down. He was glad of the seat, even though it was carved out of rock and didn't feel all that comfortable.

'What's that you've got there, Mike?'

'A Beretta Jaguar.'

'Handles well, does it?'

'I always travel with two. Perhaps I shouldn't have told you that.'

'Can I look?'

Mike handed the pistol to O'Driscoll who examined it.

'A seventy-one T. Twenty-two calibre. Very rare, Mike. Nice.'

O'Driscoll handed the gun back to Mike.

'Put it away. You won't need it. We'll end all this without a shot fired.'

'You prefer explosives, high velocity weapons and knives. Don't you, Gerry?'

'The truth is, I do. I like killing all the same, and combat, at close quarters. Far away stuff doesn't thrill me at all. I like to be close. I like to see death in the eyes of someone before they die. But it's all cause and effect. Isn't it? You see, as I prepared our two Serb friends for dinner I was thinking ahead. Just who will pay for their demise? Yes, I'll bury what's left of them or visit my pig-farming friend. Their mortal remains will never be found. But who pays the price? Someone, somewhere. I'm sure you've seen as much killing as I have.'

'Where are the others?' Mike asked.

'Safe. Unharmed. Don't worry. It was hard to get a piece of flesh to shoot at with a tranquilliser gun in the dark. But I have had a lot of practice over the years. You were all very well prepared. I think I hit dear old Skip just below his right eye. He fell silently like the others. I was really close to you.'

'What did you do to the two Serbs?'

'They sealed their own fate. The Balkans. Jesus. You were there, Mike, weren't you? Anyway, I gave them less of a relaxant. I worked it that they would just be out for long enough to wake up and then see and feel the foxes eating at their stomachs.'

Mike looked over at the bodies and shook his head.

'Can I have a cigar?'

'Oh, sorry. How rude. Here you go.'

O'Driscoll moved closer and gave Mike a cigar and lit it up for him.

'What are we to do here, Gerry? I mean, we have a bit of a sticky situation.'

'Yes, I agree.'

'If we're not out of here, with or without you, by break of day, more soldiers will follow. You can't take on everyone.'

'No, Mike, well put. But I could kill you all and leave you for the foxes. Did you hear them crying? It was hunger. I hadn't fed them anyone in a while.'

Mike sighed through his missing teeth. He stuck his tongue up and around all the cavities in his mouth.

O'Driscoll continued.

'You won't get the rest of your money if you don't deliver me dead or alive. I can lift the block I have on your transponder locators and you can leave. You'll be able to pick up each man as you go. Their locators are still on them. You have a little down payment on your fee already, as I understand it. Hard to vanish with just a few hundred thousand, to be fair. But you will last a while. You should have negotiated better man. Two million? Get yourself a better agent.'

'What were you, Gerard? Or what are you? Some kind of monster or some kind of agent? Or both rolled into one? What happened to you? You are revered and despised. What happened to you?'

'You don't have time for the answer. You don't deserve it either. You came here to kill me or capture me. I'm doing you a favour. I'm keeping you alive. And you came here to kill me.'

'That's right. What can I say? It's just business. You've

178

killed plenty and got paid plenty. That's the word anyway. So, no apology from me. Sorry I can't be sorry.'

'No. Don't. Maybe we can help each other, though. I like your style, Mike.'

'Are the other men safe? Really? Don't lie to me.'

The wailing of the foxes started again.

'Oh, the hunger. Look, Mike. The animals have the scent of blood here and will be back time and again looking for Rad and Rat long after they're gone. After that, they will go looking for the others. They'll eat them alive. Once they start at the neck, it's all over. Now let's say, once we finish these cigars, we go and get your men and I help you all out of here. Then you can take me.'

'What? Are you serious? Are you going to shout "God is great" and self-detonate and take us all out? Come on.'

'Once daylight comes, film me in your custody and arrange to get me to where dear old Seán wants me. But make him sweat until daylight. Sure, what could be better? Don't bring me to him until you all have confirmation that the rest of your money is sitting snugly in your accounts. Give him new accounts that Rad and Rat want their money deposited in. You'll be the six-million-pound man then, my friend. Swiss accounts I assume. Old habits and tradition. Or do you have an old Wells Fargo box in America? You could deposit it next to the IRA money from the Northern Bank. We can hang out for twenty-four hours, say, just to allow enough time for the money to reach your accounts. Then pick a drop-off point for me. How about it? I know the best part of the forest here for a secure internet connection. I need to go to my base anyway to get a few supplies. What do you say?'

'Gerry, don't bullshit me.'

'I'm serious. I need to get a few bits and pieces and a shovel to bury what's left of Radovan and Ratko. All the same, just one condition. Just one, I promise.'

'Right. Go on.'

'I want a shot at him. Carlin. I want the opportunity to kill him and escape one last time. It's just something I want to do. I could kill him in a more simple way but I'm happy to comply with your audacious operation. You'll have your money by then, too.'

Mike chewed heavily on the cigar with his remaining front teeth. Six million pounds was obviously better than two million.

'That puts me in a spot. What if someone finds a way to get our money back?'

'I'll pay you.'

'You will?'

'Sure. I'll act as a guarantor. Bankers love guarantors. They get to inflict their arrogant spite twice over with a guarantor. We'll find a way to do it. I'll have the money deposited for you to uplift if I don't get Carlin. Everyone's a winner.'

'What about the other men?'

O'Driscoll's demeanour changed for a moment and became more serious.

'They've already agreed. I'm just being polite and respectful towards you, Mike. You're the boss man as I understand it. How do you think I have all this information? I've some sources in Lisburn. Jesus, what a shithole. But I got the rest from the others. Rad and Rat were especially helpful. Just before I opened the veins in their legs first, then their necks. I didn't tell you that part.'

The wailing of the foxes was getting louder.

O'Driscoll let the wailing continue for a few moments.

'Mike, the noise of these wild foxes reminds me of someone I helped in prison one time. The noise seems to disturb you. I keep telling you, it's just hunger.'

'The sound does annoy me. It cut through me the moment we landed here.'

O'Driscoll paused before he spoke again.

'A friend of mine in prison, Eric, got himself into a bit of a mire. A child was crying in a car. The child was left alone. It was the pitch of the squeal that troubled Eric. It was a medical condition. You see, Eric had to stop the crying. He just had to. He didn't think he was doing anything wrong. By that I mean, well, I believe he truly meant just to calm the child. Its mother had left the car door unlocked. Eric opened it and tried to calm the infant.'

'Please don't, Gerry. Don't bother with the rest. If I fucking die here now, this is not the sort of story I want to take

180

to my grave. I have an image in my head of what happened next. I'm staring at two mutilated bodies here, with their guts and entrails all over the place. I can even smell them. The foxes might eat me. And if they don't, it looks like I'm going to be blown to bits or cut to bits by you. I'd prefer to think of Beyoncé sitting on my face and wiggling about before I die than the images you're inflicting on me.'

'You keep that Beyoncé image strong, Mike. Good on yee. But look, it's not what you think. He didn't harm the child. But he nearly killed the mother all the same. She came running out of the hairdressers screaming at poor Eric. He stood there biting into his hand until he drew blood. Then he started screeching. The blood was everywhere. He tried to calm the mother down but she ran away into the path of another vehicle speeding into the car park. The police then arrive and it's a mess. Eric tried to replicate for me the screaming of the child and its mother. I can tell you, it resulted in a bit of a headache more than once. I eventually got through to him and we became great friends. Eric's capacity to engage with a criminal investigation was non-existent.'

'Is there a point to this story? I need to know.'

'The pitch of the foxes will drive you mad. That's for starters. Then you might want to start eating yourself before the foxes start on you. So, what's it to be, Mike? That's the point.'

'What have I got to lose? I produce you and get my money. I deliver you and whatever happens on delivery ... well ... whatever.'

'Exactly, Mike. Do we have a deal, then? An invitation to treat? An agreement? A binding contract, as our dear old friends in the legal world would say? Do we?'

Mike nodded his head in agreement.

'Can I have another cigar? And will you dispose of those two fuckers? I didn't trust them anyway.'

'Sure, Mike. No problemo. Here you go. Another nice big fat cigar. It was the cigars that kept the smell of their intestines at bay. A pipe might have been even better. I would have been some sight waiting here smoking a pipe. And it was easy, wasn't it? You can switch your transponder back on now. I'll turn the jamming device off and we can go and get the others. Just as soon as we finish our cigars here.'

181

'So you will let us film you captured and deliver you to Carlin?'

'That's it.'

'I expect he wants to kill you himself and then we dispose of your body. So fucking predictable really. Maybe he wants to make sure you're dead. He hasn't told us where yet, but we are to deliver you to him at some point tomorrow.'

'Well, you do that, Mike. You have my full consent.'

CHAPTER 40

Valberg was just about to fall asleep for the first time in two nights when his mobile phone vibrated. A text message from a withheld number read: 'If you want to find me, travel to the mock Temple of Vesta. Gerry.'

Valberg had to think for a while before it hit him. He remembered his father taking him to Mussenden Temple at Downhill Demesne on one of their fishing trips to the lake at the top of Benevenagh Mountain. The small circular building on the cliffs overlooking the Atlantic Ocean was modelled on the Temple of Vesta in Rome by Bishop Hervey back in the 1780s. The site was now a National Trust property.

Valberg became totally consumed with thoughts of O'Driscoll again. He realised that Mussenden Temple would be just the sort of place O'Driscoll would lure him to as there probably wouldn't be any security cameras there. It was precariously perched on the wild edge of the land on the Downhill coast, ready to tumble into the sea.

The text could have come from O'Driscoll or anyone. Perhaps O'Driscoll was finally captured and Valberg was heading to a trap. But he didn't care. There was no chance of sleeping now. He'd be at the location in less than an hour. Doing anything, no matter how dangerous and unpredictable, was always better than trying to sleep.

In a begrudging attempt to follow procedure, Valberg forwarded the text to Constable Bell and added a few words on his own plans to follow up on it. He then started up his motorbike and set off under an incredibly bright full moon.

While driving carefully, although lost in thought, Valberg reminded himself that time had a way of resolving so many things. Experience had taught him that once the dust of battle in a given situation or problem had subsided, things become clearer. Circumstances are never clear to combatants in the heat of a battle or just when arms are taken up. He was in a reflective mood driving towards a destination he had fond memories of.

In the smooth moonlit drive with little traffic, Valberg felt calm and assured as he replayed events in his head. He remembered a tear-laden Mrs Rankin telling him the sad story of the disappearance of the two young girls along the coast he was driving towards. He could see their mother tightly clutching the photograph she had of the girls and he thought of the torment of their father and the brutality of his death.

Valberg was consumed with thoughts of the dead children. The bodies of the children were never recovered. Perhaps they could even be somewhere in the grounds of Downhill Demesne. Anything was possible, he thought.

Everything fitted now. This was the endgame. This would finish for everyone tonight, Valberg hoped. A hope he knew was dangerous, as nothing seemed to ever work out the way he imagined it. So perhaps it was best not to think too much and instead simply enjoy the drive.

It was a particularly beautiful evening.

CHAPTER 41

Valberg parked his bike on the grass verge outside Down-hill Demesne. He checked his weapon and flashlight and made sure the two mobile phones he had brought with him were on silent.

He replaced his leather jacket with his Canadian Army coat that he kept in the bike's side pannier. Sidney Rankin's blood was still soaked into it, but it was his most comfortable piece of outdoor clothing. Underneath he wore a tight-fitting Kevlar vest.

Valberg felt sufficiently armed and ready for anything.

Valberg could smell the fresh sea air. The moon lit up the area in front of him. His boots crunched on the pebble path to the left of an impressive entrance with a statue of a large animal atop each of two tall pillars. Lion's Gate, the sign said. He then only had to push open an unlocked wooden gate to gain entry to the grounds of Downhill. He shone his flashlight downwards onto the path on his way to the main building, heading slightly uphill.

The outline of Downhill House ahead was breathtaking in size and construction. A solid stone monster lay asleep and alone, with no protection from the elements endlessly sweeping over and through it from the Atlantic Ocean. The building was spectacular in the moonlit evening and in the crisp air.

What a waste of a magnificent edifice, Valberg thought. What secrets lay behind the walls? The house was now a shell. Valberg wanted to walk through it. Walk through the mysteries of its construction. He could see the outline of a

185

path around the house but could not remember if it would lead to Mussenden Temple. So he decided not to take it.

He recalled walking straight through the building before with his parents, so he thought that would be the safest course now.

In the dead of night the area was desolate. Valberg felt like a speck of dust blowing through history, alone and insignificant. The thought almost made him dip into one of his hallucinogenic states, but he fought it immediately for his own safety. He wasn't totally successful.

Valberg couldn't stop thinking about his father's small black Instamatic 33 Kodak camera with its leather cover that captured nothing but happiness for years of the Valberg family. All gone now. The old camera was one of the treasures that Valberg kept proudly as it held nothing but joy through its lens. Its camera eye.

Valberg remembered old biscuit tins full of photographs of himself as a child with his brother Patrick, and even more boxes of images of the Valbergs from Sweden. They were all supposed to be organised into albums, but for some reason, even in Gustav Valberg's very orderly life, this was never done.

Valberg's father always carried his camera and was forever going to the chemist with rolls of film to be developed. Valberg recalled his confusion as he thought about the amount of film that his father used to go through against the number of actual family photographs in existence.

The developing process vanished in the digital age. Valberg remembered his father telling him that the Kodak camera was so sturdy and reliable it would outlast everyone. Valberg accepted his father was right about that. Well, he was right so far.

At every happy family occasion that camera was always with them. It had visited Downhill Demesne and the surrounding area. It had travelled back and forth to Sweden. It had gone to Uppsala and Stockholm, Malmo and Oland, all over Ireland, Spain, France and Germany, and especially America.

However, the photographs taken in America were disturbing, and Valberg thought this was perhaps why his father didn't arrange all his images into albums. Maybe his father couldn't bring himself to even touch the photographs of his dead son Patrick. His younger brother had died in America and Valberg knew his parents never recovered from that loss. Perhaps his father had left the American photographs for him to organise. Moments were frozen and time stood still in all those stills. Trapped forever.

In Valberg's mind the images were moving now with him towards the Temple and the shoreline.

CHAPTER 42

Valberg carefully climbed the steps to the front of Downhill House and opened another unlocked gate. Immediately, Valberg thought he had walked into a massive cement
mask as a portion of the internal structure of the building
surrounded him.

He shone his powerful flashlight upwards and got sight of
a small black sign for 'The Library'. But there were no books
here now. Just concrete and cement left to the elements as
Valberg moved forward shining his light now and again upwards. The full moon was illuminating the structure enough
for Valberg to see where he was going. Through the empty
structure he continued forwards and slightly downwards.

On approaching the exit of the old house, Valberg decided
to take out his weapon. He kept it lowered and made sure to
keep looking all around him.

Valberg saw the Temple was just coming into view ahead
of him through the old building. He could see it now with the
aid of the moonlight. His mind began to drift again.

He thought of the time his father had told him all about a
post-World War II military operation known as 'Operation
Deadlight' as they sat in the living room of the family home.
The conversation came back to him.

'It wasn't in real terms a completed operation. It was a
success of sorts but not carried out in terms of its order.'

'Why not, Dad?'

'You see the blown-up picture here?'

'Yes.'

'That was all U-boats. They were positioned at Lisahally, with others elsewhere. That's what the big poster is in my study as well. You see, Jon, they were all supposed to be taken out and, as I understand it, dropped to the bottom of the ocean. Well, sunk. Or to use the proper term, scuttled.'

'Why, Dad? Why didn't they keep them? I'd love to see inside a German U-boat now. That could have been a great museum of sorts. Even one of them. Jeepers, that would be brilliant.'

'I think you're on to something there, Jon. It could have been. But it wasn't long after the war. And you know, the blood was probably still up. Never make a decision about anything when the blood is up, son. Anyway, there was a great determination to destroy those German U-boats. They had caused so much misery. Perhaps people or things that cause so much misery end up destroyed somewhere. There had to be total elimination of all one hundred and sixteen U-boats captured. It must have seemed logical then to the Royal Navy to scuttle them. They had forty-two of them moored at Lisahally. But it was all messed up.'

'Why? What happened?'

'It seems the dreadful weather had a large part to play. They couldn't get the U-boats hauled out to where they wanted to. Also, the ones that had been moored at Lisahally fell into disrepair from lack of use I suppose.'

'I see. I can imagine that.'

'Believe it or not, some of them were shot to the bottom of the ocean. They just opened fire on them and sunk them that way. Seems almost undignified.'

'That would have been some shooting match, Dad.'

'It would have had to be to sink the damn things. And I suppose the long-term intention to destroy the German fleet was a success in that way. Fascinating, isn't it, Jon? What's even more fascinating is that for some reason the Russians and the Americans will never allow those U-boats to be salvaged. Maybe there's gold in them. More secrets duly buried.'

Valberg was imagining what it must have been like to try and sink those German U-boats miles out at sea not far from the coast he was approaching.

The full moon, glaring from the sea beyond, convinced Valberg that what was illuminated before him was done so by what he imagined to be the dead light of the full moon.

Valberg carefully checked all around him, opened the steel gates at the other end of the building and could now see beyond him with no difficulty.

As Valberg exited the ruined house, he could see Mussenden Temple was coming into view. He checked his weapon again.

CHAPTER 43

Valberg put his flashlight away, kept his gun lowered in a two-handed grip and moved forward on the grass verge. He was out in the open again.

Valberg still felt like a tiny figure against the backdrop of the building he had just left behind and in the shadow of the Temple ahead. While trying to clear his mind of random family thoughts he noticed a light flickering in the Temple and stopped to focus. The large front doors were open.

Valberg caught sight of the calm Atlantic Ocean in the distance, lit up by an incredible full moon as he jogged now towards the Temple. He stayed on the grass verge, his eyes fixed firmly on the flickering light inside the circular building.

Valberg had a sense of loneliness being so exposed. However, in a peculiar way, although he did not feel the presence of anyone physically, for the first time in many years he felt a spiritual presence, in particular of his parents, close to him.

He couldn't understand this sentiment. It caused him to run faster towards the Temple perched on the high coastline. His heart was pumping and he was having an adrenaline rush. Who would be in the Temple?

The faster he ran, the more his jumbled personal thoughts turned into sharp images in his mind in relation to recent horrific events. The sort of images that he tried to always dispel or ignore. But O'Driscoll was influencing his every move and thought. There was nothing Valberg could do about it.

He could see Billy Black. He heard again Bell's quip about the rope that was used to hang him from the bridge. He could see the whiteness of Black's naked body, and his hair,

191

together with the exactitude of the incisions throughout his body. He thought of Avril Gibson's ribcage flying through the air. He could see Father Doherty, visibly upset in Majella McLaughlin's living room. He could smell the blood of Paddy Sharkey's deathbed at Saint Augustine's Church. Above all, he sensed the thud of the explosion that killed Finbar and the intensity of the heat from the burning car. He felt himself propelling his body towards O'Driscoll, while at the same time, holding his mother's frozen dead body in the snow. Father Doherty was saying over and over, 'He is my son. He is my son. I brought him into this world.'

Valberg remembered the rat he was sure he witnessed scurrying around the floor of Long Tower Church, just before he went unconscious after Raymond Grimestone attacked him. He could feel Sidney Rankin's blood on his body and the heat of his flesh burning from the fireball ignited at the Emerald Bank. He could smell Christina's hair and felt his hands running over her shoulder blades and back.

Valberg could see Victor Bostridge's vacant dead eyes and his mouth stuffed with what he later discovered were his own testicles. He now knew it was claimed that putting Bostridge's testicles in his mouth was supposed to ensure that he went straight to hell.

Valberg remembered holding the dying hand of District Judge Bailey as he choked to death on his own blood in Derry Courthouse after O'Driscoll was first remanded in custody. He could see the depth of the self-inflicted cut to Diana White's arm as she sat passively in her car after being chased to the Donegal border. He could hear Dottie Harkin's voice in his head and thought about all the dead innocent civilian Iraqis he had watched on Mrs Harkin's fifty-inch television screen with no sound. Fathers were carrying the bodies of dead and mutilated children through the Baghdad streets as if they could be revived or their limbs put back together again.

Another flicker of light in the Temple caught Valberg's attention and made him stop and gather his breath. After a few moments he inched the last few metres towards the historic building.

CHAPTER 44

Valberg carefully climbed the stone steps leading to the Temple entrance. With his gun raised, he slowly edged past the large solid wooden doors that hung open to the night air. He at once looked up and around at the high ceiling, then ahead of him and from side to side. His gun remained carefully raised in caution.

A voice spoke from behind him.

'Do you think your father came to Derry for the weather?'

Valberg recognised the voice immediately. He lowered his weapon but did not turn around. He noticed one of the large bay sash windows was half-open, facing out towards the ocean. He could hear the sea and felt fresh air gently trickling into the Temple. He put his gun away.

'Seán, did they let you out? So it was you who sent the text?'

'Oh, if it was from Gerry, I knew you'd come.'

Valberg shook his head.

'It seems someone is getting married here in the morning. Not a big wedding, but they have it all beautifully laid out, don't you think? And then that touch with just a tiny sprinkle of white powder on the ground, harking back to the old flirtatious days at the house up there. A bit of deceit.'

'You'd know all about that, Seán. But not just a bit of deceit.'

Valberg refused to make eye contact with Carlin and instead stared at the setup in the Temple.

'Did you know your father was a member of The Special Collection Unit, Jon? The KSI? A limb of the Swedish Army intelligence corps. Did you know that?'

Still staring at some candles struggling to flicker around him, Valberg answered.

'Seán, the KSI doesn't really exist. Does it? I think the point is that you don't talk about it or even deny its existence. I've just made that mistake. Do you believe all that? Part of its function is to deny existence at all. Don't you know that? You can't talk about or even contemplate the existence of such an organisation. To do so is to betray it. Don't you know that?'

'Get rational, man. What do you think your father was doing all those years? Tax returns for failed Derry businessmen? He'd plenty to choose from. Catch yourself on, Jon. Grow up. Get real. There was a war going on and Gustav was a prime agent. The agent of agents. The mother of all agents. An intelligence officer who remains irreplaceable. The like of which we will never see again ... or will we?'

Valberg looked at the thin layer of white powder at his feet.

Carlin paused then continued.

'Well, unless you care to join us, Jon.'

'Us?'

'You've lost your way, Jon. Every day looks like the next. On and on. Make a difference. Or do you want to die and have Sigor Rós music at your funeral? Will that be your legacy? You're not afraid, are you? Where are you going?'

'I came here by design. Your design, no doubt. To this Temple. You won't have time to put a bullet in my head by the way. I'll do it myself. I'm used to being on my own. Why should I fear death? Why should I be afraid?'

'Brave man. Brave words. Do you know how gifted your father was? A magician. God, he could see round corners. How he anticipated things, I'll never know. A legend. Untouchable.'

'Not so. Not untouchable. Cancer doesn't pick and choose. It falls wherever. Random and business-like. A perfect business model for death, Seán. Whereas you and your murderous cohorts choose your targets and ruthlessly, like cancer, end their lives.'

'Join us, Jon.'

'How do you know I'm not one of you already? Do you really know who I am? Or who I really work for?'

194

CHAPTER 45

Valberg momentarily looked around and noticed Carlin had his hands in his jacket pockets.

'Do you know who you are? Do you love what you've become? What are you, Jon? Who are you?'

'I'm someone who has been watching and had enough of people like you. Aren't you supposed to be locked up somewhere? You should be.'

'I don't think so, Jon. We have happily avoided Gerard in the witness box, and any legal process. No inquiry and no criminal trials. Nothing.'

'Well, you could never tell the truth anyway. Could you? Especially if you take that oath confirming you believe in that God of yours as well. Or you could affirm and lie like fuck.'

'Jon, I've told you many times. We need people like you.'

'Oh, don't start that. It makes me sick.'

'You know. I know. We all know. This new PSNI is a sham. We need to remind them and the public who really runs this place. And the politicians? Don't start me. Just puppets for their masters in London.'

'Oh, very original. Politicians here, puppets for their masters in London. Deep thinking.'

Carlin smirked.

Valberg asked, 'And what are you, Seán? Who do you think is running and checking on you? Should you not be where Gerard O'Driscoll needs to be? In some secure mental wing, sedated and in a straitjacket. Who do you think has been keeping you and your unlawfulness in check?'

Carlin shook his head in indignation.

'Jon. For God's sake, what do you think we've been do-ing since the so-called ceasefires? We have the best intelli-gence apparatus in the world now. Every phone, computer and home bugged to death. There are more drones over here than over Afghanistan, Iraq and Pakistan. No-one moves without us knowing. We've more power now than ever. And guess what? It's all legal. I don't even have to lie about it anymore. National security protects me. I cry it once and the covers come over and protect me. I'm untouchable. And your father was untouchable. United Ireland. Don't make me laugh. United intelligence.'

'There's nothing united about the intelligence apparatus. It is, like you, unfit for purpose.'

Carlin laughed.

'You compromised so many people, Seán, and got away with murder. And now you laugh.'

'War, Jon. A war that was stinking, foul and miserable for both sides. But now we are in supreme control. As we always were. The hair on the head of anyone we choose to watch can't move without us knowing.'

'The very thing you claim to restore or uphold you oblite-rate in your modus operandi. Truth, justice, democracy, the rule of law. Just shields and slogans used by you to murder people. You break the law to try and make a law that suits you and people like you. It's nonsense.'

Carlin didn't answer.

'And what's this "us"? Who are "we"?'

'Intelligence is now becoming evidence, Jon.'

'Is that because you can't get any lawful evidence?'

'We know everything that's happening in this town ...'

'You mean Derry?'

'Derry, yes. But we have agents everywhere now. And social media gives us bonuses every day of the week. We collect, study and compile. Do you know that people even put on the internet exactly where they are? They almost complete their own intelligence files for us. My department collects, and everything I do is in the interests of national security. Your father, the architect of it all. The collection master, below the radar.'

'Everything?'

'Everything.'

'Murdering Finbar? Trying to murder me? Trying to murder the Chief Constable? Does that go down in the interests of national security? Framing Gerard O'Driscoll for murdering a child. Blowing his father to kingdom come for two Provos. Was that all for national security?'

'War, Jon. War.'

'War? You should be the one catching yourself on. You should be well retired now with your OBE, sitting on committees in quango land. Living up in Bangor or Holywood, out at your bridge clubs and bowling at the weekend. Even get your photo in the *Ulster Tatler* with every other sad bastard. And singing *God Save The Queen* when it suits you. It's a fucking world of middle managers, groups and committees sponsored by the state. You're pathetic. And you're lucky O'Driscoll never got his hands on you. Was he an agent too much for you to handle? And you let him roam the streets of Derry. That great intelligence apparatus you boast about didn't stop him. Did it? Or perhaps all those deaths were convenient. Just like Orla Harkin's and those Rankin girls. You heartless, lowlife bastard. Fuck you. You betray truth and honesty. You make a mockery of justice. Any kind of justice. It's a sham with you. When the RUC couldn't get any worse, you came along.'

'If you talk enough you'll never hear the truth about your father and that little incident at Slaus Avenue near Marina Del-Rey.'

Valberg felt like getting his gun out again. He turned around and took a couple of steps closer to Carlin.

CHAPTER 46

'Now, now, Jon. Slaus Avenue. On your way to Marina Del-Rey, just outside Los Angeles in California. You couldn't remember much really, could you? Why do you think you were there? The weather was better, but go and check the police report. Accident? No chance. You were all nearly mowed down. A real turning point for everyone.'

'You talk in riddles, like Gerard O'Driscoll. You taught him well.'

'Patrick's death was no accident. Your little brother. Don't tell me you never thought or wondered.'

'What do you mean?'

'Well, you'll not find any record of it. Anyway, now we watch everyone so well. The Collection Department has to wonder who is watching it. Or us.'

'The penny drops for you at last.'

Valberg could see Carlin wasn't listening to him.

'One of the last supreme pieces of advice we got from your father was to buy old typewriters. Hundreds. Thousands of them. They're all in underground factory bunkers now. Everyone going internet and computer mad. People will sign the Official Secrets Act in Lisburn to work in an underground bunker there. Tell them they're doing it for the Queen and to keep this stinking shithole British and they'll work for free.'

'Sounds like my father sold you a pup and slowed you up. You're an idiot. You're unhinged in a real medical way. Even over my father's dead body I tried to get you to understand. You didn't listen and you're not listening now either, Seán.'

'As I said, easy to get anyone to sign up to the Official Secrets Act now. Everyone has a price. Anyway, your father was right. Since we can watch everyone so easily, then who is watching us? I do wonder.'

'You should,' Valberg replied with contempt.

'I mean in terms of combatants or our enemies. So Gustav, God bless him, told me one day to start buying typewriters.'

Valberg sighed and shook his head.

'I'm brought all the way here for this?'

'Well, you see, we have pools of typists now who just type, And a ribbon team.'

Valberg shook his head again.

'The typists type and the ribbon team come and collect the ribbons at the end of the day and burn them.'

'So there is no trace of anything on a computer?'

'Exactly, Jon. Exactly. Untraceable. Nothing. Your father. What a man.'

'Full of shit. You really are, Seán. Full of it. You can make documents disappear or have no record of them ever existing. But people? Lives? Is it worth it? You're as misguided as a modern-day teenage Loyalist or Republican so-called volunteer.'

'You can choose to believe me or not. It's up to you.'

Valberg could now, in his mind's eye, see his father tapping away on his old typewriter. He knew his father hated computers.

'I can't believe a word that comes out of your mouth, Seán. You talk as if you're all powerful. But you will fall. No matter how mighty you think you are. You put your hand in the till. Dipped your hands in blood and murder. The state provides some sort of spurious legal justification, and off you go to eat the altar rails on a Sunday. So you can't stop yourself. Then you demonise others. O'Driscoll. Not a devil. A man, just like you. A murderer, that you helped create. Unjustified murder and unjustifiable.'

Carlin was annoyed.

'There was no old man who lost control of anything, Jon. Patrick was run over by an enemy of your father's. He drove straight into him. It looked like an accident and was reported as such. Even by your father. But, no. It wasn't an accident. I'm sorry, Jon. Another secret your parents took to the grave, I'm afraid. Then life changes for all of you. Your own brother was ... murdered.'

'How does any of this help me? Even if you speak the truth? Can we not draw a line somewhere, like the Second World War, and move on? I can't bring Patrick back, can I?'

'It just might help where you are now, that's all. But I leave it with you, and you will see I speak the truth.'

Valberg sighed. He looked around the Temple and to its ceiling and out of the windows to his left and right.

'Truth? What would you know about truth, Seán?'

CHAPTER 47

'Jon, do you know where or what your breaking point is? Have you any idea?'

'No-one knows where a person's breaking point is.'

'You look like you live your life in a permanent gulag. Stop it. Join us. You will see how powerful we are, especially when Gerard is brought here to beg for mercy before me.'

'No chance. He'll never do that. Especially not to you. You're deluded. You always have been.'

'Join us. I'll not ask again.'

'Do you think I'd go from one place of suffering to yours? Do you think I want to cleanse my soul just for the likes of you? Has the penny not dropped yet, Seán? Me, a loner. Single child. Going to university in England then joining the fucking RUC. Seriously. Think about it. Who do you think I've been really working for all these years? The RUC and then the PSNI? As a lowly drunken CID detective in Derry with no career, or prospects. Seán, you've missed everything. That's how good your personal intelligence is. That's how fucking smart you are. You imbecile.'

Carlin looked startled and confused.

'You're in the gut of a bleeding intelligence body, Seán. And it's bleeding to death.'

'You think so?'

'Stop it. Stop it. For God's sake stop it. Enough. It's over. It's me who finishes you and has been watching you. And others.'

Carlin took his hands out from his coat and pointed a Glock pistol at Valberg.

Valberg was incredulous.

'A Gaston Glock. As predictable as my cover, and you. You still carry a Glock. Untraceable, no doubt. Perhaps even with plastic casing. Common as muck and not very deceptive. Here, shoot me. Or will I shoot myself?'

'Comply or die, Jon?'

'Die. Fucking die. Kill me. Here, shoot me in the head.'

Valberg pointed to the front of his forehead. As he did so he could hear the sound of a helicopter approaching the Temple. The old walls vibrated. Powerful spotlight beams shone in through the windows.

'That's our friend now. Captured like the animal he is at Glenshane Forest, Jon.'

Valberg began roaring at Carlin.

'Shoot me. Shoot me. Fucking shoot me.'

He rushed at Carlin and bent down. Carlin, startled, stepped back. Valberg forced his head onto the end of the barrel of the Glock pistol, hard enough to make an indent on his forehead.

He was still shouting, 'Shoot me. Shoot me. We're both finished.'

The noise from the helicopter was getting louder. The Temple was shaking. It seemed as if the foundations were about to give way at last and the ancient monument would slide into the sea with Valberg and Carlin inside it.

A side door slid open in the helicopter as it levelled. O'Driscoll pulled down a mask he had halfway over his face and took aim towards the Temple.

Valberg was roaring over all the noise.

A single shot rang out.

At that moment, Bell came bursting through the doors of the Temple.

Valberg had fallen forwards onto Carlin. Both were motionless on the ground.

CHAPTER 48

The helicopter landed close to the Temple, its rotor blades still spinning and raising clouds of dust. Four masked and armed men, in full black military fatigues, jumped out and ran into the building. One of them carried a black body bag and pushed Bell away just before he got to Valberg. Bell was then pinned to the floor by Mike. He couldn't move but could see everything that was happening.

Two of the armed men lifted Carlin who had been shot through the forehead. In seconds, they put his body and weapon in the body bag, zipped it up and hustled it out to the chopper. Everything happened instantly. It seemed like a well-rehearsed routine. Not one word was spoken.

O'Driscoll kept guard at the doors of the Temple. Once Carlin's body was gone, he moved forward to where Valberg still lay motionless. He knelt down to feel the pulse in his neck then stood up to check the area. All the while, Bell was roaring hysterically for Valberg. He lost control of himself. But he was held pinned down, unable to move.

Bell tried to struggle free, but it was no use. Mike kept his right knee firmly on his chest. Despite Bell's own strength, he couldn't shift his attacker and he had a weapon pointed straight at his head. He could see brain matter on the floor around Valberg and he continued shouting wildly.

'Let me help him. Please. Please. Let me up. Let me call for help. We need an ambulance.'

Then O'Driscoll nodded to Mike, who plunged his knee deeper into Bell's chest then got up and left as quickly as he and the others had arrived. O'Driscoll looked around the

Temple again. He checked everything one last time and left, closing the huge doors behind him.

Bell tried to get up but fell over once more, as he had been winded. He struggled to catch his breath, all the while calling out.

'Jon. Jon. Jon.'

Then Bell fell to his knees, crying over Valberg and held him as the helicopter rapidly flew away over the sea.

PSNI vehicles and ambulances were on the scene within minutes, sirens blazing and lights flashing. As armed officers quickly entered the Temple they were followed by the Chief Constable, DS Wilson and Constable Hastings.

Everyone lowered their weapons on sight of Michael holding Valberg on the ground. They both had blood on their clothing and hands.

As a medical team were signalled to enter by DS Wilson, Bell refused to let Valberg go. He started shouting at everyone to go away. The Chief Constable went to Bell and put her hand on his shoulder.

'Let him go, Michael. Give him up. Calm down. You have to release him.'

Bell slowly eased himself away from Valberg and the medics rushed in to begin their work.

Bell was still sobbing. He stepped back and tried again to compose himself but he lost it.

'He had time for me. Time for all of us. Did he ever refuse any of us help? Not one of us. He listened to me. He helped me. What's this police? What are we doing? Look at us. I don't remember a war. But I seem to have inherited one. Now I'm responsible for it. Am I? My generation. Do we have to pay for the last forty years? The last eight hundred years?'

Wilson tried to calm Bell down.

'Michael. Michael. It's okay. Calm down.'

He pushed her away.

'I'm finished. I'll get a job in a call centre selling mortgages to people my age who don't want one and can't afford it. Maybe I'll become an accountant and play rugby. I'll go on Facebook and friend every bore I know. I'll pretend I'm interested in their mundane lives and what they think about.'

Wilson tried again to calm Michael but it was no use.

'Or perhaps I'll just be anonymous. Change my name by deed poll. I'll not make a difference to anything. I came to this respecting the law and look at what it has done to me. To all these people and to Inspector Valberg. At least I tried to do the right thing. I owe that to him. I hate this. Hate it.'

A female medic working on Valberg raised her voice.

'He's alive. There's a pulse. We need to get him out of here.'

Valberg began calling loudly for Finbar. Then he took a deep breath.

The medic team began moving Valberg out of the Temple on a stretcher. An oxygen mask was put over his face, but as he was being taken away he pulled it back and Bell went over to him. Valberg pulled Bell close to him and just about loud enough for all to hear said, 'Great speech, Michael. But do for fuck's sake calm down.'

Bell shook his head and smiled with embarrassment, looking all around him but especially at the Chief Constable.

'Sir. You're going to be okay.'

'Remember that Brit on the Foyle Bridge, Michael?'

'Yes, sir.'

'Great advice, don't you think? Duck and cover.'

Valberg pointed to the ground.

'That's not my blood. Ironically, bending down and sticking my head into the barrel of a gun and asking to be shot in the head saved my life. I just fucking faded to black. I've very low blood pressure and bad sleep deprivation since I came back to Derry. This was supposed to be my holiday. Happens now and again. Bloody hell. More blood. Jesus.'

'You're okay, sir?'

'Sure I am. Why do you think I texted you that message before I came here? I knew you'd work it out. I knew I could rely on you and you would let everyone know.' Valberg smiled, 'The mock temple.'

'But who was that—'

'Michael, leave that. Mouth shut. No notes. Let me talk to the Chief Constable. None of this happened.'

Valberg put the oxygen mask back on and lay back. Anna Harte took Valberg's hand as he lay on the stretcher. She walked with him and the medical team to the ambulance.

Bell said to Wilson as he looked at the Chief Constable speaking with Valberg, 'I'm still chucking this. I can't do it anymore. My holiday with Jenny is booked and we're going. The timing is perfect. I might not come back.'

Wilson responded with a wry smile.

'Jon says that almost every day as well. That he's chucking it. You're getting more like him, Michael. God help us.'

CHAPTER 49

At the back of the ambulance, the Chief Constable asked the medics to give them a moment of privacy.

'Jon, as usual we don't have much time, but this has been more than elaborate. Did you go to all this trouble just to get me here? I was just leaving Strand Road after a protracted security briefing.'

'What a coincidence. Well, it was this or meeting at a house that might be blown up. Need I remind you? You see, I can be as sarcastic as you.'

'Look at you.'

'Look at me?'

'What's happened here, Jon?'

'Open your eyes, Anna. No. Perhaps keep them shut like a good Chief Constable. That's best. Credible denials are always best.'

'All I can say is that I miss you.'

Valberg didn't answer.

'Jon, security means we can never meet. I'm sorry about that. But you vanished on suspension.'

'I'm watching you, Anna. All the time. Believe me. I hear your voice and see you on the television and the bloody internet when I'm in the mood. I read about you in the newspapers. I do all those things now. There's not a day goes by when I don't hear your voice or see you in some way.'

'Watching me or watching over me?'

'A bit of both. You have plenty watching you. Look, you're making your security team nervous. I think they're worried you're going to be attacked here near the cliff edge for God's sake. Or perhaps just being in my presence or close to me is enough to freak them out … enough to freak anybody out, I suppose. I'm trouble. Stay away from me.'

'You know it was Constable Bell who phoned in where you were going?'

'I know. I knew he would. But I didn't know you were in Derry. I didn't know you'd be here … I'm glad … I'm glad you're here and to see you, Anna.'

'We will find him.'

'Find who?'

'O'Driscoll. You know he has a condition. A fatal one.'

'Then he's all the more dangerous. So find him quickly if you can.'

The ambulance team made it clear they wanted to leave. It suited Valberg.

Anna got closer to Valberg and hugged him.

'I'm here for you, Jon. No matter what you do or who you are. I need you to know that. Stop beating yourself up. You don't have to be so tough. Let me help you. This is all nearly over.'

'I'm not coming back, Anna. I want out. I'm getting out. I'm finished. You should do the same. Get out.'

The Chief Constable stood back.

She kept her gaze on Valberg until the ambulance doors closed and it sped off with its bright flashing lights illuminating the area.

CHAPTER 50

Valberg knew he wasn't physically injured and had no intention of going to hospital. He couldn't face Altnagelvin again or any medical facility. He was content to use the ambulance as a means of escape from the Temple. He was well gathered now and, despite the pleadings of the medical crew, he insisted they let him out at Lion's Gate where his bike still stood.

Valberg mounted the bike and sped back towards Derry. He had decided to sleep in his parents' home for the last time before he sold it. The journey was uneventful, but as soon as he entered the house he had a call from Christina Maguire.

'A solicitor at this time of the morning,' Valberg said, 'I'm honoured.'

Valberg's immediate thought was whether he should tell her Carlin was dead. Perhaps she already knew.

'Jon.'

'I'm not coming back, Christina. I'll never say never. But I'm going to be away for longer than planned. I need time to deal with the estates of my parents and sell the house. At least four to five weeks. No more law firms and no more police. I'm done.'

'Well, good morning to you, too. Jesus.'

'Sorry. Sorry.'

'And so you should be. I'll just ignore your latest drama statement. When will you be back, then?'

'Why are you calling me at this time of the morning?'

'God. One question leads to another. I couldn't sleep. Are you relaxed, Jon?'

Valberg thought about the fearful night he had just experienced. He looked forward now to a lie down in his blacked-out old bedroom.

'Relaxed? I wish I could relax. I came back here for a break and the madness kicked off.'

'That's why I'm calling. I've heard a bit about it. I just want to know how you are. That's all. I'm worried about you.'

'The mistress is worried about her servant?'

'Jon, do you know what I'd like you to do to me – right now? Can you guess?'

'Is this the part where I ask you what you're wearing?'

'More like what I'm not wearing. Ask me that. Go on. Brighten up my morning. It's been a long night.'

Valberg didn't answer as he undressed and lay down in the darkened room. It had been a long night for him, too.

Christina started humming the melody of *Paint It Black* by the Rolling Stones.

'Jon. I love your gloom. I really do. I love your cyclothymic moods. Lithium is no cure for you. I love your intensity, passion and emotion. I love your dips into depression. Even when the sun is shining, you're my darkness. I see a red door, I think of you, and I want it painted black. Your attitude is more honest.'

'You sure know how to boost my ego, Christina.'

'And, I'll have you know ...'

'Right. Have me know what?'

'I'll have you know that you've also made me develop a female foot fetish. I blame you. I can't explain it. Women's feet – especially in black nylon or stockings – really does it for me at the moment. It's my new thing. If you were a normal person with Skype or Facetime, I could show you what I'm not wearing.'

Valberg thought he had experienced most of Christina's sexual fetishes with her over the last year. But her female foot fetish took him by surprise, although he was glad of it and the conversation. He also began to contemplate a bottle of wine. But he would leave that and the foot fetish for now.

'Christina, can we leave your foot fetish to another time? This perhaps isn't the moment. But keep humming that tune. Or even sing it to me. It's getting me aroused.'

'*Paint It Black* was about a girl's funeral, you know,' Christina replied and started singing the words very slowly. Valberg was getting more sexually excited. He didn't think about the funeral of any girl. He was relaxed and making himself tension free.

Christina knew all the lyrics to the song. She sang some of them and hummed the rest.

'So when will the moment be when I see you? I just can't let you wander off AWOL style. I need you. Please come back ... Jon? What are you doing there?'

Valberg could only imagine Christina straddled over him. He could smell her and felt her dyed blonde hair falling on his face. Her breast and teeth implants were perfect. Her black Christian Dior underwear fitted perfectly, too. As Valberg had got into the habit of having sex with Christina while she kept her underwear on, he couldn't fantasise about her any other way. It was so tight to her skin it looked as if it had been painted on. He remembered that she had insisted on giving him some of her used lingerie to take home, but he was so aroused at the moment he didn't want to have to get up out of bed to find it.

'Jon? Are you there?'

Valberg didn't answer.

Christina asked in a more demanding tone, 'Jon Valberg, what are you doing there? You naughty boy.'

Valberg ended the fantasy in his head. He just realised that Christina had stopped singing.

'Sorry, this last year has been good for me, working for your law firm. Yes, there are a few cases I'd like to tidy up for you, but not now. I'll explain later when I see you.'

'Will you? Really?'

'I promise.'

'Did anyone ever find my coat?'

'Your coat?'

'That crazy day in court at the remand hearing. When my client was unlawfully put in custody. Remember?'

Valberg ignored the sarcasm.

'I'll ask Constable Bell about it.'

'Oh. I know. The sweet cute cop who'll be in CID soon. I like his girlfriend, too.'

'Christina, please. Not now.'

'You like her as well. You saved her from a whole disciplinary procedure. She didn't take out her weapon. Remember that, too? She cuffed my client on her own in the police station. A very brave girl. That was very good of you.'

'She didn't deserve any disciplinary action.'

'Is it her you call out to sometimes? Jenny? Does she move you?'

'Christina, don't.'

'That young constable must have his two-year probationary period as a temporary investigator well up now. He'll pass his CID exam with flying colours. But can he find my coat?'

'Let me speak to him.'

'Give him my personal number.'

'No. I won't.'

'Why not?'

Valberg laughed.

'You'll corrupt him. And his girlfriend.'

'Jon. Come on.'

There was a moment of silence. The only thing lighting Valberg's bedroom was his phone.

Valberg asked, 'What's it like being an agent for MI5, Christina?'

CHAPTER 51

Valberg took some comfort in the delayed response from Christina.

'Do you mean agent as in the legal sense? An agent of a client and an advisor? Or an agent in their employ? Be more specific, Jon boy.'

'No. You know what I mean and what your firm does.'

'We don't do anything illegal. Sure you know that. You've been around. You've done your inspection ... Inspector. And you're part of it now. On the payroll.'

'I have been around, for sure.'

'Did we pass the test?'

'You did.'

'That's something, then.'

'Anyway, I am going AWOL and I do need to talk to you. I may even have a business venture in mind.'

Christina raised her voice. 'Oh fuck. So you're retiring from public duty. Don't bore me. I was enjoying this until now. You sound like a commercial client. Don't tell me you're going to reinvent yourself and open a new business. I don't want to hear that you're going off to find yourself. Don't bore me like every other bore I'm surrounded by.'

'I was thinking more of a fishing shop in southern Spain somewhere, bought with my inheritance and savings. I've got my payment from you as well as you've just reminded me. A small fishing-tackle shop. I don't need much space. That's all. Something like that.'

'Well, I suppose it would be good cover. Great location, too. Easy access to everywhere.'

There was a further pause between them.

'Can I get back to my female foot fetish again and get to feel all tingly once more? I'm bored here at work.'

'You're at work?'

'I can't sleep.'

'But it's—'

'I know what time it is. I'm at my desk and London looks beautiful at the moment. So, when will I see you?'

'A few months maybe. After the summer. It'll take a while to get things sorted here and I'm locked into a Law Society vulture-grabbing firm. I've no choice. I'm just going to let them take care of everything. So, after the summer, perhaps. How does that sound?'

'Perhaps? I get a perhaps? You've explored every orifice and pore in my body and I get a perhaps.'

'Not perhaps. Sorry. I will.'

'Damn right you will. You have my numbers. And the legal game is over.'

'It is. I forgot about that.'

'It has caused devastation, heartbreak and bewilderment; and that's just for the legal profession in Derry and Belfast. It was their ticket out of the recession.'

'Your firm doesn't need such a ticket.'

'That's right. I'm glad for everyone all the same. All a bit over my head, the whole bloody thing. Is there anything you can tell me? It all collapsed so well. National security and all that.'

'I thought you could tell me. And both your clients off the hook.'

'We agreed never to speak about that.'

'Okay. Just saying in passing. It must have been some Chinese wall all the same.'

'Jon, don't.'

'I mean, for Princeton, Braithwaite and Sotomeyer to represent O'Driscoll and Carlin.'

'Don't go there. We agreed. Don't let that red mist descend over you or we will have a row again. And custard.'

'Custard?'

'Apple tart and custard. When I'm back in Derry. Back to Austins café with a window seat. When?'

'Soon. You really have come a long way, Christina.'

'Or you could get that nice constable to take me.'

'As long as you don't eat him. Okay, on one condition, then.'

'What's that?'

'Tell me how it came to be that your law firm represented Carlin and O'Driscoll?'

Christina didn't answer for a while. Valberg waited.

'Right. This one time. I'm supposed to say "lawyer to lawyer". But you're not a lawyer. So I'll have to trust you. This one time, Jon. Then will you leave it?'

'Okay. This one time. Was it in band camp?'

'I haven't watched *American Pie* in a while, but I suppose it was like this one time, in band camp.'

CHAPTER 52

Valberg had always meant to extract the truth about Christina's firm representing Carlin and O'Driscoll. He dared not ask any other member of staff in his time there about the position. He knew that all good information eventually came to those who wait.

He didn't expect to have Christina on the ropes about it in the current circumstances. He thought it might all come out in a row or in some other way, but not this way. Not now.

'Look, Jon. Big law firms. Big money. Thousands of clients and staff. Offices all over the world. Every one of our offices kitted out in palatial grandeur. While there is a worldwide economic meltdown and lawyers vanish, Princeton, Braithwaite and Sotomeyer buck the trend and grow. We've bought more real estate in the last ten years for ourselves than in any time in the history of the firm. Everyone else is renting. We are buying and renting out. Visions of splendour and all that comes with it. Looking the part is very important. The law takes care of itself.'

Valberg grunted. 'I know. I've seen it. Like the devil taking care of its own.'

'Graduates don't compete to work here. They kill each other. We represent, on a percentage basis, very few private clients. And you know some of them. You see, the beauty of representing governments and organisations and multinational companies is that any conflict of interest – when and if it arises – is easily explained away. What's more, we get the trickle-down of grunt law matters from individuals in trouble. How can we refuse to represent them when the company or government they work for is already a client of ours, paying millions of dollars, sterling or euros in legal fees? We just can't say no.'

'A conflict of interest in a law firm, or for a lawyer, is usually miraculously cured with the payment of legal fees. Is that what you're saying, Christina? Greed?'

'Survival. That's what all this is about. Survival and business. It's never personal.'

'Nice lecture, Christina. But what's the answer to my question? I know all about big law firms. It's the connection between you, Carlin and O'Driscoll I need to know about.'

'Like an RUC Special Branch agent, I was compromised. I'm not going into the details, but part of my brief was to develop a personal relationship with Carlin. He made my fucking skin crawl. But I didn't have a choice. You know full well his connection with the security services and you certainly don't need a lecture from me on that. He was a slime dog but a grunt from above. If you represent MI5 you need to take on a grunt or two.'

'And he was your grunt? Your trickle-down problem from above that a more senior partner in your firm – no doubt nameless – told you to take on?'

'In a nutshell, Jon, yes. That's it. National fucking service.'

'So a managing partner bags the cash from someone like Carlin, and a salaried partner ... no disrespect ... deals with the grunt.'

'It's that or you're out. And they pay me so much. So I thought, I'll do this and get out. I genuinely didn't know he was on our books as a trickle-down grunt. I already knew Gerry by then. Well, long before.'

'And did Gerry O'Driscoll know then that you were—'

'What do you think? Of course he fucking knew. Who do you think was bagging more cash to one of the managing partners?'

Valberg contemplated and took stock of what he was being told. He never got near a managing partner in the law firm. His only contact was Christina.

'Jesus. He has controlled so much and continues to control so much.'

'Gerry?'

'Yes. Gerry.'

'Now that's it, Jon. No more.'

'Not even how it came to be that you knew Gerry O'Driscoll long before?'

'No chance. Now stop it.'

'Fair enough.'

Valberg paused then said, 'You need to know, then.'

'Know what?'

'Carlin is dead. He was killed this evening. Although I did notice that you talked about him in the past tense.'

Christina didn't respond.

'Did you hear me?'

'I heard you. You know what, Jon? I miss you. Did I say that already?'

'Yes, you did.'

'Please come to me. Come back to London. Bores surround me lately. I need danger in my life again.'

'I will.'

'Could you not say that you miss me, too?'

'I could.'

'What's become of us?'

'I'm not really sure.'

'Don't use your fortune to try and overthrow the king.'

'What?'

'The last Derryman who tried that had a Lundy experience all of his own with a Senor Moreno.'

'Who are you talking about?'

'Robert Boyd. I'm not talking about Carlin anymore. Don't mention his name. There's even a street now I think named after Robert Boyd in Malaga and some sort of memorial to him on Malaga beach. I'm surprised you don't know, or are you just messing with me?'

'Ferdinand, wasn't it? King Ferdinand. Yeah. Just messing. I've heard about that.'

'You do know. Ferdinand the seventh. And it ended in abject failure, blood and death. Robert Boyd was betrayed after sinking his fortune into a doomed escapade. Don't let that happen to you with your fortune. Your queen's ransom. Don't squander it all on a fishing-tackle shop in Malaga.'

'I've no interest in overthrowing the King of Spain, that's for sure.'

'So, Jon. When? Where? When will I see you?'

'Let me take care of a few things first. The house and everything. I just want all that over and time to deal with personal business.'

'Okay. I'll wait to hear from you. You know our little arrangement has worked out very well. The clients love you. The men trust you and all the women want to have sex with you. Great for business.'

'The success is in trying to help.'

'Even better when wealthy clients are willing to pay.'

'I know. So the security services must be very wealthy, then. They're paying your firm very well. And you.'

'And perhaps you, too, Jon. Don't get too cocky. There's a time and a place for that.'

'I better let you get back to your work while I try to get some sleep.'

'You? Sleep? Right. You will be in touch?'

'I will. Bye.'

'Bye, Jon.'

Valberg started to think about the arches on Christina's feet, inside her black stockings. He didn't have a foot fetish before his telephone conversation with Christina, but he was certainly developing one now.

CHAPTER 53

Bell and Jenny Hastings were on holiday to Tenerife together; they were officially a couple now. It was three in the morning and Bell was wide awake. And annoyed.

Bell hadn't gotten anywhere in his attempts to find out about the bomb at Spencer Road that Valberg had asked him to follow up on; officially and unofficially. All the police officers who dealt with the original investigation were either dead, retired, or simply refusing to talk to him.

Bell was wise enough now not to take the lack of co-operation personally. Ex-RUC officers, generally, wanted nothing to do with the new order. A call, in particular, from the Historical Enquiries Team or the Police Ombudsman Office usually resulted in a feigned stroke, heart attack or the sudden onslaught of Alzheimer's disease. It always worked. Many were bold enough just to refuse to co-operate with the HET or the Police Ombudsman, or anything in relation to the past. This was made pointedly clear to Bell, sometimes politely but generally impolitely.

What Bell also realised was that this collective amnesia and illness had nothing to do with what Valberg had asked him to look into. It was just the culture now and the norm to refuse to co-operate.

It was all really troubling Bell and he couldn't sleep.

'Jenny, I don't get it.'

'What is it, Michael? It's the middle of the night. Jesus.'

'I tried everything and everyone I know. I thought about it all day at the pool.'

'You weren't at the pool. Your head was in lockdown somewhere else.'

'I know. Sorry.'

'What is it you don't get?'

'That bomb in Spencer Road. I don't get it. I don't get the target. Well, I get the rationale of the commercial heart of the Waterside and all that nonsense. But it's a strange one.'

'Look, Michael. You're not in CID yet.'

'I know, I know. But Jon asked me to look into it.'

Michael got up out of bed.

'It just doesn't make sense.'

'Right. Here we go. Are you going to start about the JFK assassination again? If you are, I'm going into the bathtub to sleep or out on the terrace.'

Bell stared at Hastings through the darkness of the room.

'It doesn't make logical sense, Jenny.'

'Well, why don't you tell him what you have told me a million times? That you can't find anything out.'

'But that's it. That's the problem. That doesn't make sense.'

'Michael. I'm tired. We've that boat trip tomorrow. I'm really looking forward to it. I can't wait to see the dolphins. Please come back to bed. Please relax. Please, Michael.'

Michael turned away from Jenny, still in deep thought.

'Michael.'

'What?'

'Was anyone killed in the bomb?'

'One man. A Mr McKillen. Not even from Derry. From County Cork or somewhere. A piece of masonry hit him on the head as he was walking by. Miraculously, no-one else. A complete miracle in a no-warning bomb. But a complete freak for him and his family.'

'Was there an inquest?'

'I assume so. But probably perfunctory.'

'Oh. There you go with your big words again.'

'Why are you asking me about an inquest?'

'When we get back we'll both go to the Public Record Office in Belfast. Mr McKillen's inquest file will be there. Away from the police archives that you can't get access to. Never know what could be in there.'

221

'You're right, Jenny. The report on the bombing and that should be there at least.'

'At least. Now come back to bed.'

'Right. Will you come with me?'

'No problem. I've got a card and all and I've been there at the Public Record Office about a few things.'

'It's something anyway, Jenny.'

Michael got back into bed.

'Jenny?'

'What, Michael?'

'When do we go home?'

'The day after tomorrow.'

'Right. Okay. Thanks. The day after tomorrow. Right, that's Saturday. We can go on Monday to the Public Record Office. It's probably not opened on a Sunday.'

'Jesus Christ,' Jenny said with a sigh.

CHAPTER 54

Valberg was on another sleepless cycle. A lot of it had to do with the torturous events surrounding the administration of the estates of his parents and the sale of the family home.

He had been in and out of the law offices of Mains, Graham and Jobbing multiple times for the last number of weeks, signing and resigning documents and forms, affidavits and statutory declarations for all manner of legal things including tax and title deeds. He was at a point now where he would sign anything Mr Mains put in front of him without even reading it.

Two Grants of Probate had to be extracted from the court for the estates of both parents in order to complete the title to the family home to allow it to be sold to a property developer. Valberg didn't want to know the details of the purchaser, he just wanted rid of the house.

Valberg then had to decide what to throw out and what to keep. He knew there would have to be a clear-out of the house, to include his father's personal belongings and papers. It was as if his father was still alive, with the existence of the papers and the fishing tackle. He wasn't bothered about the fishing gear, but he certainly was cautious about going through the papers. What other secrets lay in there?

One day, Valberg was for just burning all the paperwork and files, and the next he decided he was going to meticulously go through everything. Ultimately, he knew in his heart, in true compromise fashion, that he would box up all the paperwork and files carefully to go through when he was ready.

What he didn't contemplate was the time this process would take. In his head it seemed straightforward enough. But the reality of physically packing up everything was enormous. Added to that, he refused all offers of help. He wanted to do everything on his own and it took weeks. There were some days of physical inactivity when he was too depressed to move anything. Then there were moments of manic activity into all hours of the night and morning. It was demanding work for one person to do. The only help he sought was when he invited different charities to collect furniture and other such items he was sure he wanted to dispose of.

The clear-out was slow and depressing. There was nothing cathartic about the process at all. It was the complete opposite for Valberg. It was emotionally exhausting as well for him. He found it hard to let go, but there was nothing he really wished to keep apart from the papers and personal possessions.

Nearing the day of completion of the sale, Valberg's head was pumping and he was physically drained. He felt alone and strange as he prepared for what would be his final night in the house. But, try as he might, sleep would not come to him. He lay tossing and turning all night and greeted the morning light totally shattered.

Valberg thought about his time working with Christina. Hotel life, in a luxury suite, paid for by someone else had truly been a blessing. Sleep was rarely a problem then. Added to that, when he was away from Derry, and particularly in a room at the Savoy in London, he had the best sex he could wish for or fantasise about.

Valberg badly needed to get some sleep now so decided to book into the City Hotel again for a few days. It had worked the last time. He had felt really relaxed after the three days and nights he spent there so he thought he would try the same thing again now, but with less alcohol. He didn't have the same motive on this occasion, though. Back then he really wanted to drink himself senseless. Now, one or two bottles of wine would do. Sleep was the goal.

CHAPTER 55

Valberg checked into the City Hotel on the evening of the closing of the sale of his parents' home on 24 June. His only luggage was a disposable plastic bag containing two bottles of Brunello wine and a blackout blind.

The law firm who handled everything for him had Valberg's bank account details. They assured him that all balance funds, to include the net proceeds of sale after all deductions, would be deposited in his account within the next five days. All done and dusted. Valberg felt a sense of betrayal in selling the family home. However, he knew it had to be done.

As he stood in the hotel foyer, Valberg wondered if there would be a young, malcontent, dissident Irish republican sitting about, waiting and willing to put a bullet in his head. Or if Gerard O'Driscoll could be in disguise there watching him. Both possibilities were real and dangerous.

Valberg had a good look around. Some faces he recognised, most he didn't. What he was most terrified of was someone recognising *him*. But it didn't happen. He felt invisible. No-one took him on apart from the female hotel receptionist checking him in. The public were more focused on their Bacardi and Cokes. He wasn't the Derry celebrity he thought he might be.

In particular, Valberg was looking for any PSNI personnel who had been tasked to keep an eye on him. He could easily spot a police officer in civilian clothes. Their hair and demeanour would give them away instantly; especially their hair. But the gathering in the hotel this evening, Valberg believed, didn't contain any members of the security services.

He barely looked at or spoke to the girl checking him in and just grunted responses to her. He had one last look around the foyer and then left for his bedroom.

Valberg was content enough with his room and hung the 'Do Not Disturb' sign outside. He locked the door and wedged a chair against it. He removed the bottles of wine and black-out blind from the plastic bag and placed them on a table by the window. Anxious not to be disturbed, he unplugged the telephone from its socket in the wall.

Valberg suddenly felt a wave of despair sweep over him.

He pulled off his jacket and threw it on the bed. His personal protection weapon fell out from the inside pocket and he grabbed it. He forced the weapon up under his chin. Then he pushed it into his head and started to grind his teeth.

At that very moment he wanted to die.

He moved the gun to his forehead, just to feel the area again that Carlin had his Glock pistol pressed against. Then he immediately put it in his mouth and was certain he was going to pull the trigger. Suicidal ideation had just come on him suddenly from nowhere. His bipolar disorder was putting him into a rapid descent.

If he didn't kill himself now, then he might never do it. The maverick in him was rising. He was becoming unpredictable again. His heart was beating and his mind went blank. He had let so many people down. He was really just a burden on everyone. It was time to end all this now.

He pointed the gun upward toward his pallet to ensure that the bullet shattered his brain, as he couldn't bear the thought of a mistake and just blowing the front of his face off, surviving and then finding Jesus.

He believed his million-pound fortune would be divided equally between the surviving Valbergs in Sweden as he had no other living relatives that he knew of and he was intestate. But the touch of the barrel of the gun on his pallet made him momentarily gag and he thought he might vomit.

Then there was a knock on the door and a young female voice calling his name.

'Mr Valberg. Mr Valberg. Excuse me. Sorry to disturb you. Mr Valberg.'

Valberg took the gun out of his mouth. He'd only been in the room a few moments. He hadn't even checked the curtain position to gauge how much light could get in. Clearly he wasn't thinking straight. This was yet another dangerous symptom of severe sleep deprivation and his illness.

He gathered himself, removed the chair, and opened the door, holding the gun now behind him, wary of who might be calling.

The girl at the door was holding Valberg's mobile phone.

'Mr Valberg, I'm really sorry, but you left this at the reception desk. I was calling after you but you walked on, so I thought I'd bring it straight up. I knew it was yours as you took it out at reception and set it on the counter while you were looking around you. I phoned the room but couldn't get through. These things always get lost in hotels and I'm sure you'll need it. Sorry again to disturb you. I wanted to get it to you before you got settled.'

Valberg stared at the phone as if it wasn't his own. He was trying to remember taking it out when checking in but he couldn't. He also immediately thought, what if he had taken out his gun and had casually left it at reception and forgot about that?

'It rang, Mr Valberg, but obviously I didn't answer it.'

Valberg said, 'You're a lifesaver,' and took the phone from her with his free hand. He pushed the gun into the back of his jeans and steadied himself a bit more.

'Sorry. I was rude to you at reception, wasn't I?'

'Oh, not at all, Mr Valberg. It's okay.'

'And what's your name?'

'I'm Sophia.'

'Sophia. I love beautiful names and Sophia is beautiful. Thank you. Of course, none of us can survive without these damn things. You really are a lifesaver.'

'Ah. No problem. Goodnight, Mr Valberg, and sleep well.'

'I'll try. Thanks again, Sophia.'

Valberg closed the door, locked it and put the chair back up against it, solid again. He looked at the phone. It was a Spanish number calling him. He switched it to silent and threw it under the bed. He was hyperventilating. The carpeted floor seemed more attractive than the bed. He felt the pistol sticking into his back. He always hated putting a gun in his jeans or trousers; it was uncomfortable. He took it out and held it as he lay sprawled face down on the carpet. He started whispering repeatedly, 'My life is finished, my time diminished.'

He continued to lie on the floor and was dribbling at the side of his mouth. He remained still, holding on to the gun. He felt paralysed. He really wanted his father to come and help him. He just wanted to hear his voice.

'Oh, baby, baby, fuck me, fuck me,' was what he heard instead.

With his left ear pressed firmly to the hotel room floor, Valberg began listening to the grunts, groans and vocal exchanges of a couple in the room below having sex. He remained solid on the floor as if paralysed from the neck down.

Now the bed was banging as well, which convinced Valberg it definitely was a couple together and not a porn movie on the TV.

As the noise faded below him, Valberg thought he saw something moving under his own bed. He was also convinced he was hearing a scratching noise, like nails on concrete. He was shivering involuntarily and believed he could see in his peripheral vision flakes of snow falling outside. The scratching stopped.

'If only you had called, Jon. You didn't call. I rang you. Where were you? You let me down. I loved you, Jon.'

'Mum. Is that you?'

Valberg put the gun into the back of his jeans again.

'You have brought shame on me. Hell does freeze over. Good to see that you are warm and I am cold. You shiver like a little girl but you are all cosy on the floor. Not like me.'

'But I feel cold. I miss you.'

'Can you lift me before I freeze to death again?'

'I'll try. Hold on.'

'All alone, son. The headache was the worst. You complaining about a sore head and stress all the time. Try kneeling over the grave of your father and brother in a snowstorm, in the cemetery. Big baby. Stop your whinging. Get up, man.'

'Let me try.'

'For God's sake get up. Two years ago to the day ... at least we got the opportunity to walk over the Peace Bridge together the day it opened. Remember that?'

'I do. I will never forget.'

'Your father's not coming. He's in a rage. He can't settle. You will never hear his voice again. Never. His life, and now his death, is a fountain sealed. Get yourself to the lowest place. Here, try to stretch your hands and catch at hope.'

'Mum. Stop it. Are you there? I'll save you.'

Valberg pulled himself closer to the bed and stuck his head under it. Whatever was there was gone.

CHAPTER 56

All Valberg saw under the bed was his mobile phone. He reached for it and could see Antonio Domingo had been calling from Malaga. He was on friendly terms with him at this stage as they had spoken so much and Valberg knew that Domingo was not averse to telephoning him at strange times. Valberg had also assisted with the investigation into the death of Carolina Munoz who had been mutilated and murdered.

Valberg recalled the first time he had seen Carolina. It was at the post office in Puerto Banus and he had immediately been captivated by her. She was beautiful and he was always in a trance-like state in her presence. He really missed her.

In time, she brought Valberg much comfort and they became very close.

He momentarily froze again with his head just under the bed. He had the phone now and the gun was still secure in the back of his jeans. His mother had gone. The couple below him must now be peacefully asleep.

But through the bottom of the bed, Valberg could see a pair of battered white trainers with the laces removed. He could also hear someone banging on the radiator beside the trainers. There was a groaning and weeping noise from there, too, and the clang of what sounded like a chain rattling.

'You put her in jail. So you killed her. It's your fault. And everyone else you fucked over and let down will be here soon.

230

They're waiting in the bathroom, Jon. But don't look at me. Don't touch me. It's your fault I'm disfigured.'

It was Carolina. She was chained to the end of the radiator. Valberg remembered Domingo had told him Carolina had been found dead, still manacled to a radiator with her face cut to pieces.

Valberg's legs wouldn't move. He crawled around the bed.

Valberg could now see Janice Sloan. She had killed herself with the laces from her trainers as a remand prisoner. Valberg had given evidence many years before at a remand hearing that resulted in the girl being wrongly placed in custody. Valberg believed she was now kneeling at the radiator, dead, with her body only being held upright by the laces from her trainers tied around her neck to the radiator.

Carolina was sobbing.

'I try. I try to reach her. Part of my torture was that she come here. I watch her die. From bathroom where the others are. She take running shoes off, laces out and tie them all together. She say Hail Mary and call for you and her mammy. But you no come for her either. She die slow. I try to put fingers in my ears to stop the sound, but bad.'

'Carolina?'

'Don't look at me. Don't look at me.'

Valberg could see Carolina, covered in blood. Her face was buried deep into the radiator away from Valberg.

'Do not look at my face. Urko's boys do this to me. Because of you. They rape me. I loss count now. I am sore everywhere. They rape me when they cut my lips off. And rip my face to bits. All your fault. You cannot save the girl. She is dead for a while. Who is she?'

Valberg remembered his mother saying to reach out and try and catch hope. But this was the death of hope. This was the graveyard of the possible. He remembered Domingo had told him that the Carolina Valberg had described to him was not the Carolina the Spanish police found. Her body and face had been mutilated and her coffin closed at her wake. Valberg was offered, but refused to read, the post-mortem report which included photographs. He only imagined what she might look like after Urko's sons were finished with her.

'You do not come to my funeral. Why is that? Ashamed of me, Judas? My daughter. My flesh. Who will look after my flesh?'

'Forgive me. Forgive me.'

'Only if you stop trying to look at my face.'

Carolina turned her body and face away from Valberg, who was lying on the floor; almost close enough to touch her if he could.

Valberg felt weak and spoke softly.

'You asked me about the girl. You see, I thought ... was convinced . . . at the time her fingerprints would be on the knife. No prints on the knife, but blood on my hands. I tried ... I really did.'

'Not hard enough. Try harder. Pray for us. You will see the dead no more, Jon. Take care of the living. The girl say something about, if you came, to go back to where you find her and forgive yourself for letting her down. Something like that I think. I am not sure.'

The phone lit up. A text message from Domingo. Valberg noticed the date – 25 June; the date of the opening of the Peace Bridge two years ago and the date of the conviction of O'Driscoll for the murder of Orla Harkin long before that.

Valberg pulled the gun away from his jeans and rolled onto his back. He thought about killing himself again, staring now at the ceiling. But his arms were weak and he couldn't draw the gun up to his mouth. He didn't want to shoot himself in the stomach or chest and risk a slow death. Or worse, survival.

His attention was now drawn towards a child standing over him in a white First Communion dress. He recognised her smile immediately from the large blown-up photograph of her at her home. It was Orla Harkin.

CHAPTER 57

'Orla. Orla.'

Valberg put the gun behind him to shield it from the child he believed was standing over him. He thought he was moving his arms, stretching them out towards Orla, but they weren't moving at all.

'You didn't talk to Mammy. You left her. I didn't like that, Mr Valberg.'

'I know, Orla. I know. I'm sorry. Forgive me. I'll make it up to you.'

'How can you make it up to the dead? Is that the story of your life? Anyway, it's okay. The dead speak. Only in short bits. We forgive you. The dead see. The dead wait. We don't return. That's all I have to say. Listen to the secret voices.'

Orla joined her hands together, clutching a pair of rosary beads and a small prayer book that had a cross on the cover. She began praying in whispers. She then put her right hand out towards Valberg and smiled. She was wearing her white gloves that complemented her First Communion dress. She helped steady Valberg to his feet.

By the time Valberg was standing, Orla and everyone else had gone.

He went straight to the bathroom, turned the light on and looked around anxiously. No-one was there. He looked back around the room. The bed wasn't touched. The two bottles of Brunello remained unopened.

Valberg rushed over and got down on one knee, biting on his right-hand knuckles, and pulled open the mini-bar door.

Nothing was touched there either. He had not consumed any alcohol.

He stood up, feeling energised, and realised he must get out of the hotel room and get some fresh air. It would be daylight soon. He put on his jacket and stuffed his gun into the inside pocket.

He hurried downstairs and saw Sophia at the reception desk. She smiled at him and he approached her.

'I just need some fresh air, Sophia.'

'Okay, Mr Valberg. Be careful all the same. I think it's going to be a beautiful morning.'

He moved quickly out of the hotel towards the Peace Bridge. He wanted to jog out the line to where Orla Harkin's body was found. He didn't feel he could run too fast, but he would try.

CHAPTER 58

Valberg felt that if he exhausted himself properly he would stop hallucinating and be able to sleep. The images he created in his head got so mixed up and confusing that he found it hard to distinguish fantasy from reality.

He stood at the entry to the Peace Bridge and looked over at Ebrington Square. He remembered coming upon Chief Superintendent Kells at the very spot he was standing at now, two years ago, after O'Driscoll had eluded everyone in Derry.

Valberg noticed two unmarked police cars driving along the Foyle Embankment. He walked briskly along the riverside walkway until he came to the area before Craigavon Bridge, opposite which he had chanced upon the screaming, blood-soaked Janice Sloan as a young enthusiastic policeman. Not for the first time, he wanted to be back in that time so he could pick up the knife he had found at the scene and throw it into the River Foyle.

He moved quickly on, noticing a marked police car go through the traffic lights in the direction of the Foyle Valley Railway Museum. He crossed the road under the bridge and could see that the disused steam-train engine that he had stood on to watch Billy Black's body being removed from the lower deck was now surrounded by a green wire fence, no doubt to protect it.

It had been an effort to walk at such a brisk pace to get this far, so Valberg decided to compose himself before the final leg of his journey out the line. He walked to the railings at the riverside and looked over at Victoria Park. He stood with his hands on the rusting metal, just past the museum, soaking in the view. Then he noticed the rubbish and discarded materials exposed in the mud below the bridge by the retreating tide and shook his head in disgust.

He really wasn't sure how far he was going yet, but it would be enough to tire him. Something was dragging him towards Orla Harkin's final resting place along the river and he was determined to get there. Perhaps he might even lie down in the area where her body was found and sleep. Anything was possible in the muddled state he was in.

The fact that it was the morning of 25 June also resonated with him. It was an important date for so many reasons. He found it hard to accept that his mother was gone. His father, too. The family home, legally gone as of yesterday.

He looked down the river and could see the tide quickly moving out. In order to stop hallucinating and dwelling on the past again he decided to exorcise the demons in his head by trying to run hard and fast. He was wound up, ready to launch himself as swiftly as he could as he gripped the railings in front of him.

With one last look all around him, Valberg then took off running as fast as he could remember in recent times, along the pathway out the line and away from Craigavon Bridge. He wasn't sure of his exact purpose, but it seemed the right thing to do. His heart might explode with exhaustion, but it was worth the risk. He had to move. He couldn't stand still.

After a speedy start he settled down to a more deliberate and manageable pace. He was enjoying the run as the sun was just starting to rise behind him and reflected on the river.

Valberg didn't care how bizarre he might appear to anyone who might be out at this early hour. He felt like he was running away from a crime scene and realised that if the police were to spot him they might pursue him on the reasonable grounds that he looked suspicious.

He kept going and before long he spotted the little pathway to his right that led up to Letterkenny Road. He also came upon a wooden pallet fence to his left that he knew from recent police reports had recently been constructed in the vicinity of where Orla Harkin's last resting place was.

Valberg started to slow down and realised how out of breath he was. He reached a walking pace and was panting heavily but more than content with the feeling of utter exhaustion that he had been trying to achieve. He hadn't felt this way for ages. Slightly bent over and still breathing deeply, he walked the last short distance to where Orla Harkin's body had been found.

As he reached the spot, Valberg saw the outline of some-one sitting hunched and unmoving close to the riverbank to his left.

He was sure he wasn't hallucinating now.

CHAPTER 59

Valberg couldn't make out the identity of the person sitting on the embankment. Whoever it was had their back to him. The slight-framed figure didn't turn around but spoke while facing out along the River Foyle.

'Agent Deadlight, I presume?'

Valberg was stunned to realise who was in front of him. The voice was weakened, but he immediately knew it was Gerard O'Driscoll's. The same way he had recognised his commanding voice in the past.

He was shocked to see O'Driscoll in such a state. It looked as if he had lost half his body weight. He was gaunt and bony. His clothes hung on him. Valberg could now clearly see him in the brightness that was beginning the day. His mind couldn't engage with his mouth. He was perplexed but did not fear for his safety. In fact, he did not even feel the need to draw his gun.

'Thanks for ducking at Mussenden. It gave me a clear shot. I didn't want to have to shoot through you. Get your breath. I've only a few left in me. Finally. Here we are. Alone. The Nemesis Project I told you about – all over. My little personal mission all done. The end of Nemesis. It was just a little personal title I gave to the operation. I mentioned it in my note to you I left at the Peace Bridge. God, that was two years ago. Hard to believe. Now look at me. I've faded to grey in the last month. It started rapidly.'

'Gerry? Gerry, is that really you?'

Valberg continued to try and get his breath. He thought he was being kind to O'Driscoll, querying his identity.

O'Driscoll let out a large gasp of air.

'It's me for sure, Jon. I'm all done. It's all done. My little mission.'

'The Nemesis Project? I remember you mentioned that to me in your note that Kells gave me. From the Peace Bridge. I remember.'

'It's the Nemesis endgame now. And you have arrived. Thirty-one years too late.'

Valberg paused before he answered, regulating his own breathing. He could see O'Driscoll was composing himself, too. His speech was laboured but not slurred. He spoke quietly but with confidence.

'Better late than never,' said Valberg.

O'Driscoll just about managed a smile. Each time before he spoke he drew in a lot of air. He was breathing heavily as well through his nose. Valberg was going to give him all the time he needed to speak.

'What a beautiful place and a beautiful time of the day, Jon. I've been watching the birds skim along the water. You brought the sun. It must have followed you on your back towards me. You know, more should be made of here.'

As the physical effects of his run started to settle, the emotional effect of seeing O'Driscoll hit Valberg hard. He stared at him in disbelief. For once, this was not his imagination playing tricks. The certainty of death and his own mortality were brought sharply into focus. Despite all the blood and killing Valberg had witnessed over the years, O'Driscoll's physical state moved him more than anything.

Valberg attempted to speak. He was still slightly breathless.

'I never thought ...'

O'Driscoll started coughing heavily like a chain smoker. It was as if he had glass in his lungs. It was a dreadful noise. He coughed so loudly that it startled some birds resting on the riverbank and they flew up and away. The terrible strain on his lungs brought up some blood which he wiped into a well-soaked hankie.

'Gerry, how did you get here?'

O'Driscoll smiled thinly and looked out over the Foyle.

'I always had, how shall I put it, some help. I insisted I

be left here. That's all I've got to say on the matter. I made some good friends recently on a trip up Glenshane Mountain. They have been very obliging, I must say. Don't have me waste my last moments of life in a debate with you about how I got here.'

Valberg was losing his composure.

'You knew I would … I would …'

'Come here on this day? I know, Jon. Don't be so hard on yourself. Or others. But you're here by chance really. The stars matched up. I always wanted to come here … to die. My health deteriorated suddenly and badly over the last few weeks. In the complete absence of medication, this is what happens. What you see is pretty much what you get. I stopped taking the drugs just about four or five weeks ago. Not for the faint-hearted.'

'Being faint-hearted would not be one of your traits. Now we're both together, Gerry.'

Valberg looked around him again. He knew that everything from an emotional point of view was going to catch up on him now. He felt it coming. There was a tide rising inside him that he couldn't quell. Part of that emotion certainly was for O'Driscoll. Valberg was once again overwhelmed with thoughts of all those who had died recently and those he had let down.

'At Orla's resting place, at this last moment, we are alone. Your eyes, Gerry. Jesus, they're sunk in your head.'

'Our lives could have been so different. If there's one thing I wish I could change … well, I wouldn't have come to this beautiful spot all that time ago. Or would I? My innocence ended the moment I sat down. Just here, where I am now. It hasn't changed at all, has it, Jon?'

'No, Gerry. The Craigavon Bridge stopped inept councils and crooked government idiots from ruining here I suppose.'

O'Driscoll tried to laugh.

'They still have time. This country, well, false state, is static. We're the Pakistan of Europe. It doesn't move. It has eaten itself. The Pakistan of Europe – a so-called country with a stupid name.'

'Are you okay there? You look as if you can barely sit up, Gerry.'

'Just about, Jon. You could knock me over with a twig. Hopefully it will stay calm with no breeze or I might blow away. Just disappear into the water.'

Valberg moved closer towards O'Driscoll whose breathing was getting even more laboured. His terrible coughing spasms erupted again.

CHAPTER 60

Valberg looked at the Foyle and the water flowing and slapping quietly on the riverbank in front of him. He also stared at O'Driscoll. Valberg realised that many of the things he wanted to ask and berate him about may not get answered now. He had always imagined being alone with O'Driscoll and trying to drag the truth out of him. But not now. The powerful courtroom-type cross-examination Valberg had in his head about his own father, and all the terrible events that had happened, was now never going to take place. Perhaps it would always be for the best for most secrets to be taken to the grave. It would be easier on everyone. That was something he believed his father would agree with.

The setting was peaceful and calm. Valberg looked all around him. He was convinced he was being followed. Or both men were being watched. Valberg rarely escaped that feeling. There were plenty of sheltered places in this lush summer countryside to observe from.

Valberg put his hands on his head and tried to compose himself. After all that had happened, he pitied O'Driscoll. He could see the obvious pain and discomfort he was in. O'Driscoll was dying in front of him.

O'Driscoll regulated his breathing and the coughing stopped. He tried to draw in as much air as possible.

'Jon. Is this the end for you as well? Surely Division Forty-Two is no more and Operation Deadlight is complete? Carlin was dropped to the bottom of the ocean at the right spot, I hear. Flown out in a helicopter and dumped. A successful Operation Deadlight this time. Better than the Allies. Totally complete. Down where those U-boats should have been sunk after the war. Carlin and others caused havoc. They were out of control. No discipline. Couldn't let the old criminal days of the RUC go.'

O'Driscoll looked at Valberg.

'But you've reported on all that now. And the new PSNI and how they are shaping up.'

O'Driscoll looked away again. He then tried to shake his head but he was in obvious distress.

'Terrible that in an individual, Jon. A lack of discipline. Perhaps worse in a team. Awful.'

Valberg could hear a distant police siren. He moved closer to O'Driscoll but was reluctant to touch him.

'There's not long, Gerry.'

'Oh, is that the cavalry or a cadaver dog for me? As you can see, I've lost my will to survive. I've had enough, too.'

Valberg didn't answer and continued to stare at O'Driscoll with growing pity in his eyes.

'So you are exposed, Jon.'

Valberg looked out towards the river.

'You were the man brought in to clear out the trash. Or at least report on it. MI5. What a joke. They missed you. Fuck. If I were to find out you'd been working all this time for MI5 I would plunge myself in the river. If you were that predictable, I'd have died sooner. That crew you worked for were so secret, MI5 couldn't even pick them up.'

'You know I'd never work for MI5. Somewhat too predictable, don't you think? Every police hack searching for an OBE got on that train.'

'So undercover, Jon. You feigned everything so well. You were a method actor, or more so, a method agent. A one-off. Like a great writer or musician. Or perhaps martial artist. Despite the number of so-called agents out there. To beguile the time, you looked like the time. Well done.'

'Not everything, Gerry. And not everyone either. I didn't bluff you. My cover became less credible this last couple of years, thanks to you.'

'Sorry about that, Jon.'

'Oh, that's nothing now. I have myself to blame for most of it. My dips into depression and mayhem became too real and personal. Behaving like a policeman made me despise the RUC and the PSNI. It's a fucking shambles. God, this place is a mess. For fuck sake, I knew the day I stood staring at Billy Black's body my number was up. Something stirred in me then. I just knew it.'

'It was obvious you were suffering. To me anyway.'

'Your killing spree exposed me. I'd spent years in that role, effectively going nowhere. I was so undercover I got too deep and drowned. Leading my own secure unit, just myself. As far as I know. Once all this mayhem started with you, I got lost. Mentally and then physically, I was in the wilderness. I even lost contact with—'

'Your handler?' O'Driscoll laughed and Valberg smiled.

'A handler. Fuck, what a joke. The person I sometimes reported to. I never thought of him as a handler. I'll need to re-engage to disengage from him and the Division. But Black's death ended all my contact for the last couple of years. I just went into hibernation.'

'Agents do that. Sometimes for longer than two years. But there's no way out. Just a job you had to do. Someone to watch over the fabulous PSNI. The whole intelligence thing is one monster of a machine, gathering information. You were one part of it and I was another. I was the violent practical part of it. Maybe we are more alike than you think. What a lovely war.'

'My life was so secret and secure I was forbidden to talk about it. You know how I felt at times, Gerry?'

'How's that?'

'As if I was doing something wrong. That I was just spying on colleagues and reporting on them. It was dealing with you that sent me on a downward spiral. Feeling guilty about things I hadn't done.'

'I know that feeling.'

'Anyway, it seemed the first and only rule of Division Forty-Two was not to talk about it and to deny its existence. It didn't even have a formal name. Division Forty-Two was just a nickname. It was ultra-secretive.'

'So secretive, Jon, even MI5 didn't know about it. I'd like to say that that's some achievement, but no. And don't take it the wrong way. When you have had the time I've had to think about things, you can see how every hopeful Brit from here thinks they've got a papal blessing or keys to the Kingdom of Heaven when they get a call from MI5. Perhaps a carry-over from Special Branch days. The good old days for Carlin and the like.'

'Don't make me laugh. MI-fucking-5. I could never be part of the idiots they recruited from here. All the same, I did get too fond of the wine and women. Very predictable. Very RUC. Very MI5, I suppose. I became a template in obviousness, I fear. Identified and signed up. Just like you. It was even predictable of me to lose contact with the person I reported to over this last while. That, in itself, is something that is so bloody run of the mill.'

'At least you weren't answerable to the same lunatics I started out with at the Force Research Unit. What a monster that was. At least your father developed something unique, if I may say so. Isn't that right? Give that to a dying man, Jon.'

'He crafted an organisation that is nameless. Unidentifiable. One division and one operation. No legal accountability and invisible. The thing is so complex in one way and so simple in another. I answer to no-one, effectively. There's a debrief now and then. Singularly lacking in recent times, yes. I had all the money and resources I needed. But no name. No office. Nothing. Someone, or some organisation, needs to watch all the intelligence services. The Iraq débâcle taught us that.'

'Division Forty-Two became deeper than the darkest corners of British intelligence, Jon. It's like the intelligence machine has come alive and morphed into this group your father helped to create. Not artificial intelligence, though. Nothing artificial about your father.'

Valberg didn't mind opening up to O'Driscoll. But he was reluctant to talk too much about his father.

'The best thing about you, Jon, is that your mind was never for rent. Perhaps, until now. It's the best defence. A quiet one.'

There was nothing to hide now for either of them. O'Driscoll was rapidly disintegrating in front of Valberg. It was Valberg's assumption, however O'Driscoll organised it, that he wanted Orla's last resting place to be his as well. Another way of professing his innocence.

That's really why O'Driscoll was there.

Valberg looked around him once more.

'The siren has passed, Gerry. Maybe we do have more time.'

CHAPTER 61

O'Driscoll was sickly grey and almost jaundiced looking. The colour of death in Valberg's view. His ankles looked terribly thin, like his wrists. The scar on his face seemed to have grown. His teeth looked yellow and his head wasn't shaved anymore; it was obvious it had all fallen out. O'Driscoll shouldn't even be sitting here, thought Valberg. He should be dead and buried already.

O'Driscoll didn't look like the mercenary he was in so many ways, and Valberg didn't feel like the policeman and agent he was. They both, it seemed to Valberg, were a study in contradiction and despair.

O'Driscoll spoke. His voice was slow and laboured, but clear.

'Now that this time has come, Jon, I have a flood of memories of people dying in front of me, who in the very last milliseconds of life fought hard to survive, genuinely believing they could. Well, that's how it looked. But I don't feel that way. I'm not fighting to live.'

Valberg could only think of O'Driscoll's victims.

'I remember in particular in Spain, a man I shot at least four times in the body. Then shot again and again, because he was scrambling for life in front of me. It took a bullet to the head to stop him. It took a small pack of wild foxes to help me stop his sons. But that's a whole other story for another time, another place. If there is one.'

'Perhaps it was the release of his life. An adrenaline rush or nature releasing endorphins that caused the man to resist death so fiercely in the way you say.'

247

O'Driscoll gently nodded in agreement. Valberg thought O'Driscoll's neck might snap if he moved it too much.

'Perhaps so. Even in the aftermath of explosions, horribly mutilated bomb victims think they are going to survive. They dare not look at what's left of their body.'

'It doesn't bear thinking about.'

'I once watched a mother cradle her son who was shot in the head. The child was dead. No doubt about it. His brain matter lay scattered beside him. Right at his little head. I watched it all through binoculars safely on the hillside. His mother attempted to push the brain matter back into the gaping hole in the child's head. What must have she been thinking? That there's still hope?'

'There has to be, Gerry. Or we are all doomed.'

Both men looked out over the river again and remained silent for a while.

O'Driscoll's breathing was getting slower and more laboured.

'You know what, Jon?'

'What?'

O'Driscoll took his time before he answered.

'I've often thought – perhaps wished – that if you had been a police detective instead of a schoolboy when all this started, then maybe all the mayhem wouldn't have happened. If someone like you had investigated my case it would never have got to this. I'd never have ended up in Angola getting what has turned out to be a fatal blow to my head. Or getting that White girl – Diana – into so much trouble.'

'Diana? Diana White?'

'Yes. I took the heat for her. I talked her out of killing and murder. Do I get any credit for that? I was only teasing you on the phone at Ebrington. Sorry.'

'Where were you that day?'

O'Driscoll immediately answered without hesitation.

'A back, disused room at the Tower Hotel. Great line of sight for firing, too, at Ebrington Square. About a metre in, with two different weapons. Silenced. The rifle at Foyleside was a decoy. It fired blanks now and again and made a lot of noise. Reminds me of some people I used to know, in fact. Anyway, I had a remote control device on it for exploding.

248

I waited until the town was cleared before detonating it. I set it up the same way the Provos attacked Downing Street with the mortars. Remember that? My Jeep had an improvised sunroof. Very simple and effective, don't you think? I even had time to conceal all the equipment in the room then walk out the front door like a tourist as usual.'

'And Diana wasn't involved?'

'Diana is completely innocent I can assure you. That's one of the reasons why I decided to leave prison. To protect her. I thought it better if I kill Bostridge. Eh, let's kill all the lawyers, Jon. Shakespeare had a point. You nearly strangled the poor fellow to death before me.'

'So it suited you, it seems. Victor Bostridge was the son of Sir Ronnie Bostridge, your trial judge.'

'Yes. That's correct. The law of Karma follows everyone. What goes around comes around and all that. I should know. So leave Diana out of it all. She just got upset with the reality of what happened. I'm sure she freaked out. That's all. Pin Bostridge on me, too. She didn't do a thing. I'm sure there's an element of some moral or emotional guilt on her part. But what more harm could come to that poor girl? Better me than her. She'll confirm all I say when you eventually speak with her. Tell her I was asking for her. I did so enjoy my chats with her. And dear old Sid Rankin's son, Dominic, too.'

'I will. If I see her again. And what about Dominic? Son of the man you obliterated from the face of the earth.'

'Now, Jon. Careful. I'm very weak here. Don't stress me. Don't be rude. I did give a banker a bullet in the head. Will I get a posthumous award for that one?'

'I can still smell Rankin's burning flesh. I held him in my arms. There was death in his eyes—'

'Please stop. Not now. Look, Dominic had his breakdown long before the events at Ebrington. He will never be able to participate in any investigation. Sure fuck all is going to happen in the legal world anyway with all this. That was murdered as well. The law. Dominic could never have been involved in the operation at Ebrington. If you want, check him out and you'll see he was detained in hospital at the relevant time. He's innocent. He had a number of, shall we say, consultations with me in prison and after I decided to leave, but that's it.'

O'Driscoll was attempting to speak quicker now just to get resting again and draw in more air.

'That poor family have had an awful time.'

'As I said, Jon, if only you were the man on the ground in charge of my investigation. That would have been something.'

Valberg wasn't in the mood for an argument.

'I understand,' Valberg replied. 'I'll take that as a compliment.'

'Do, Jon. It is.'

O'Driscoll groaned and was clearly fighting back serious pain.

'Well? Shall we? Would you mind?'

Valberg had tried to be tough with O'Driscoll but he couldn't maintain that attitude. He was just too tired and emotional. He couldn't stop the tears building up in his eyes. He was thinking about the futility of all the killing in the last two years in Derry. What a waste of human life. The emotional ripple effect of murder was never-ending. Staring at O'Driscoll, dying before him, seemed like a further unwarranted assault on his senses that he could do without.

'What is it you want, Gerry?'

O'Driscoll's breathing was very shallow now and it took him a while to answer.

'To read together, Jon. Would you do that with me? *Personal Helicon*. Please. The last time I read it here was all those years ago. Pity you didn't join me then that afternoon. What a difference that would have made. A witness to my innocence.'

O'Driscoll attempted to take something from his outside coat pocket but couldn't. Valberg could see O'Driscoll's right hand trembling with the exertion.

'Here, Gerry. Let me help you.'

At that precise moment, Valberg felt a deep wave of sympathy for the shell of a man before him, now facing his final moments on earth.

'Shall I call an ambulance, a doctor? Have you a phone, Gerry? I have to get you help.'

'No, Jon. No. Let me die here. Please. Leave it.'

With Valberg's help, O'Driscoll managed to pull out a small copy of *Death of a Naturalist*. He started coughing uncontrollably again. Valberg had to hold him in case he toppled over. He then embraced him.

When O'Driscoll steadied himself, Valberg joked through his own emotional state, 'Gerry, more blood on me.'

'Probably the last, Jon. Let's hope so.'

The two men went silent.

'Can you help me over, Jon?'

'Where?'

'Just behind you. I want to lie down where she was. On my back, too.'

'Okay. I'll try.'

Valberg lifted O'Driscoll to his feet. All he could feel was bone. Valberg thought O'Driscoll's legs were going to come off. In the process, the bloodied hankie and poetry book fell.

O'Driscoll was listless but started to whisper as he was being helped: 'Others had echoes, gave back your own call/ With a clean new music in it. And one/Was scaresome, for there, out of ferns and tall/Foxgloves, a rat slapped across my reflection.'

As Valberg eased him down gently on the soft embankment O'Driscoll let out a long sigh. It seemed like his last and Valberg looked at him.

'Gerry. Gerry.'

O'Driscoll acknowledged him with a slight puff of air from his bloodstained mouth. His eyes were staring at the sky.

'Come on, Gerry. Finish it.' They both spoke together after a pause and a long stare at each other: 'Now, to pry into roots, to finger slime/To stare, big-eyed Narcissus, into some spring/Is beneath all adult dignity . . .'

O'Driscoll's breathing got more laboured. The brief physical exertion had taken the last ounce of strength out of him.

Valberg held him tightly and pulled him up. O'Driscoll whispered in his ear slowly and clutched Valberg ever so slightly: '. . . I rhyme/To see myself, to set ...'

O'Driscoll paused and then they both said together: '... to set the darkness echoing.'

With that, O'Driscoll let out a gentle breath and he was gone.

Valberg felt O'Driscoll go limp. His light hold on Valberg eased and his skeletal hands fell down towards the grass. Valberg gently eased him back down again onto his back as he cried softly.

Valberg stared at O'Driscoll's lifeless body.

CHAPTER 62

Valberg took in the scent and noises that surrounded him in the early morning light. He joined O'Driscoll's hands together and closed his eyes. He thought of the horrors those eyes had seen over the years and the pain those hands had inflicted.

Valberg noticed a blue flashing light in his peripheral vision and looked up. Several police vehicles were arriving up the pathway along the river as a group of officers scrambled down the embankment from the Letterkenny Road. It was a sizeable force led by David Kells. Unusually, none of them produced any weapons. Kells ordered everyone to stay back as he approached Valberg.

'We followed him. And we followed you from the City Hotel. You need to know. We also allowed those who placed him here to leave.'

Kells looked around the area.

'I am presuming they did leave.'

Valberg looked over at O'Driscoll's body and didn't make eye contact with Kells.

'I need to know what you've done, David.'

'Not now, Jon. Don't make a scene in front of other police officers. I allowed him to come here. To be placed here. You remember that.'

Valberg continued to look away from Kells.

'It was you, wasn't it? All this time. He got everything from you he needed. Including my bloody phone numbers. That always bugged me. You told him all along. Where I'd be and what I was doing. His Angolan diamonds couldn't save

253

him, but they must have helped you. I read a report about that trip he had for the CIA. No Patten money and a doomed escapade as a security consultant in the Middle East for you. You got your own bonus. Is there anyone in the old RUC who has not been compromised over all these years? No wonder he knew where I was all the time.'

'I'm retiring.'

'Of course you are, David. The sooner the better.'

'And you will report and be debriefed.'

'Of course I will. But I'll do you a favour.'

'What's that?'

'I won't mention you when I report and debrief. Fucking joke. Isn't it? I'll not squeal on you. You fucking overstepped the line. Didn't you?'

Valberg turned around slightly, still making no eye contact with Kells.

'You were good to me I suppose. You trusted me, David. You really didn't have a choice.'

Kells shrugged his shoulders.

'And Carlin fell off his sailing boat in an accident off the Irish coast, out in the northwest Atlantic. It's just made the news. His boat was found adrift and empty. There's no sign of his body.'

Valberg now looked at Kells directly.

'Of course there's not. There never will be.'

'And we will take this body now to the morgue before it's flown out of here.'

Valberg sighed. He could see Bell and Wilson standing in the distance, staring over. He knew he owed them some explanation but wondered how he could do it without breaking the Official Secrets Act.

Valberg turned his attention back to Kells.

'David, there's one thing that has always puzzled me – now that I see her – Linda. Can I ask you something?'

'Go on.'

'I pretended, more than anything, to be suspicious of her.'

'You sure did.'

'Perhaps unfairly.'

'I agree.'

'So is there a logical explanation for her familiarity with O'Driscoll when we interviewed him at the police station?'

Kells nodded his head in the affirmative.

'Yes. I've watched all the CCTV footage from the custody suite before you arrived. While you were on the phone to the Chief Con and Headquarters, and God knows who else.'

'Right. And what did you see?'

'I could see and hear everything. The whole custody suite is bugged, not just the consultation rooms for the solicitors. I watched all the processing of O'Driscoll. And the fact is Linda, with the help of the custody sergeant, made O'Driscoll at least two cups of tea. At least two. It's all so simple really.'

'That explains it, then.'

'It does.'

'I double-checked with the custody sergeant. Linda knew all about no sugar and a little milk well in advance of you arriving and the interview taking place. The tapes were destroyed in that fire in the storeroom. Old style analogue recording saved you. Everything melted.'

'Yes. I recall.'

Valberg shook his head at Kells and said, 'Give me a moment.'

He turned away from Kells and looked at O'Driscoll's dead body again.

Kells continued talking.

'Okay, Jon. As these things go, we need time to close off the Letterkenny Road in both directions and set up a checkpoint. For the dissidents we will intercept any moment now in a car full of guns and explosives. Just in time for the news. You know, the usual. We just need another security alert – which no-one will question – and all this will be taken care of.'

Valberg turned around sharply and nearly lost his temper.

'You mean covered up, David? Yeah, the usual. You do that.'

Kells nodded in agreement and signalled to everyone to stay where they were while Valberg went back over to O'Driscoll. He dropped beside him on one knee with his back towards the police and facing the River Foyle.

'I wish I had faith, Gerry. I really do. Where are you now?'

Valberg placed his hand on O'Driscoll's head and looked around again, catching sight of the copy of *Death of a Naturalist* that had fallen with the bloodied hankie. He lifted both. As he went to place the book in his own pocket a small photograph fell out. It was of O'Driscoll with his father, Paul, in better and faraway times. They were smiling, arm in arm. Both content and happy. Valberg could see that it was taken at the exact spot everyone was present at now. O'Driscoll's mother must have taken it, Valberg assumed. He also realised that, despite O'Driscoll's violent life, he was the one in his own family that had the most peaceful death.

Valberg used the bloodied hankie to wrap the book and the picture.

'Bye, Gerry. As my father used to say, safe journey.'

As Valberg got up to leave, the police swarmed forward and turned the site into a crime scene with demarcation tape, although no crime was suspected here. Forensic teams already in place were allowed access. The whole area would be cleared.

Valberg looked on momentarily. Nothing had changed. Life trundled on. The PSNI were setting up another sham investigation area as a security alert for the media and to justify the closing of Letterkenny Road.

He refused all offers of a lift back to the City Hotel and returned on foot the way he came through the cordons of police, taking no notice of the hive of activity all around him. Constable Bell tried to make eye contact with him but Valberg was too drained to respond. He walked on and felt a sense of shame ignoring him.

Valberg was determined never to set foot in Strand Road station, or any other PSNI facility, ever again in his life. He felt like saying loudly 'mission accomplished' with a hint of regret and mendacity.

Life was nasty, brutish and short. It was always better, and safer, to trust no-one and believe nothing.

CHAPTER 63

A bright midsummer sun was rising steadily over Derry, shining on Valberg's face as he walked quickly back along the Foyle Embankment towards the City Hotel. His mind was blank as he looked around him, taking in the bustle of another day beginning.

Before long, Valberg found himself standing near the reception desk of the City Hotel with a puzzled expression. He was certain he could hear the voice of Anna Harte, but she was nowhere in sight. He looked around the foyer then realised she was being interviewed on the radio which was playing in the background.

The Chief Constable was giving details of a successful police operation that took place in Derry overnight that had resulted in the PSNI thwarting a major bomb attack on some unspecified target in the city. She was apologising for any inconvenience to the public, particularly in the Letterkenny Road area, but insisted that lives had been saved as a result of the actions of the PSNI and that the police would not allow terrorists to derail the city's cultural celebrations. She stated the police were intent on ensuring safety for members of the public and was adamant that the rule of law will, and must, prevail at all times.

The news report confirmed that the area around the Letterkenny Road junction with Foyle Road remained cordoned off and closed to traffic in both directions at the moment. It was likely to be that way for a large part of the day. Army technical experts were at the scene and a substantial suspect device, intercepted in a white Ford Transit van, was being examined. Police had arrested two men while a number of other arrests were made in the city as well overnight. All those detained were currently being processed for interview at police stations in Antrim and Belfast.

'Mr Valberg. Mr Valberg. Did you have a nice walk, Mr Valberg? Where did you go?'

Valberg had been listening with incredulity to the news report. He knew Anna Harte could only be as genuine as the information fed to her – which was fabricated and clearly designed to cover up what was really going on out the Letterkenny Road.

'Mr Valberg. Are you okay there?'

Valberg immediately thought of the fresh blood splatter from Gerard O'Driscoll on his coat and wondered if the receptionist could see it.

'I'm only noticing for the first time that you have a name tag, Sophia. And I asked you your name earlier. Sorry.'

'It's okay. Did you have a nice walk?'

'Yeah. Great. I walked out the line along the river. I needed to. I think I'll get some sleep now.'

'Well, good morning now, Mr Valberg. I'm off duty but I might see you again. I'm on nights the rest of this week. Have a pleasant stay.'

'Thanks, Sophia. You have a good day.'

Valberg turned away and walked upstairs to his room. Once inside, he found his phone and could see a number of calls and text messages had come in from Antonio Domingo. For an instant, a dark part of Valberg wished for it to ring and to hear O'Driscoll's voice baiting him again.

Valberg stared at the Peace Bridge and the early-morning joggers and walkers, oblivious to what was really going on in their home town. But Valberg had had enough exertion for one day. He pushed off his shoes and was glad of the comfort of the hotel room.

He sat down at the table and rang Domingo.

CHAPTER 64

' Jon. How are you, my friend?'
'I'm fine, Antonio. I think I'll be heading your way soon again. Perhaps via London and then on to LA. Who knows? You were looking for me?'

'Just a few things, Jon. I thought you should be told and brought up to date on.'

'Okay. Hit me.'

'Just so you know, we are not proceeding – or perhaps more correctly, we have been requested not to proceed – to look into the death of the political man from Derry, Mr Mc-Flynn, any further. The guy who was found dead in Malaga with his arm removed and a knife in his head. I'm sure you don't forget. Just over a year ago. The investigation is as good as closed.'

'That doesn't surprise me at all, Antonio. McFlynn was just another casualty of the corrupt situation here. Anyway, thanks for letting me know. There have been some developments here, too, Antonio.'

'Yes? Tell me.'

'We can talk in more detail when we meet, if that's all right?'

'Sure. No problem.'

There was a pause on the line then Domingo spoke.

'Jon, the tests are back.'

'The tests?'

'Carolina. The blood samples. The tests, too, from your vial. Remember?'

'Oh, yes. I had no problem with that. I knew you had to check everyone who had contact with her. I gave my blood gladly.'

Valberg paused.

'Now you have reminded me about her, Antonio, I won't sleep. I was just going to try. I've had a bit of a long night and strange morning. We will have to meet and talk soon. There are some things I must tell you.'

'I would love that, Jon. You are always welcome, my friend.'

'Okay. I'll be in touch. I promise.'

Domingo cut in quickly before giving Valberg a chance to hang up.

'Maria, Carolina's daughter, was asking for you. She asks for you all the time.'

'How is she?'

'She's fine. But misses you.'

'I can't do anything about that.'

'Well, you can. And perhaps should.'

'Should?'

'You are, of course, eliminated in our investigation here in relation to her mother's death. That all took longer than we anticipated. But you are not eliminated in another matter. Well, it is certain.'

'What is certain? You mentioned the certainty of death when we first met in Malaga. I'll not forget that in a hurry. I'll add taxes to that as a result of recent events in my life.'

The line went silent.

'Antonio? What is it?'

'It is certain that you are Maria's father. Her natural father.'

'What did you say?'

'There is no doubt about it, Jon.'

'But surely ...'

'And don't bother checking dates and times. We've done all that already. Worked everything out. Perhaps even to the place and evening of conception. Easy enough with the help of Passport Control and Interpol to trace your movements.'

'*Blodigit helvete.*'

'Maria is your daughter, Jon. She has your eyes. Congratulations. Jon? Jon? Are you there? Jon?'

Valberg couldn't believe it. Immediately he wondered, as he had struggled to forgive the sins of his father, would his own daughter forgive him for his many transgressions? He felt he was failing as a parent already.

'Antonio. The only thing I can say is that my father would have loved that. You ... well, she, has made me think of him. He really would. He would have been so proud. It would have meant so much to him.'

'Maria Josephina is your daughter. Why do you think her mother let you even near her?'

'I can see that.'

'I will put you in touch with a lawyer here and you can make everything official. In fact, remember that female officer I spoke with when we first met in Malaga?'

'Yes. I remember. She was a bit distressed.'

'Well, she will contact you. She has been dealing with Maria and Carolina's case.'

'What is her name?'

'Officer Genoveva Royo-Villanova.'

'Great name.'

'She is a great officer, I can tell you. Any problem, call me.'

Valberg was in shock. He went silent.

'Jon? Jon? Are you there?'

'Yes. Yes. That's a bit of a shock. But in a positive way, I think. But me? A father? I dunno. I don't think the social services here would allow it. I'll phone you again sooner rather than later.'

'Okay, Jon.'

'Is she all right? Is she safe?'

'She is safe, Jon. She will be ready for you when you are ready for her. You are a fortunate man to have a daughter.'

'I've a few things to sort out. I promise. I really do. I will be in touch. I'm Europe bound on my bike. That's what I think I'll do. Travel.'

'Like a Ghost Rider?'

'Yes, Antonio. Like a Ghost Rider. Packing up my phantoms and hitting the invisible road. I'll call you. Or call the officer. I may be off the radar for a while so tell her I will be in touch.'

'Goodbye, Jon. For now. Speak soon. I'll text you the officer's personal number. We all know you will need a bit of time. We need time as well, so give us a week or so before you get here.'

'Bye, Antonio.'

Valberg's first thought, as he sat down on the edge of his bed, was that a motorbike wasn't going to be practical for a young child. He'd drive down through Europe anyway and buy an apartment in Malaga. It was the first step in his life towards some sort of normality.

Or was that normal? Would a normal person not just get on the first plane to Spain to see his daughter? But he could sense that Domingo didn't want him there immediately. So a week or so would be fine.

Valberg recalled that Domingo wore a fresh bandage on his hand when he first met him and told him that his own daughter had died. In all the time they spoke since, he never broached the topic with him. It was Domingo saying that he was very fortunate to have a daughter that made Valberg wonder about what had happened to the girl. He made a mental note to ask him one day.

Malaga seemed like the city to invest in now, Valberg believed. It would be a good place to settle and the climate was fantastic.

Valberg decided to call Domingo back.

'Antonio. Does she know? I forgot to ask.'

'Know? No. We haven't told her yet. The girl has been through enough recently. The child can't take any more pain or disappointment. I mean, I wouldn't let that happen to her. Neither would Genoveva.'

'Right. I understand. I promise I will call. Give me some time. I need time.'

'Okay, Jon. No problem. Soon, eh? Maria Josephina has always felt attached to you I am told, without realising you are her father. Or perhaps she has sensed that.'

'She is a clever girl. Bye, Antonio.'

'Take care, Jon. Bye.'

Valberg went over to the bedroom door. He put the Do Not Disturb sign on the handle outside and locked it. But he didn't secure it with a chair this time. He checked the curtains. They worked perfectly fine, blocking out all light. He undressed and got into bed. His body shut down physically and mentally.

Valberg fell into a deep and welcomed sleep at once.

CHAPTER 65

The Italian sun was high and bright in the sky in the early morning of the second day of July, the date of the first Palio horse race in Siena.

But Valberg had other business to attend to first. He had to make a telephone call he had been avoiding for a long time. Now he was ready and in the right frame of mind to confront the task.

Having travelled to Italy, via London, Paris and Berlin, he was planning his almost perfect day in Siena before his long journey to Malaga.

Valberg loved the heat. In another time, he thought, he would have been a genuine sun worshipper. He felt it burn his face and he was content. It was a far cry from the rain and heavy grey cloud that seemed to permanently hang over Derry.

He was looking forward to seeing Maria Josephina and was thinking about her a lot. In truth, he was apprehensive about meeting the child again. He even called Doctor Crawford to get some help and guidance. Valberg thought that was a very normal thing to do. She had counselled him not to rush into things and he was happy to comply as he needed time to adjust to the reality of being a father. He had been in touch as well with officer Villanova in the last week. She told him she needed more time to deal with the courts and social services and to prepare Maria for the meeting with Valberg. This delay suited his travel plans perfectly.

Sitting by the sea, Valberg called a number he had vowed to himself he would never ring again. It answered after just a few rings.

'Agent Deadlight? At last. I've been waiting on your call for some time now. Will this be our last friendly talk? I hope not.'

'I hope so. Don't take it personally, though. I just couldn't call you. I couldn't do it. My head was fried. Anyway, I'm out. Finished.'

'I have heard that so many times. Not just from you. But in my previous life in our dear old, decrepit and antiquated MI5. That organisation is imploding. But your last exit stage left was May two thousand and eleven, if I am correct.'

'The O'Driscoll affair sucked me back in. I knew when I arrived at the bridge that day that it was no ordinary murder. Something stirred in me. I was moved in a way I hadn't been before and—'

'And, of course, you were dealing with your father and his deteriorating health at the time as well. I understand. I know all about Mr Black and what has happened since.'

'I'm sure you do. Everything became much too personal as you know. I was angry and confused.'

'I understand that, too. Events were unexpected. But you adapted. You had to and … well, circumstances played out.'

'You got everything. Everything and everyone. You even crashed the legal process. I don't think MI5 could have done that. And now everyone is a spook.'

'How will you spend your inheritance, agent?'

'I'm giving most of it away. I don't want it. I might open a shop that specialises in fly-fishing. Or a wine shop. Somewhere. I'm not sure.'

'Your father worked hard for it. It's your inheritance. You deserve it.'

'Division Forty-Two should cease. As of now. In this moment. That's what we agreed. Enough is enough.'

'You're never really out. But okay. As agreed. The operation is over anyway. You need not call this number anymore. The line will be dead if you do. I was just waiting on you to check in after all that happened. Or check out, so it seems now. And plausible deniability exists as ever for PSNI Headquarters. None of the Chief Constables you have worked under know anything. Well, anything they can truly say on oath if ever summoned to do so. It had to be that way. For past and present. And we know you are close to the present occupant of the post.'

'I won't be calling you again. This is over now.'

'Okay.'

'What did you do with all the information I gathered over the years on the RUC and PSNI? On people and operations. Some of it was pretty mundane.'

'It wasn't just information and intelligence going nowhere. Don't think that. Certainly not mundane. You know we had more of a military and security theme to what we developed with the help of your father. You had to go through the tedium of continuing to be a police officer with no prospects. You fitted the role perfectly of the disillusioned RUC man with a drink problem. Very predictable. Like the goddamn awful weather there.'

'Perhaps I fitted the role too well? That's what I think. I became a bore. I even complained about bankers ruining the world.'

'Perhaps. But any information gathered is never useless, no matter how mundane. One never knows the hour when it is needed. That's the beauty of information.'

'But for years? Collecting all that stuff on RUC members and mentally challenged MI5 runners. Derry is full of them. It melted my head.'

'What was the alternative? You were loyal to yourself and to your father. Someone had to watch them. The distraction of criminal investigation in a corrupt and dangerous police force was the easy part for someone like you. We've always needed people of your calibre. Checks and balances and all that.'

'Will you leave me alone now?'

'Alone? That's why we selected you. You were always alone. Although, perhaps not now that you have a daughter to care for. But yes. It's over. We'll contact you if we need any help. I'm afraid MI5 still have agents that need watching. They have morphed into victims. They turned themselves into cry-babies. Sometimes I'd like to say to the Irish: "Where's your British stiff upper lip?" Every politician works for them. Some don't even know it. We need people like you. So can we contact you again if needs be? Is that in order?'

'Not really. But what choice do I have? Everyone is a writ-er, a celebrity, a victim or a British agent these days. Very common. Although, your secret department may not be as secret as you think. Rumours have been circulating about the existence of your nameless group for a while now. The Big Brother of intelligence, as perhaps you would like it to be there. You treat MI5 like the little sister it is. Not even as a subsidiary with a corporate veil.'

'We know that.'

'Then be careful.'

'We will. Payment has been made to the usual account in the usual way. The same account the solicitors made a rath-er large deposit to, we hear.'

'Did your boys in MI5 give you any help? Is Princeton, Braithwaite and Sotomeyer still the legal recruitment agen-cy for a failed intelligence service?'

'I'm not getting into that. No-one knows you or I exist in the capacity in which we talk.'

'Okay.'

'One . . . a few . . . last items, if I may?'

'You may.'

'Some operational matters have been concluded recently in your absence. Would you like to hear?'

'Right. Go on.'

'That young policeman, Bell.'

'A good officer.'

'He's done great work on finding the bodies of those Rankin children. Just a few days ago.'

'I thought he would. What happened?'

'My understanding is that he discovered Mr Haslette, the solicitor, had an allotment.'

'An allotment? He had nearly half an acre of a garden. Why would he want an allotment?'

'Exactly. He owned a little plot near a forest towards Mus-senden Temple that was well-kitted out with a good size shed, too.'

'Right. What happened then?'

'Bear with me.'

'Okay. Go on.'

'I think, under supervision from other senior officers,

Bell located Mr Haslette's legal title to the allotment and thought it would be a good idea to dig it up. Just on a hunch it seems. But a hunch that was trusted. Superintendent Kells gave him a map of the area that was discovered with all Mr Haslette's belongings.'

'And what was found?'

'A great supply of the best vegetables money could buy, I'm told. That's all. But then there was the shed.'

'What about it?'

'One of the older men who was a regular grower there said Mr Haslette used to spend quite a bit of time in the shed – sometimes crying. Even on sunny days. Apparently it was no ordinary shed and had a cement base. So Bell had it demolished and the floor dug up.'

'I can see where this is going.'

'I'm sure you can. Their bodies were rather decomposed after all this time, of course, and the remains were intertwined with the roots of nearby trees. But their clothes were in quite good condition and they each had a plastic doll beside them. I've watched the photographic and filmed evidence. There had been a rumour that the children were obliterated in that huge car bomb that killed Sergeant Wilson's father years ago. You know the story that they were locked in his parked car and vaporised when the bomb exploded. But no. Good news and bad news. At least their mother will get a proper burial for them now. Great work by Constable Bell.'

'Yes. Great work. Another loose end tied up.'

'Indeed. The young policeman is to be commended for his tenacity. His menacing tenacity, if I may say so. He reminds me of someone.'

Valberg wondered if the two girls were now to be interred with their father. Should he call Bell and Wilson and suggest they arrange to open Sidney Rankin's grave? This would avoid the formality of an order being obtained for exhumation. The coffin could perhaps then be opened unofficially. Ever since Mrs Rankin had told Valberg she only buried her husband's notebooks, as there was nothing left of him after the bomb, Valberg was intrigued to know what exactly was in the coffin. Could those secrets of the grave be unearthed? But was it worth it? Was there any point in literally digging up the past? Surely enough was resolved now. Valberg was drifting like the current in front of him. The sea was hypnotising him. He knew if he were in Derry he would be insisting on opening Sidney Rankin's coffin.

'Are you there?'

'Sorry. My mind was elsewhere. Sorry. What about Dominic, their elder brother? Is he still around?'

'He had a severe breakdown. He never recovered from what happened to his father. Still hospitalised I understand, and not by consent. But the mother has made it through it all and maybe she will get some sort of peace now.'

'Let's hope so. I will make contact with her. I'm holding something for her and her son.'

'There's one more thing about Bell.'

'What is it?'

'We know he was at the Public Record Office recently. With his girlfriend. His work colleague. Jennifer Hastings.'

'And?'

'We checked the file he looked at and he may have discovered something. You need to know.'

'What is it?'

'He was looking at the inquest file of a Mr McKillen, who was killed in a bomb blast on Spencer Road in Derry many years ago. There was a reference to your father being the real target of the bomb still in the file.'

'I know about it.'

'It should have been removed.'

'What should have been removed?'

'Well, it should never have been there in the first place.'

'What shouldn't?'

'The details of your father as the target. His work for us may have been exposed. I only mention it in case it ever comes up. We've removed all references to him now. We had effectively destroyed all the old RUC files, but Bell was shrewd enough to go looking for this old inquest report. Very astute.'

'There's nothing can be done now. I bloody well asked him to research that bomb. It's my own fault. Anything else?'

'May I make an observation?'

'Go on.'

'You've never asked to meet me, like other agents. That's the observation by the way. Now a question: why was that?'

'I didn't need to. You'd refuse anyway, Mr Mulholland. Wouldn't you?'

There was a moment's silence.

'If that is my correct name . . . how do you know it?'

'I had a good teacher. I'll find you if needs be. The more things change, Mr Mulholland, the more they stay the same. Bloody hell. Agent Deadlight is no more.'

Valberg was just about to hang up.

'Wait. Wait. If Agent Deadlight is no more, what about the secrets of Deadlight? Are they safe with you? I hope there isn't a book or a WikiLeaks moment coming. Very un-dignified.'

'You were lucky with WikiLeaks. Very lucky. Nothing really. What a mess that could have been.'

'We don't write anything down that's intelligible. All coded in shorthand and never committed to a computer. Like good lawyers. It wasn't luck. You know that. Your reports to me, all verbal, and logged in a code only the both of us know. Why not become a lawyer, agent? I think you'd be a good one.'

'I'm finished with the law. I've lost any respect I had for it. I'm not very fond of lawyers. Most of them anyway. But enough to make me keep away from the professional side of their lives.'

'So, agent. Let's cut to the chase. Is it safe?'

'Everything is safe – in my head.'

'I need to know.'

'Of course. You mean collusion, criminal conspiracy, cover-up, death squads, abandoned MI5 agents, inept and purposely shambolic police investigations, lies, deceit, untold breaches of the rule of law and the creation of a legal system that has ossified and turned into a world of form-filling, paper-chasing, bureaucratic, pedantic pettifoggers? Forms to fill and shoot to kill. Will I go on? That's enough, isn't it? Oh, and then there's the monster of monsters. Special Branch and their legacy. Will I move on to the bad stuff now? It would be a great book, now that I come to think of it. What a police force. You wouldn't have gotten away with it in South Africa or Chile.'

'Hardly original now, that viewpoint, is it? You were a new type of agent in a new time. An agent within, conducting a *voir dire*. Trial within a trial. You weren't exactly a British provocateur, or some sort of Military Reaction Force undercover agent now, were you?'

'Well, I hope not. All the same, if you're trying to hide your secrets, Mr Mulholland, you're hiding them in plain sight. There's an arrogance that you need to be careful with. It's something special to the English. Did you not get that theme in all my verbal reports to you? In all our many telephone calls?'

There was no reply.

'Your secrets are safe with me. The one thing about growing up in Derry is that you learn to take secrets to the grave. Did I ever strike you as a whistle-blower? Close down the Division and put an end to this now. For me, anyway. I want no more part in it, or of it.'

'Agreed. And thank you.'

'We'll meet some day, Mr Mulholland. You can thank me personally then. Goodbye.'

'Goodbye, agent. For now.'

EPILOGUE

Valberg hung up. He was annoyed with himself that he hadn't ended his conversation with Mulholland on a more friendly basis, especially in view of the number of times they had spoken on the phone in previous years. He had a gnawing feeling he would be in contact with him again. Valberg also realised that if his 'contact' was not satisfied he was going to keep quiet then he could be killed at any time.

As he was about to destroy his burner mobile, it vibrated. A text message.

'Jon, got ur number. Long story. It's Amanda from Journal here. Have to see you urgently. Need advice. Have material re Fr Doherty. Need to show to you. And other stuff. It's important. Film and audio. No-one knows. Promise won't go public until speak with u. Promised Fr D would wait a month or so after he died. Call me or txt back please. Rumour there's some sort of agent or double agent on the loose.'

Valberg had had enough. It could only be more bad news. He didn't respond. He took out the sim card and smashed the mobile against the rocks he was sitting on. He threw the remnants of the phone, the sim card and his personal weapon as far as he could into the Mediterranean Sea.

It was time to change into his diving gear and swim with Christ of the Abyss. Then a three-hour bike ride to Siena for the Palio that evening. Valberg's plan for the next day was to head for Malaga via the Italian, French and Spanish coastlines to meet his daughter.

Alone.

It was a beautiful July morning.